THE GROUNDING OF GROUP 6

JULIAN F. THOMPSON

AN AVON  FLARE BOOK

THE GROUNDING OF GROUP 6 is an original publication of Avon Books. This work has never before appeared in book form.

AVON BOOKS
A division of
The Hearst Corporation
1350 Avenue of the Americas
New York, New York 10019

First Avon Flare Printing: May 1983

AVON FLARE TRADEMARK REG. U.S. PAT. OFF. AND IN OTHER COUNTRIES, MARCA REGISTRADA, HECHO EN CANADA.

Printed in Canada

UNV   10   14   13   12

For Polly,
best and most of all.

Chapter One

THE PEOPLE in their group, Group 6, were all sixteen, all five of them, and none of them was fat. Coke and Sully both were boys; Sara, Marigold, and Ludi all were girls. Nat Rittenhouse was twenty-two, the leader of the Group, and meant to be a teacher. Even if he looked more like Sir Galahad after praying with his sword in the chapel all night, as Ludi thought.

The lack of flab should not be too surprising. The sort of folks who could afford the Coldbrook Country School were (a) not often known as "folks" and, (b) fanatic anti-fats. Anxiety, depression, even drugs were more acceptable; at least they were contemporary, Now, the *"fleurs du mal du siècle,"* as Sully's mother put it once, while sipping *kir* and "rapping" with Mc-Corker. But teenaged fat offended them. It was even more annoying than overhearing your child refer to "my life-style."

Coke told Sully all about it, once they got to know each other better.

"It gets them in the image, if their kids are fat," he said. "Same as this one time my father had to rent a car at Cincinnati airport, I'm pretty sure it was, and all they had was some great, fat, four-door American monstrosity, painted powder-blue on navy, or something like that. It really freaked him out. Like going to a movie with the cleaning woman would.

1

Suppose somebody saw him, and thought that it was his?"

Sully nodded, looked away. When he was younger, his mother paid Porfirio, the doorman weekday nights, to take him to the Jets' home games on Sunday afternoons. "*Arriba*, Tawd," the little mustached man would cry. And pointing way downfield at Wesley Walker: "*Miray! Miray! Miray!*" The doorman had no business watching football if he couldn't root in English, Sully thought. Sometimes he'd try to start a conversation with the person on his other side.

"You know, it isn't just that parents want their kids to *look* like names of cars, like Jaguar, Cutlass, Wraith, like that," said Coke. "They like it if you *act* like one, as well. You know what I mean? Quick and clean and quiet? Economical and start right up?" He often spoke a little laughing sound between his sentences. "And easy to park. Heh-heh. And, yeah, no breakdowns. Trouble-free." He paused, and wrapped a strand of long black hair around his forefinger, and sighed. "If there ever was one thing my parents really liked me for—I did say 'if,' remember—it's probably that I'm not fat."

He certainly was not: six-one, one sixty-two were his dimensions. He had a pointy chin and nose and slightly slanted eyes. He didn't much mind looking like a fox in those respects, but being almost whiskerless depressed him. "Damn lazy little follicles," he'd say, pulling at the longest one of maybe twelve black hairs that sprouted here and there upon his cheeks and chin and throat. "Let's get those little protein-rich behinds in *gear*," he'd say. And Marigold would laugh and ask him if his mother ever had an Abenaki chauffeur.

The five of them were made a group—Group 6—by chance, or whim, as far as they could tell. The new kids all had rendezvoused outside the Plaza the first day of September, at high noon. There was a bus to get on there, to take them on a ride some seven hours long, no stops. Nat Rittenhouse stood outside the bus and checked their names off on a clipboard; the clipboard had the number of your group beside your name. Before she'd gotten on the bus, Marigold had pointed to the name, E_____ R_____, she'd gotten from her parents, and said to Nat she didn't use it anymore. "Um, well, what do we call you, then?" he asked, and she said "Marigold," and so he crossed that old name out and wrote in Marigold above it. He didn't give her any knowing smiles, or funny looks, or arguments—not even a "Marigold *what?*" *Most* peculiar for a teacher, Marigold decided. And then, when three names on his clipboard never did show up at all, he'd only shrugged and told the driver, "Roll em . . ." instead of acting really pissed, the way a teacher would.

He also didn't look like any teacher Marigold had ever seen before. His head—with long, long, *long* blond hair and blond goatee and vaguely hazel eyes—was strictly *Rolling Stone* material, she thought; the rest of him was out of *Standing Timber,* or whatever lumberjacks and other backwoods bumpkins read. He was about her father's height— six feet—but put together differently: with stronger-looking, more elastic stuff, and a much better sense of proportion. His clothing made her think of words like "galluses" and "brogans," words she kind of liked but wouldn't bet a fortune that she knew the meanings of.

Coldbrook—seven hours later—was the last place on a gravel road that wandered on and on, and up and down, for maybe fifteen miles. There weren't many houses on the road, and some of what there were were mobile homes; a few of them had barns nearby, and pastures, which held cows. Most of the

3

houses had several cars outside them, one or two with their hoods up.

The Coldbrook Country School, however, had a split-rail fence, and a half a dozen dwelling houses sheathed by narrow clapboards, white, and wooden shutters, gray, and roofed by cedar shingles, natural. There were also sheds and barns, both red and white, and black-topped walks, and one huge, level field that still was green. There wasn't any sign. Whatever's at the end of a dead-end road can get away without one, oftentimes. "Well, I guess this must be it," is what the people reaching it will almost always say. And so, in this case, it would be: the Coldbrook Country School. One other place that you could usually find it was in the back of *The New York Times Magazine*. It had a heading to itself: "Schools, Co-Ed, Innovative-Alternative." The write-up in the ad was very promising.

The way it worked at Coldbrook was that new kids got to school before the others did and then went hiking out in groups. Each one had a teacher for a leader. They'd camp and roam around the hills and hollows for a certain time, and start to "get acquainted with the school's unique philosophy." Orientation, this was called, and "vital to one's function at the school." Apparently, the school believed that "each and every new experience must start at a Beginning." Quotations from the catalogue.

So, when that busload got to Coldbrook, they didn't get assigned to rooms or roommates. Instead, Nat told them all the number of their group again. First thing off the bus, they went into a dining hall, where there was soup and sandwich stuff, and after that they trooped on over to a barnlike place, the school's all-purpose room, where there were cots that they could sleep on in their sleeping bags. Groups would be embarking in the morning, they were told: reveille at six A.M.

4

* * *

Because it was the sort of school it was, Coldbrook seemed to make the *kids* apply to go to it, instead of being sent there by their parents—though fees were payable by anybody's check, or cash, or many major credit cards. (Or, if a customer insisted, in lots of other currencies, like real estate, or vintage wines, or paintings, jewelry, rare books, and glass.)

The first page of the Coldbrook application asked the kid to print his name, or hers, address, and date of birth. And parents' names, or guardian's, and siblings' names and ages. Also, other schools attended, subjects taken, interests/hobbies, and activities. That page was colored tan and was printed on 100% recycled paper.

The second page was olive green, a nice light shade of olive. On top it said:

Please write your name in full, again, including any nicknames you may have. Underline the name you like the most.

Below that was a line: _____ that stretched across the page.

Then it said:

Please tell us anything about yourself you want to, including why you chose to come to Coldbrook. If you really don't want to write anything, don't.

The rest of the page was blank.

Here are the ways that each of the five student members of Group 6 dealt with page 2 (olive green) of the Coldbrook application.

5

On the name line, with a fine-point Bic, Coke wrote, or, rather, printed:

Coleman "Coke" DeCoursey

His answer to the second part was in even smaller print:

I guess I'm pretty much your average misfit malcontent (genus suburbianis). My father thinks I'm smart and also wise; *I'd* say that he's half right, as usual. When I was little I liked school a lot. They seemed to teach the sort of stuff a kid would want to know. But in the last few years its gotten more and more irrevelant, so mostly I tuned out, sometimes with a little help from my friends (the Flying Cannabis Brothers and etc). I don't think that I'm a burnout, but if I was I wouldn't know it anyway, I don't guess. Anyway, my old man's gotten more and more fed up and last year he handed me a big fat book and told me I could choose any school he'd circled on the page he'd turned down, or he'd pick one for me. Well, seeing as I never thought I'd look that great in uniform, I did, and here I am. PS. I'm spending 6 weeks this summer at something called the Institute for Basic Motivation. That was my mother's idea. But I'll probably see you regardless.

Sully filled in the name line thusly:

Arthur Robey Sullivan, Esq. (Sully, Linus)
<u>Loni</u> <u>Anderson</u> (joke)

On the rest of the page he wrote, in ill-formed cursive script that slowly sank across the piece of paper:

usually one of the smallest in my class. *likes:* reading, sports, outdoors, mom, apple pie. *hates:* phonies, liars, New York City!, math. really want to get totally away from New York. like the way Coldbrook lets you make your own decisions (courses etc) and teaches you self-suffientcy.

Sara typed her form:

> *Sara* Slayman Winfrey

And in the other space:

At this point, I have two major interests in my life: native American peoples, and all aspects of outdoor living. Eventually, I think I would like to live in a native American community, probably in some isolated part of Arizona, or possibly the Dakotas. After I graduate, I intend to go on to college, major in Biology, and then study to be a doctor.

Before I got into that mess at my last school (which I suppose my parents had to tell you about), I was on the Student Council—10th grade president—and captain-elect of the hockey and the swimming teams. I was also on the Honor Roll, legitimately.

Coldbrook seems like the perfect place to make a fresh start. My father tells me not to count on it, but I still think I can get into a good college and a fine Med School, with Coldbrook's help.

Marigold used an orange crayon. The only name she wrote was:

Marigold

In the middle of the space she had to tell about herself and why she'd chosen Coldbrook (if she wanted to), she put:

Moi?

In the same orange crayon.
Ludi wrote in dark green ink, in an italic script:

Louisa Rebecca Locke   ("*Ludi*")

And then:

My best friends always have been chickadees. Perhaps you'll find that strange, but if you do, I promise you: you don't know chickadees. When I was four, my mother died. My father was, and is, a pigeon-fancier—possibly she died of that—so in a little while he brought a plump young squab back home, and married her. She cooed at me a lot and ate French toast for breakfast. We never fight . . . or kiss. I read a lot, and write, and paint—but often not the books I should be reading, and poems instead of paragraphs, and saints instead of still-lives. I know that I could get good grades, and want to, in a way. But it never has seemed worth it, yet.

Coldbrook looks so beautiful! I really want to go to it, and I *am* going to try to fit in and "do a job," as my father likes to say. You'll see.

They slept atop the canvas-covered cots, uneasily, the girls up on the stage at one end of the room, the boys down on the wooden floor with all the lines on it: like blue for badminton and green for volleyball

8

and black for basketball. The cot assigned to Coke was on a foul line, a fact that wasn't lost on him, for sure.

At six o'clock, a voice came through some speakers and waked up everyone who hadn't been already, by morning light or nerves. "All right, good morning, everyone," it said. "Breakfast coming up in twenty minutes. Please find your group and sit with it; the tables all have numbers on them. Twenty minutes, please."

All the members of Group 6 were early; some of them were talkative. Coke did gagging noises, said, "My God, a hearty breakfast," when he saw the dark grain cereal, and plates of eggs, and slabs of heavy toasted bread with honey. Marigold announced that she'd had only juice and coffee in the mornings—better make that *afternoons*—since school let out in June. Sara just relaxed and ate. Good nutrition was a thing with her; she even liked the way "nutrition" sounded: sort of wholesome, munchy, down-to-earth. One of the basics, along with sleep and exercise, she thought. Her body was the one creative project in her life so far, the only one that she'd been proud of, anyway. Her mother was quietly pleased that Sara "had such a nice figure"; Sara liked the fact that she was strong and hard and supple. Sully asked her for the butter, and she looked him in the eye as she was passing it, and nodded. He also ate the cereal and also wore wool socks and boots that had been broken in and taken care of. Sara liked the way he looked: his unstyled shaggy haircut, his snub-nosed freckled face, and eager, quick blue eyes. He wasn't tall, or real sophisticated, or brawny-hairy yet, but she'd seen muscles on his smooth-skinned arms and legs that pleased her, put her at her ease. Sully had a friendly look about him, Sara thought; working with the same small set of facts, Marigold decided he looked "young."

9

Ludi hardly thought how Sully looked at all. She ate a piece of toast, and then another one, with Constant Comment tea. She didn't like to talk at breakfast, but she smiled at everyone. Ludi had a head of soft black curls; her face was small, and what she called "guh-nomey," with its round, dark eyes. The little smile she wore meant she was happy and at peace, but other people felt approved by it, as well, and therefore gentled.

Nat also sat with them. In between the mouthfuls that he took, he looked around the table, focusing on each of them in turn. He told them, sounding shy and careful with his words, that he was also new to Coldbrook Country School, but that he'd spent the summer here, in Coldbrook Country. ("Cool as a mountain stream," said Marigold.) "Not at the *school*, you understand, out there." Nat waved his hand to mean the hills and valleys all around the school. "Just camping—*you* know—living with Big Momma Nature." He dropped his eyes and smiled. He didn't tell the Group he hadn't spent a penny of the money that they'd paid him, yet. The checks remained tight-folded in his wallet, seven hundred fifty bucks apiece. He'd get the third, for fifteen hundred, after it was over.

Sara, filling silence when it came, asked him where he'd gone to school, and he said, "Um. Well, UVM," and she said, "Where?" and he said, "Oh, Vermont." She nodded, muttered "Good," wishing he'd said Williams.

"So what're you going to teach?" Marigold asked him. She giggled as she said it, which made her feel like an idiot. If she wasn't really on her guard, she'd break out in that stupid nervous giggle, still; just like a twelve-year-old or something. She might as well hold up a sign, "Beware of teeny-bopper." Not that the thought of anyone who looked like Nat teaching a class didn't have a humorous side to it.

10

Going by appearances, he'd have a class in Chain Saw I, she thought, and Senior Grateful Dead, and How to Make a Toadstool Taste Like Tenderloin, and maybe, as a lab instructor, Oral Sex. She'd have to write her friend Odetta Neeskens that, when she got back from camping. O.D. would get a chuckle out of that. Her real first name was Wendy.

"From what I understand," said Nat, "that may depend on you, at least to some extent." He cleared his throat and moved some clots of scrambled egg around his plate. "Um. I think that I could teach some literature—American, I guess—and psych. Religion, if anyone was interested. Philosophy, maybe. Oh, and how to use some basic tools, and playing certain instruments, and woodcraft. I guess that gets worked out when we come back. I'm still a little vague on how it's all negotiated." Nat laughed, and also seemed to blush. "Everyone says not to worry, so I don't."

Ludi, looking at the blush, did not believe him.

Sully simply heard the laugh and what Nat said. It sounded good to him. A little vague, but one thing at a time, he thought. Whatever it was, it was a lot better than New York. "When do we head out?" he asked. "And how far is it, where we're going?"

"Um. Well, almost any time we're ready, so I understand," said Nat. "We'll have to organize our packs, and then I'm meant to check us out with the Director. Give him—well—our flight plan, sort of." He nodded briskly to himself, and leaned way forward, lowering his voice, and looking very much like Sully, suddenly. "I'm going to take you to . . . well, it's the best, my favorite place I found all summer." He gave a little chuckle. He had a silly name for it, this place; he wouldn't tell them *that* until they'd started. Spring Lake Lodge, he'd christened it. "You'll see. It's quite a good ways off. I hope . . . well, I hope you're ready for a hike." He lifted up his

11

eyebrows, and his light eyes went around the table, stopping for an instant on each face. Ludi felt he wanted something from them that he wasn't getting, something more than their attention, that's for sure.

Nat didn't know he looked that way. What he did know was that no one in Group 6 was living up to expectations. He'd steeled himself to meet a hateful bunch of kids. "You've got the dregs, of course, the ultimate bad seeds," Dean Luke Lemaster told him. It was the night before he went down to New York. Luke used a lot of other words, as well: obnoxious and belligerent, arrogant, deceitful, shallow, lazy, selfish were a few. Hopeless. Luke used all those words and pulled his nose; he had been at Coldbrook many years. "It's a type as old as history, I guess," said Luke Lemaster wearily. "Long before you had Group Six you had that type of kid. Guys like Hitler, for example—they were that same type, I bet. Others of them we can teach up here. They learn. A Six-er never would. Grounding is the only way. It's not their fault, I guess." He pursed his lips and nodded, looking off at nothing, looking old.

They did what Nat called "organize our packs" out on the lawn behind the kitchen entrance. Nat stacked a pile of food and certain pots that he could carry, asked if they would divvy up the rest. They looked at one another, little smiles in place.

Cole was tallest by a lot. Sully turned and looked at him, and so did Marigold. Sara looked down at the ground, and Ludi picked a piece of grass and put it in between her thumbs, and cupped her palms and blew in them, and made a raucous, cawing sound.

"O.K.," said Coke. He wore a floppy leather hat, and frayed, stained painter's pants, and beat-up running shoes. "It doesn't look as if there's room in anybody's pack but Sara's, so—heh, heh—I guess it's up to her to . . ." He nodded solemnly in her direction.

12

Her pack was only two-thirds full; the rest of them were stuffed.

"We-e-ll," she said, slowly, "I guess I can take a lot of it . . . ." She bent and picked up packages of food.

"No, wait," said Marigold. "I can't believe . . . If you and Nat have that much room, we must be doing something wrong. God knows *I* don't know what . . . ." She started digging in her pack. "Sara, help me." She tossed out sweaters, underpants, designer jeans, a pair of sandals, different colored turtlenecks and leotards. She emptied all her stuff out on the lawn, then stood with hands on hips and stared at it. The way she looked, she might have just thrown up. "Will you get a load of that crap?" she said, and slapped herself on the outside of her thighs, and turned to Sara. "What would *you* take, out of that?"

Sara kneeled and started to divide the things in piles. The others moved in closer; Coke and Sully saw that Marigold wore skimpy nylon underpants with sunsets, lightning bolts, and rainbows on them.

"It's really hard," said Sara, working fast. "In September you can roast one day and freeze your ass completely off the next. But there"—she moved one pile beside the pack—"that should pretty much allow for anything. It's only—what?—two, three days, or something? I learned a way to pack stuff I can show you, but still I always seem to need whatever's on the bottom first."

When Sully'd seen what Sara did for Marigold, he said, "Well, shoot, I guess I packed a lot of extra, too." He looked at Nat. "Have we got time to go back where my trunk is?" He didn't know the name for where they'd spent the night.

Nat said he didn't see why not, and Ludi said she guessed that she'd go, too. "No fair Sara gets to carry all the marshmallows," she said, and looked at Nat and laughed.

13

Coke watched Nat, as he watched Ludi walking after Sully. Then he turned and watched her, too. She sure seemed strong for such a flat-chested little thing. Maybe she was into gymnastics or something, he thought. "Coma*neetch*," he said out loud. "Shaposhni*kova*."

"What?" said Marigold. She had her hands back on her hips, and now she lifted up one foot to nudge Coke's pack frame with her toe. "You're next, big boy," she said.

"Hey, look," said Coke. "The thing is this, no fooling. My stuff takes up a lot more room, 'cause I've got such long arms and legs and such humungous feet. Counting every article of clothes as one, I bet you *still* got more things in your pack than I do." That didn't count the bottle of white rum he'd rolled up in a towel, or any of the packs of Camels that he'd stuck in here and there. Marigold might thank him later, though with his luck she'd probably turn out to be a pot-head. Women were always apt to like whatever you didn't have, or couldn't stand, or really were afraid to do.

"Well, then," said Marigold, "to make it fair you'll have to tie some pots and pans outside your pack. Here, gimme thet thar skillet, Sary. This'll be like *Treasure of Sierra Madre.*" She laughed. "You see that on TV? With Humphrey Bogart?"

"Wait a minute. That was on a donkey, wasn't it?" said Coke. He did like Marigold; she didn't seem to give a shit, and she had bolts of lightning on her underwear.

"Close enough," she said, and grabbed his leather hat and put it on, angled toward the front, across her bangs. Once, when she was plucking on her eyebrows and smoking some outrageous Ghani, Marigold decided once and for all that she really did look like Pat Benatar, but younger, of course, with just a *trace* of baby fat still, and *definitely* a softer style.

14

Now she wore a pair of lime-green running shorts that showed her legs from ass to ankle. Her legs were not too bad, she knew. Odetta and herself had pledged preventive war on cellulite, which ran—or, as they giggled, "jelled"—in both their families. "Flab-patrol, flab-patrol," Marigold would say, jabbing at the back of one of O.D.'s thighs with an iced tea spoon, as they sunned beside her pool. "I think you'd better send a lard-guard over, on the double." Both of them did exercises that they'd read in magazines, before they went to bed, but neither of them said so to the other. Who wanted to admit she writhed around on the floor?

Marigold also wore white leather running shoes with green stripes and green laces, and socks that didn't go above her shoes, with little green pom-poms on the back of the ankles. And a white zippered sweat shirt with green trim, over a white embroidered camisole, and a perfume by the name of Ishtar.

Sara watched. She'd hunkered down into a comfortable position, sort of like a baseball catcher's crouch, but weighted to one side, and resting on a heel. Her face was strong and pleasant, deeply tanned, with heavy brows and perfect teeth. She'd done her dark brown hair in braids, drawn down from a center parting, tied with bright red yarn. She always had a piece of rawhide looped around her neck, with special knots in it, and she had just the start of squint lines in the tan around her eyes.

Sara thought that Coke and Marigold were different from the friends she'd had before, but she'd expected that, and so it didn't bother her. She'd known the kids at Coldbrook would be . . . well, *alternative*. A little wild, most likely. She often told herself she wasn't into judging her own tribe, whatever it turned out to be. When other kids would ask her, as they had for years, "What do you think of so-and-so?" she'd mostly shrug and smile and say that she or he was "nice," or sometimes that she didn't know them all that well.

What she really thought she thought was quite a bit more complicated—sort of her philosophy of life, she liked to feel. She'd figured out that everybody started out as good, and if they *acted* bad, that wasn't really them. There wasn't any point in saying someone was a jerk, a nerd, an asshole; that wouldn't be the truth. People's *actions* could be bad, unnatural as Sara thought of it, but if you dwelt on what a person did too much, you might confuse the action with the person. That would then be bad of *you*, and an example of the fact that every bad action grows out of another bad action. The thing that she believed was that if you hung around a person some, and paid attention, well, pretty soon you'd see their real, good self. That's the way it worked for her a lot. Certainly with kids. Sooner or later, most kids seemed to get to like her; they wanted her to be with them, and even looked to her to help them certain ways. Their goodness came out in the way they acted, then. It never entered Sara's mind that people liked her for her looks, or brains, or tolerance, or because she was so good at sports. She noticed older people mostly seemed to think that people *changed* from good to bad, or that some people were good and others just weren't. Adults seemed to hate a lot, almost get off on hating someone. A lot of them were so *un-natural.* Sara didn't know who she should blame for that, so she blamed civilization.

Nat now looked at Sara, squatting easily by her pack. She seemed like such a classic All-American— strong and healthy, quite good-looking, really. Her faded blue-jean jacket stretched across her shoulders, her khaki pants pulled tight around her sturdy thighs. He couldn't understand why she was here at all—and even more why she was in this group. The same with Ludi, even more so with Ludi, come to think of it. And Sully, too—*and* Coke *and* Marigold. He realized that all of them, in different ways, reminded him a bit of someone else: Nathaniel Palmer Rittenhouse.

Whoa. He felt the sweat start on his palms. My God. Could it be that he'd been missing something obvious as hell? With Group Six taken care of (as the saying goes) would Coldbrook School want N. P. Rittenhouse . . . well, *anywhere?*

Now he walked across the campus, met with the Director, Dr. Simms. "How about I take them up the other side of North Egg Mountain—you know, where all the boulders are, along the brook?" he asked.

Doctor jotted down the information in an open notebook. "That should be quite fine," he said. His eyes twinkled behind his rimless glasses. He looked like a family physician in a Norman Rockwell illustration; in fact, his degree was a Doctorate in Occupational Guidance from a nonresidential correspondence university over a dry cleaner's, in Boca Lustra, California. " 'Shoulder to shoulder, and bolder and bolder, ta-tum, ta-ta-tum to the *fray,*' " he sang softly. "And you will . . . disappear on Monday morning . . . ?" Doctor asked.

"Yes," said Nat.

"Then we can say 'good-bye,' then," Doctor said. He stood and handed Nat the little bottle and offered him his well-made, clean white hand. "I thank you for your services to Coldbrook—and to humankind. And I'll mail your final check on Tuesday morn."

"Yes," said Nat, squeezing Doctor's hand with what he hoped looked like a cheerful, righteous smile. He turned and left the office.

By his rough reckoning, the boulders back of North Egg Mountain, by the brook, were maybe twenty miles from Spring Lake Lodge.

Chapter Two

KIDS WHO don't have hideouts often grow up fast. A hideout tends to keep a person tethered to his childhood, to a world that isn't organized and ruled and limited by grown-ups, a world where nothing you can think of is impossible. Children not disposed toward hideouts sometimes get right into "life"; when they say, "Let's pretend . . . ," they are the Teacher, Doctor, Mommy in the game, and everyone gets bossed around. They're the ones you read about who never had a lesson but just sat down and played the stock market one day, very much as if they'd done it all their lives.

Nat was not that sort of kid at all. Spring Lake Lodge was number ten or twenty, maybe; the latest and the best of many secret places that he'd had, beginning with his bed. When he was five, he'd taught himself to do a sort of horizontal surface dive: tucking up his legs, he'd make a half a sideways somersault and, pulling with his arms and wriggling, go way down deep beneath the sheets and covers, to the cold, black bottom of his bed. That was a cave, and only he knew there was air space under there. In it, he was free from their control, away from all the rules and customs that the older people had. There he could, for instance, take off his pajamas, if he wanted to. Nobody would know, as long as he got dressed again before he came back up. Once his mother almost caught him, and he had to lie there, faking sleep, sure that she could hear his stealthy heart, his bottoms pulled up barely to his knees.

Later on, there was a tree house, with a Scottish shortbread tin for contraband. The Milky Ways and peanut butter cookies that could see him through disasters of all sorts were stored—say, "stock-piled"—in that tin. It took the sort of discipline and strength a Spartan youth would have to keep from eating them, to save them for a time of greater need—when he had had to run away from home, or if, returning home from school one day, he'd found his house destroyed by an explosion, or a nuclear attack. Or if a friend, or even someone that he hardly knew, like Amy Robinson from down the block (oh, how he loved her: braid and bottom) were ever beaten, badly, with a belt, at home, by some fat, pig-faced person like her father, why, she could come to him for help, and he could give her something good to eat and care for her.

In his teens, in boarding school, he'd wandered in the woods beyond the soccer fields until he found a newly fallen tree, one branch of which was perfect for a ridgepole. Over that he'd woven lengths of wild grape vine and draped the poncho that his roommate never used and didn't miss, all camouflaged with brush. A sturdy metal strong box rested on a sort of shelf he'd chiseled in the trunk. It contained a corn-cob pipe, and matches, and a pouch of Dutch tobacco. Also, special fruit-nut chocolate chunks, Sur-Vital Bars by name, and a couple of magazines which had a lot of fascinating articles and great cartoons, as well as color photographs of people by the name of Shauna, Reine, and Sylvie.

College wasn't all that good for hideouts, other than his room. And rooms were almost public, al-ways sitting right where other people knew they were, and everyone had his or hers, a great deal like

19

your own. About the best that he could do was have a different atmosphere. It helped to have a roommate who thought that everything made just as little sense as he did, but who also didn't see the point of carrying on about it. The roommate had to like to get up early, give and take a foot massage, and stay in pretty decent shape. A shape which wouldn't be the same as his, the way a girl's would not be.

But Spring Lake Lodge was very much the best he'd ever had. It took the game of hideouts one step further: with it, the world of make-believe became alternative reality. "Why not?" it seemed to say to Nat. "Why not?"

They used up six full hours getting there. He'd had to start them in the opposite direction, almost, heading up a trail that was the way to go if you had North Egg Mountain as your destination. Doctor watched them go. He knew they'd travel on that trail until they reached a logging road, on which they'd take a right, and go another mile or so. Then, if they were smart, they'd leave the road and travel cross-lots. The road ran up around the hill, and you could save a lot of time and distance cutting through the woods. That was the way to go to North Egg Mountain.

The people in Group 6 went off the logging road at more or less the place that Doctor would have bet they would. They disappeared into the trees. But then they made an arc along the slope and came back to the road. To say they "dove" across it would exaggerate the matter slightly, but surely they moved quickly. Soon they reached another logging road, on which they took a left. "Oh, what a gorgeous day," Nathaniel said, and took a big, deep breath, with which he almost trotted down the road. Group 6, still fresh and anxious to be good, and not be left behind and lost the Christ knows where, went with him.

Nat ignored the pants and grunts he heard behind

him for a while, but Marigold's "Ouch—fuck!" had more than just a trace of angry accusation in it—sounded downright personal, in fact. He took them off the road and stopped beside a brook.

"Fucking blister." Marigold limped past him and addressed the brook.

"I hate myself," Nat said. "I didn't think." He reached into a pocket, then another one. "Um. Shit. It serves me right, I guess. I must have dropped my handkerchief." Marigold, still staring at the brook, slow-silent-mouthed the words "Poor baby."

Nat said it must have been a little while before, when he had wiped his face. He'd just run back and pick it up, he said, slipping off his pack. "You know," he said to Marigold, "that hanky is a kind of special one. It's real close to my heart. I wore it with a cowboy hat and six-guns when I graduated. Um. Everyone cracked up, except my parents."

Marigold looked at him from the corners of her eyes. He looked so miserable she had to smile. He pursed his lips at her and turned away. The truth was always best: he'd slipped that handkerchief inside his shirt, about a mile before.

Nat jogged back down the road until he got to where it straightened out and he could see for quite a ways. He lay down on his stomach and peered between some ferns a full five minutes; then he nodded, rose, and jogged back to the Group.

"Find it?" Sully asked, and Nat could truthfully reply, "Yes, perfect," and wave it at the five of them. Marigold said, "Gross," but made it sound like "Good." They started out again.

Now Nat led them in an easy circle, slowly back, above, around the school, but even when they'd gotten past it and were heading for the Lodge, he didn't go directly. Partly, that was habit: all summer he had taken different routes, so as not to make a path. Now there was a greater likelihood of trackers, and a

21

larger, careless group to leave a trail. Then, too, there was his own uncertainty: did he really want these kids to know the way? And so they zigged and zagged—beside, across this brook, along that deer track and stone wall, even on the Old Stage Road a ways, the little you could see of it. ". . . it ran from Seton down to Mohawk Falls," he said, "and carried mail and passengers one day a week. It's hard to realize that there were farms all through these woods, but you can still find lots of cellar holes. Most of this was open pasture then, can you imagine it?" He swung his arm around. It *was* hard to imagine. He liked it better this way, much.

Ludi listened, leaning up against a birch, her long-lashed eyelids closed, her cheek against the smooth white bark. She heard again the horses' hooves, the leather-squeak and rattle of the harness, the clatter of the wheels, the coachman yelling, "Yah-Yah-Yah!" Ever since they'd joined the road, she'd heard the sounds in places; now she could allow them fully, knowing they were real. She opened up her eyes and saw the stage, coming from the uphill side, toward them. It had four horses, not well matched in size or color, and only one man on the driver's seat. He wore a little soldier's cap, with a strap around his chin—a thin man, lacking teeth, but not ambition, clearly: "Yah-Yah-Yah!" he shouted at his team, and shook the reins. "Honeytown at sundown, by the Jesus!" Ludi smiled and watched the stagecoach rocking as it passed. All that happened in the merest blink of time.

She never mentioned anything she saw or heard. Hadn't, well, for years, except for times she didn't think, and just assumed that what it was was there for everyone. When she was small, she thought that everyone was just the same, and saw the same as she did. And she saw lots of different things. Some of them were like the stagecoach, things left over from

22

another time—echoes, shadows of the past that you might stumble on, perhaps the way you'd find an arrowhead, a broken pipe, a piece of pottery. Other things were *indications,* you might say—things she saw that made her know her stepmother was pregnant (with a boy), or that it wouldn't be a good idea to walk across that hayloft. Or how to tell the red socks from the green ones in her bureau drawer, even when the lights were out.

When she was *very* little, she had told her mother what she saw—except for one thing—and her mother never told her "no," but only nodded, narrowing her eyes as if to try to see herself, or possibly remember. After Mommy died, she'd told her father certain things. At first, he didn't seem to mind so much, and said, "Now, there, there. That's all right," a lot. But in a while he started to get cross with her and said she'd better "cut that nonsense out." He told her only crazy people saw things. Did she want to have the neighbors think that she was crazy? She saw some funny things around her father when he said that, but maybe she was seeing things.

So, starting at that time, she just stopped mentioning the things she saw. She knew that she could make them not appear, and simply see the world her father saw, but she decided not to make that sacrifice. His liking her would not be worth it. That meant she stayed the way she was, a little vague and dreamy. She'd oversleep, or not pick up her room when she was told, or not be waiting by the car when it was time to go, or fail to do her homework—all because she'd been involved with something that she couldn't mention. She drove her father past the limits of his patience, which weren't generous or flexible to start with.

"You are so goddamn out of step with everything!" he shouted at his daughter.

23

"That kid just drives me up the fido-fucking wall!" he told his second wife.

Ludi was the one thing in his house and life that simply didn't work right, and gradually he came to hate her.

When they finally got to Spring Lake Lodge, it was late afternoon. Group 6 was draggin' ass, Coke thought. He wasn't sure he liked his role as much-the-biggest boy, with three girls in the group. It kind of took away his right to be the bitcher and the drag. Marigold had started in to whine right after lunch—God, *he'd* been really stiff—but she'd done it in a way that made it not sound serious: "How much longer is it, Daddy? Are we almost there yet? Can't we get some ice cream *now?*"

The other three just chuckled and kept going. For all Coke knew, they liked this sort of thing, this so-called student-centered school that really was a boot camp in disguise. Coke had no illusions. At this point he was pretty sure that any school—shit, almost any *place*—that he'd have access to would be a place he'd hate. His feet felt really hot. He tried to take his mind off them by watching Marigold's behind, and fantasizing scenes in which she showed him where the lightning struck. His pack did weigh a ton.

Then, quite surprisingly, he heard Nat say, "Well, here we are," and there they were. It hadn't seemed that they were getting anywhere. And where they'd gotten to was not exactly what he'd thought that it would be.

Spring Lake Lodge was hidden in a spruce grove, quite a big one, on the top of, oh, perhaps the thirty-fifth small wooded hill they'd climbed, or partly climbed, that day. They hadn't been on level ground since they had finished scrambled eggs—or so it seemed to Coke. The Lodge, which Sara had imagined as a Swiss-style building (with a porch) and one enormous room (with fieldstone fireplace) and maybe even moosheads on the walls, was just a tiny, squatty little cabin, pretty much the kind that's called a trapper's "tilt" some places. Most of it was logs, at least; the ones along both sides stacked up with butt ends heading forward, so as to make the cabin's front a good bit higher than its back. That way, the flat, unpeaked shed roof would slant from front to back in such a way that water would drain off, presumably. The roof did not impress Group 6. Underneath were slim spruce poles, set close together; over them was plain black roofing paper, double-layered, and other poles lay over it. The roofs the members of Group 6 had known before were either tiled (like Sara's was) or shingled, using slate or cedar—even asphalt in the case of Ludi's father's summer home's garage.

"My God, it's logs and . . . tar paper!" cried Marigold. "A shack!" She laughed hysterically. O.D. would have a cat with wings! She rolled her head around and stuck one hand upon a hip. "Eighty-five a night for this? There *must* be some mistake. I told the travel agent 'rustic,' yes, but what that means to me is, like, a darling claw-foot tub and no Jacuzzi. And patchwork quilts instead of satin comforters. Maybe, on the tables, nice thick porcelain, and waiters dressed like lumberjacks. But, this . . ." She flipped the other hand: take it away.

Nat listened, watched the others look at it, at her, at it again. They all had painted something cheerful on their faces, the sort of smiles that people use to cover major disappointments, even fear. The sort they wear before they cry, sometimes.

He looked at Spring Lake Lodge. It still looked good to him. He'd framed two windows on the east and west sides of the house—the door was on the south—and covered each of them with double sheets of firm, clear plastic. The door was made of boards

25

he'd fashioned with his chain saw and had a wooden latch; it opened in, because of snow. Inside, there was a small cast-iron stove; he'd brought it up in pieces and assembled it right there, with stove cement. Underneath the floorboards there was insulation, half a foot of it. Likewise, overhead he'd stapled three-foot strips, the kind with silver backing—it was not as deep, three inches only. People could survive a winter in that hideout, if they had to.

A little ways in front of Spring Lake Lodge, he'd made a nice stone fireplace that he used after dark, but never in the daylight, and down a little slope there was the Lake itself: a vast expanse of water maybe twenty feet by twelve, and fully four feet deep at the far end.

Spring Lake was his creation, and having never made a lake before he loved it even more than it deserved. Once upon a time, it was a wet spot in the woods, a swampy bit of ground that never dried. Nat was sure that wet spot held a spring, and so each day, when he was finished with his cutting, trimming, hauling, notching, building, or whatever, he'd do an hour's worth of shovel work, standing naked, save for sneakers, in the muck, digging out the clayey loam and prizing out the rocks. In time, he got to mostly gravel, and the water bubbled sweetly, coldly, out of it. He figured, and was right, the water had run underground and popped out farther down the hill. Now he dug a little channel for it, so it could make its way aboveground. Spring Lake was a water source; he liked that.

The members of Group 6 had all put down their packs by the time that Nat looked back at them again. Now that there was no more hiking, they were stuck for something else to do. At least nobody cried. Sully shrugged and started toward the Lodge; Sara sat down on the ground, pulled up a leg, and started doing stretches. Marigold and Coke walked down to check the water. Ludi stood right where she was, one hand upon her pack frame. Having seen a place, she liked to feel it, too—"the way it came together" is the way she would have put it. This place seemed very beautiful to her.

"Can I go in?" Sully called that down to Nat, his hand upon the door latch.

"Oh, sure. Go on." Nat smiled and waved him forward. "Make yourself at home."

They all heard Sully saying "Wow" from just inside the cabin door—and so they all had something they could do: go and see what he was wowing at. They crowded in the door and soon were saying "Wow" themselves. Spring Lake Lodge seemed almost full of double-decker bunks, or wooden shelves about the size and shape of bunks, as Sully thought of them.

There was some other space inside the cabin, but not too much, if someone had a hoopskirt on, for instance. Two sets of double-deckers took up all the farthest wall, the north side of the cabin; another set was on the left-hand wall, beside the window, which was very near the front. The little stove was on the right-hand side, a good safe yard out from the wall, which also had *its* window, right behind a good-sized wooden box. So when the five of them were all inside (and also one half-opened slab-wood door) there wasn't space to swing the smallest cat.

"It's twelve by twelve," said Nat, from in the door frame. "That means the bunks down there are only six feet long. It's lucky that a lot of us are—um, well—middle-sized. Coke's the only one that better sleep on this side." He pointed to his left. "These are six foot six." Nat heard his voice take on that stupid tone it used when he was filling silence.

Marigold climbed up into an upper on the end, and stretched out, leaning on an elbow. "*Extra*-firm, I'd say," she said, pressing on the rough-sawn spruce

27

with one extended finger. "Well, I'll say this for Spring Lake Lodge—it's intimate, all right. Would anybody like to see my vaccination *now*, just to get it over with?"

Nat said, hating it, "Well, what I thought was—is—that girls could undress first, and get into their sleeping bags, before we came on in. Then we could take our stuff off in our bunks. And in the morning we could get up first, and dress, and clear on out—you know—like that. Or maybe some of you would rather sleep outside." He shrugged. "Whatever." This was not the sort of scene he had imagined, but he didn't know what was. "I made a little outhouse over there a ways. It's—um—it's got a pretty gorgeous view. Every time you use it, toss a scoop of lime down in the hole, O.K.?" He spoke offhandedly, and didn't look at anyone. Let them find the rubber toilet seat themselves; he'd worn it round his neck to bring it up, of course.

"I like the signs," said Ludi softly. After she'd come in, she'd carefully looked all around the cabin. To her left, beside the door, there was a row of wooden pegs; above them was the biggest sign. It said: "Which of your father's 'well-known facts' will be tomorrow's ignorance?" Like the others, it was written on a nice white piece of birch bark with (perhaps) a magic marker. Next to it was one that said: "Please, please, please grow, but never change." The one above the door was "First check out your feet, then choose your dance." The one in the corner, just to the right of the door, seemed to have been badly tacked at the top, so that it had flopped over, and you couldn't see the words. Ludi lifted it, and looked, and read "Expect surprises."

Nat turned in time to see her smiling. She looked completely happy, standing there. He took a long, deep breath and rubbed his hands together.

"Now, how about we get some supper organized?" he said.

At the Institute for Basic Motivation, Coke had talked about his life in grade school, where it all went wrong for him. He said he thought he knew the reason why.

"It was my hair," he told the people on his Self-Esteem Assessment Team. "I simply couldn't make it stay in place. That, and the fact that I didn't have any hips, so my shirttail always came out. Those two things were all it took. They said I was a mess. A *mess,*" he repeated bitterly. He'd slouched down in his chair and pursed his lips, and shook his head, as if in morbid retrospection. Ms. Pembroke, MSW, the leader of the Team, felt sorry for him, he was almost sure. He thought she maybe had a point. "Once my mother got the maid to sew the front tails of my shirt into the back tail. I had to step into the thing, and, well, you can imagine how . . ." Coke kept talking till he saw their eyes begin to glaze. "I felt like telling them to stick a hairball up their hatch—hey, sorry, Angela, but I said *hatch,* heh-heh—and blow it out their Azores." He smiled his evil smile at Angela, a girl with one crossed eye, a member of the Team, who said vulgarity was sinful, mortal-sinful, even for a Protestant, a Jew, or an "acrostic." "God doesn't give a hoot who He strikes down," she told them.

It had been a fact that, in the second grade, the members of his class had called him Cole-the-(toilet)-Bowl (he'd started "Coke" in adolescence), and that he'd never had the friends his parents wanted him to have. Instead, he'd hung around the fat and silly ones, the other failures, the ones who put the green peas in their nose at birthday parties. He'd hated skating, but his father got him up at three and four A.M. to go to peewee hockey, where he'd spend an hour leaning on his stick and sliding on the leather edges of his hockey boots. According to his father, he was chicken, and so his mother took him to a farm for riding lessons. Colonel Mrs. Atkins took one gander at his bird's nest of a head, his shirttail, and his slouch and shuddered. Coke cleaned a lot of stalls that year, which wasn't all that bad. A person with a pitchfork gets respect of sorts, and anyway, the view from Dobbin's back was not that thrilling.

The year that he'd enrolled at Coldbrook, Coke's parents did a funny—not amusing—thing. They left his name out of the Social Register.

For all his sneering at the Social Register, he'd liked to see his name in there, underneath his parents' names, with all their clubs and addresses and phone numbers. He'd had a line all of his own. There was a heading: "Juniors," and then, like, "Coleman, III, at Short Hills Country Day," or whatever cruddy school had taken him that year.

He'd found out he wasn't in almost by chance. The Social Register beside the phone down in the den was still the one they'd gotten in the year before; that had his name in it. The new one, it was buried in a drawer, the second one of Mother's bedside table. He sometimes looked in there for pornographic novels or his mother's latest down. This time, instead of dirty books, there was the Social Register, *that* year's. Of course he'd opened it to *D,* and there he wasn't. It was really quite a shock.

The year before, his father'd told him he was disinherited, but Coke had figured he was sounding off. Old man with a horn. Like, let him eat somewhere with someone famous also in the place, and later on it's "Had a bite with Jack and Sally Lemmon down at La Grenouille—he's an old Exonian, you know—and he said something kinda good about the NRC. . . ." His father's friend would wait, his fingers on his own trombone, to offer his own score by

30

"Lenny" Bernstein (never-*steen*). To tell your kid that he was disinherited—well, that implied you had a lot of money, so his father'd like the sound of himself saying it. "You can't even *drink* like a gentleman," he'd said, as part of that same rant-and-rave. Coke had blown a lunch, or actually a *brunch,* up at the country club, beside (not *in*) the pool that Sunday noon. Of course someone had told his father. But leaving him out of the Social Register and not saying anything about it—that was different. It didn't have to do with money, or the future. It was personal, immediate: "You don't exist; you're over with," it seemed to say. Coke hadn't asked his parents what the story was. He almost didn't want to know, or think about it, even.

There was another thing he didn't like to think about, but had to. That was the future, his, and what he'd do in it. He realized that he was almost seventeen and also (almost) had no skills at all, none that had to do with self-sufficiency, survival. It wasn't only that he couldn't shoot a bow-and-arrow or a gun, or fight with any weapon but his sharp and dirty tongue. He also didn't know how you would plant a string bean, skin a rabbit, make some maple syrup, catch a fish. At Spring Lake Lodge, he didn't know the proper wood to get, or how to start a fire in the stove, or how to cook a meal or even clean up after one. In all his life, he'd never even *seen* a dish get washed, as far as he remembered. Nat gave them all a lesson that first night, thank God. "I want to show you how to do this when there's no hot water in the tap," he'd said. "Otherwise we'll have a plague of rumble-guts up here." Coke acted cool, but never paid such strict attention in his life. Score: skill one. At least a possible. Potential, anyway.

By after dinner, Nat had cheered up pretty well. Group 6 had gotten used to Spring Lake Lodge with quirky suddenness. One moment they were looking like a coin on edge: unstable, odd, impermanent; the next, they'd got their pads and sleeping bags spread neatly on the bunks, with packs stored underneath the lowers, and towels all hanging on the nails set in the bunk posts. Sara had a way of saying things, Nat noticed. "D'you think we ought to . . . la-la-la?" she'd ask. Or, "Who knows how (or where) to . . . cha-cha-cha?" She more or less persuaded them to follow her, by letting them go first.

When all the supper stuff was washed and put away, they sat around the outdoor fireplace and talked, looking at the tent of sticks, with bark and spruce chips piled inside, that Nat had made but not ignited.

"Don't you love to sit around a pile of sticks? I can look at one for hours." Marigold leaned forward, chin in hands. "They're so mysterious, romantic— you never see one stick exactly like another, either." She rolled her eyes at Nat. "Yes, that's a hint, beloved leader."

"Well, um," Nat said. "The thing is—maybe there's another group up here some place, and if they see the smoke, well, first thing, they'll be coming over here, and we won't have a secret place to, well, hang out in, anymore."

Sully asked about the stove, and Nat explained that it made much less smoke—provided that you opened up the draft, and burned dry wood, and had your cabin nestled in a grove of good tall spruces.

Sara said, "I love it that we have a secret place." She took a stick and made a tic-tac-toe board on the ground. "I noticed"—she talked a little softer—"that we sort of doubled back and . . . changed direction quite a bit when we were coming here," she said. She looked around at Nat and bit her lower lip, and then she smiled and asked, "Was that so other kids—like, other groups—would think that we were somewhere else, or something?"

Nat tried to keep his face the way it was. Maybe add a friendly little grin. "You've got a compass."

"Yeah," she said. "Is that all right? I didn't mean—you know—to be, like, wise, or anything."

"Sure," he said. "That's fine. I'm glad that you know how to use the thing."

"Somewhat," she said. "I'm not real good. I need a lot of practice."

"Right," said Nat. "Anyway, what I've been thinking is, tomorrow maybe we could spend the day on something that I'd sort of hoped to do before you even got here. That's build another room onto the Lodge." Every face lit up, without exception. "I think I've got a rough idea of how we ought to go about it. It'd only be a small one, just enough to have two sets of bunks in. . . ."

He got them all involved in planning what they'd do: how they'd cut right through the west-side wall and have a door where now there was a window. The window they could put back in the new addition, so there would be *some* light in it, and so on.

The Group became excited; another skill, thought Coke. Even Sara hadn't done this kind of thing before. And only Sara noticed that she'd never got an answer to her question: how come they had headed north to end up south of where they'd started from?

"You met Nathaniel Rittenhouse, I think," said Dr. Simms to Mrs. Ripple.

"I did," said Mrs. Ripple. "Slovenly. A callow youth, was my impression. I feel so sorry for the family." Mrs. Ripple was a stocky little woman, wearing good thick Carhart jeans, of russet brown, and boots from L.L. Bean. Her yellow oxford shirt, plain collar, also came from Bean's; she had her circle pin on it, as usual. Mrs. Ripple learned that there was such a

33

thing as standards at the age of reason—which was four, according to her mother—and she had then lived up to them for fifty-seven years. Even if she did say so.

"I might have seen him, too," said Homer Cone, trying to remember if he knew what "callow" meant. Homer Cone taught mathematics when he wasn't planning parties, which he loved. He was a round-headed man who could draw a close-to-perfect freehand circle on the blackboard. His favorite other sports were shooting pool and bowling. "Sort of pale, 'm I right? Looks like he crawled out from under a rock some place?"

Doctor said, "Not really, no. To give the devil his due—doo-wah—he looks like quite a healthy specimen. Of haystack." Doctor chuckled. "Oh, my, yes. Yes, indeed. The hair right down to here, the little scraggly beard." His fine white hands moved all around his face in flowing gestures. "He came up on the bus with them, and he was camping in the woods some place all summer. 'Summer—oh, Indian summer . . . ,' " Doctor sang.

"*I* never seen him, I can tell you that much," said the other person in the room. Leviticus Welch had already lost more teeth than Doctor and Mrs. Ripple and Homer Cone put together, although his age (now twenty-one) was only an eighth of theirs. "Sounds like a gah-damn hippie to me," he said. He was one of the fairly small number of people from around there who worked for the school (even the kitchen help came from out of state, "so's they could make those keeshes that the kids all eat") and the only one Doctor had ever taken a shine to, it seemed like. Before Leviticus worked for the school, he'd worked at other odd jobs and for the "Yew-nited States Army," but after a while he hadn't seen any more sense in being in the army, and sitting down in Georgia, than there'd be in working as a travel agent in a place like

34

Sing-Sing prison. As far as Levi Welch was concerned, working at Coldbrook was a job a man could do, like lots of other jobs. Those people didn't bother him, and he didn't bother them. They was all supposed to have been to college, and Jesus, some of them was smart, but lots of them didn't have any more sense than a three-year-old, and not to mention memory. Doctor liked to tell the kids that "Mr. Welch, here, is a real Maine guide," and Homer, there, could never seem to learn to say his name right: Lee-vie. What he'd always say was "Leevee."

"You can't judge a book by its cover, Levy," Homer Cone advised him now. "Do you believe the world is flat, deep down? I bet you do. Or *did* until you saw those pictures from the moon? 'm I right? Ah-ha—you see that, Doctor? I got him that time, didn't I?"

Levi Welch had had to smile; that was the truth. Homer Cone reached out and clapped him on the shoulder. He'd noticed Levi hated to be touched, so he would often dig him in the ribs, or throw an arm around his neck, or slap him on the ass good-naturedly.

Levi thought that Homer was a mite peculiar, maybe, but there was no getting away from the fact that he was smart—the way he'd almost read a fellow's mind. But, on the other hand, he had no sense, and didn't know a sugar maple from a beech, or care, and couldn't find his cock in his pants on a cloudy day. Yet he could shoot a .30-.30 rifle just about as good as anyone he'd ever seen, except for him when he was shooting good, and maybe old Miz Ripple there.

"Well, never mind all that," said Doctor. "The thing that matters is that Mrs. Ripple knows young Rittenhouse by sight, so there'll be no mistake. What he's agreed to do is take care of . . . things, on Monday morning, after which he'll 'disappear.'"

Doctor had a taste for intrigue and elaboration, little games and ironies. He smiled and looked from face to face.

"The children will be back of North Egg Mountain," he went on, "where all the boulders are, beside the brook. Levi knows the place, I'm sure." The young man nodded. He'd taken out his monster Bowie knife and laid it on his thigh. Levi's hat, which rested on the other knee, and shirt and pants, were all of patterned camouflage material. It made a person blend in anywhere. "I said good-bye to Rittenhouse," said Doctor. "He understood he's not to come back here. He knows the country. How will he proceed?"

Doctor, Homer Cone, and Mrs. Ripple looked at Levi Welch.

"You mean, which way'll he go?" Levi screwed his mouth around and, picking up his knife, he put the point of it against his head and scratched. A flake or two of dandruff fell to his shoulder, there to disappear. There was only one possible way for a fellow to go, if he had any sense at all, but there wasn't any point in saying that, or answering too quickly.

"Well, you could go *any* way, o' course," he said at last. "But if it was me, the chances are I'd head upstream a little ways to where that old bridge used to go, then cross on over, take that logging road up there along where Davis used to sugar—that's all good road in there—and come on out by Hilton Hollow, zip right up to town, and catch a bus to Mexico or somewheres."

"And would there be a place along that route where all of you could . . . meet him, easily enough?" asked Doctor. Homer Cone and Mrs. Ripple both leaned forward very slightly in their chairs.

"I've thought on that already," Levi Welch replied. "An' look . . ." He took the knife and ran the point of it along a pants leg, knee to thigh; a stout

36

green worsted pants leg, Homer Cone's. "Let's say this here's the stream, and here's where that old bridge was. . . ." He tapped the knife point high on Homer's thigh. "Well, right up here, you get some scrubby spruces"—he quick-like set the knife on Homer's fly—"with ledge rock right behind them. . . ." It climbed to Homer's belt. "Well, we could hunker down right here in them small spruces. . . ." The knife point started down again.

Homer cracked. He crossed the leg that had been nearest Levi Welch, which ruined Levi's landscape and made him pull the knife away. Homer tried to make it seem that he was merely shifting in his chair: he leaned on his left arm and got his weight on his left hip. But Levi knew he'd won, and gotten even for that dig about him thinking that the world was flat. And Homer Cone knew Levi knew. He wished he could have farted at him then, just the way a boy could in his eighth grade class. Bip Barkley was his name, and he could fart the way some other kids could burp, just when he wanted to. His family had moved to Homer's town that year from God-knows-where, and moved away the next, to Seekonk, or some place like that.

"I think that all sounds fine," said Mrs. Ripple. Levi Welch, in her opinion, was nothing but a skinny scum-squat, while Homer Cone was little better than a poop-splash. Mrs. Ripple never yet had said a dirty word. To use profanity, she'd learned, was to be childish and disgusting. Thinking was an adult occupation. "But let me understand about the children in Group Six." She shook her head. "Group Six. I always feel so sorry for the families. Nathaniel Rittenhouse will do as he's been . . . asked to do, we must presume. What then? From what you have described, I have a picture of a rather trackless section of the woods. I wouldn't want some coy-dogs finding them, or bobcats, either. And neither, I am sure,

37

would Doctor." She turned toward that small, antiseptic person. "Believe me, Doctor, I'm not trying to make waves . . . but it seems to me we have a duty to the families to see—"

" 'See, see, rider, see what you done done . . . ,' " sang Doctor suddenly. "Indeed, dear Mrs. Ripple," he went on, "you make a most important point. But one I have anticipated. My thought is this: that quick as Rittenhouse is . . . well, seen off, then Levi here, and Homer—and yourself—might go on back to camp with him. As we've been told, it isn't any way at all. Then Levi here could hike on back to school and get the Rover, and four-wheel-drive back up the logging road to where the old bridge was. It shouldn't take that long to load 'em in and zip right back to you-know-where. Drop 'em in the Letter Box, let's say, and bingo-Bridget, we're all done!" He beamed around the room. "All six of them are grounded, neatly and completely. Levi, here, can pick up all their gear on Tuesday. I think it's Goodwill's turn, way down in Albany, this time. 'Time after time, dah-dah-dah-dah that I'm . . . ,' " sang Doctor.

Mrs. Ripple nodded, clasped her hands together. She could hardly wait for Monday dawn. Good works had such a domino effect, she'd always noticed.

"I can't believe what time I went to bed last night," said Marigold at breakfast Sunday morning. "And now just look at me. I mean, *staying* up to watch the sun rise, that's one thing. *Getting* up to watch it is another." She put both fists up to her temples. "Quick. Someone get a cow. I think I want to *milk*. Oh, Coke"—she seized and shook his arm— "what's happening to me?"

The hike the day before had tired everybody out, and they had all slept well. Except for Nat and Sara, they were all completely lost, but none of them was scared. It seemed, that morning, that they'd known each other much, much longer than they had.

They started working shortly after sunup. Nat felt that they could risk the chain-saw noise, considering the hour, and the distance from the school, and the fact that there were two large hills between them. And he was fast. Marigold was right; he could have taught a class in Chain Saw I, or II, or III. By lunch the logs that made the walls were notched and dropped in place, and people had the spaces in between them mostly chinked with mud and moss, inside and out. That afternoon they got the window in and laid the roof, and took two double-decker bunks apart and re-assembled them.

But then they thought that it would make more sense to have one double-decker and a "studio couch" in each room. "Whew," said Coke, "at first I was afraid I'd have to sleep—heh-heh—with *them.*" He wrinkled up his nose and aimed it at the girls, who held their own and chorused retching sounds.

When the job was finally finished and admired, everyone was hot and smeared with spruce gum. Marigold asked Nat if he would take a walk with "our two mascots," so the women could avail themselves of what she called the "out-of-order hot tub."

"It's really cold," said Nat.

"Oh, that's all right," said Marigold, "we frontier women have a taste for hardship. It was forty-three below the day that I had baby Zeke, camped out beside the Snake. Worst part was I had to break the ice to do a wash right after."

They heard the "frontier women" squealing in the water, from just around the knob, behind the spruce grove, but when they made their way back to the Lodge, they were informed that the water was both "bracing" and "refreshing."

"Well, I guess it's our turn," Sully said.

"Oh, sure, go on," said Marigold, not moving. "*We* don't mind."

"Well, in that case . . . ," Coke undid his belt as he said that. Sara and Ludi laughed, but quick got up as well. Marigold stayed planted, sitting, smiling up at him.

"Go on," she said. Coke unbuttoned his top trouser button, took ahold the zipper tab.

Nat watched the duel. Their smiles were frozen now, no fun at all. Man and woman overboard.

"Go-*wan* yourself," he said to Marigold. "Go-*way*. What sort of boys do you think we are?" He made a face. "Momma don' 'low no voyeur-action here." Marigold got up and brushed her seat off; it was play again.

"That's sexist," Ludi said to Nat. "We're not voy*eurs;* we're voy*euses.* Feminine gender. We'll thank you to address us properly, henceforth."

"*I've* never been so offended in my life," said Sara.

"That's right. Enjoy your wallow, M.C.P.'s," said Marigold.

And away they went, tossing drops of water off their hair and sniffing.

That night, before they went to bed, Coke realized that he felt good enough to ask a little bit about the future. He had washed the supper dishes by himself, and now he knew that he could do it. Someone else could do it next time. Maybe he'd help, and maybe not.

"So what's the story with this place, exactly?" he began. They had a little fire going. He aimed the words at Nat. "I mean, I think I understand what's happening right now. We're meant to meet some other people, learn to get along with everyone, even if they're gross or perverts"—Marigold stuck out her tongue at him—"and maybe even do a job together." His eyes flicked up toward the Lodge again;

40

seemed to everyone the new addition really made a difference in the place. "But still," Coke said, "I'm not sure I get what happens when we go on back to school. I mean, I read about the classes and that stuff in the catalogue. But then there was this other crap—about the school's philosophy, and making 'men and women of the future,' whatever that means. And how you—that's us—are meant to set some goals with our advisor? Well, who's our advisor? You?"

"Um," said Nat. "I guess I am."

"Well, what sort of goals are they talking about? I mean, there was some stuff in there about Coldbrook giving us the tools to operate our lives. Like what? And who really decides what *my* goals are?"

"I'm not completely sure myself," Nat said. "But what I understand is Coldbrook promises your parents—or whoever pays the bills—that it'll teach you . . . attitudes that they—your parents and the school, that is—feel will get you ready for . . . the world." He shook his head and picked a pebble from the lug sole of his boot.

"Which could be college or anything, right?" said Sara.

"Yeah, I guess so," Nat replied. "I guess the deal is, Coldbrook says they're going to treat you like an adult and see that you turn into one."

"Wait a minute," Coke said. "What all this sounds like to me is that the school's already decided what my goals are, right? Christ, if there's one thing my old man *despises,* it's my attitude. That's just the word he uses, all the time."

"But doesn't every school believe it knows what's best for all the kids that go there?" Sully asked.

"Sure they do," said Marigold. "So first you try to find out what the story is, wherever you end up. That's what Coke is asking, right? What are they going to lay on us, down there? And I'd like to

41

know—*or what?* What happens if you don't? Or can't? Or won't?" She turned to Nat. "Up here, it's like you're grounded to begin with—so what else is there? Tell us, Great White Father. Give us your advisories."

"I'm just not sure," Nat said. "No one's told me what happens to people if they don't. Seems like they're pretty sure that everybody *will.*" Except for Group 6, of course.

"Well, maybe they *do,*" said Sara. "When I read about that goals business, and meeting my advisor every week, I kind of figured that was just to keep me up-to-date on where I stand." That didn't sound too bad to her at all.

"I can't wait for all that stuff to start," said Sully. He turned to Nat. "Doing this is neat, don't get me wrong. I love it here. But I'm like you, I think," he said to Sara. "I really want to get reports and all of that. I've got a lot to prove," he said to Coke.

"Yeah, I know but . . . ," Coke began. And then he shook his head. All that anyone could do was wait and see.

"Nat," said Ludi.

"Yes?" he said.

"I've been thinking of your signs up there." She nodded toward the Lodge.

"Well, what about them?"

"Is that the sort of stuff that you believe?"

"Sure," he said.

"I mean, deep-down—no shit?" She sounded serious.

"I do," Nat said.

"O.K.," said Ludi, and she smiled at him. "I think we've got the right advisor."

That made him nervous. He gave her one quick, semi-grateful smile and looked away.

* * *

Shortly after that, they went up to their bunks. The girls had chosen the new wing as their domain, even though the food and stove were elsewhere. Coke named their place "The Ladies Room."

Chapter Three

SULLY WASN'T anything like Coke: his hair had never been a problem, and neither had his shirttail coming out. Adults never hassled him about the way he looked at all; if anything, the opposite. In other words, they called him "cute," meaning (Sully learned) a lot of very strange and adult things by that unwelcome adjective. To them, he looked like Huckleberry Finn, brought up to date, with money—the sort of kid they'd like their kid to play with (for a change). The one that all the parents hoped they'd got, when they heard, "Well, now, it's a boy."

But other kids were not so quickly drawn to Sully. Though he was strong and agile, he wasn't big enough or rash enough to be an early choice at games. And his mother was pretty weird and he didn't have a father and teachers seemed to treat him better than you'd think they would, considering his grades. Especially Mr. McCorker, of course. And on top of that, Sully wasn't cool. He said a lot of jerky things and didn't seem to know some stuff concerning girls and you-know-what he should've. Kids told their mothers he was—like—well—"awful immature."

Sully was very much aware of all the reasons people had for thinking him a little nerd, or worse. He didn't like the way he looked or acted, either; his mother drove him up the wall, and his teachers made him feel like crawling in a hole somewhere. Except for Mr. McCorker, whom he felt like killing, any time in any way, no kidding. He considered himself the most uncool person in his class beyond a doubt, except for Fabian Fremont, who still had pajamas with feet on them, everybody said.

All this self-awareness meant that Sully had a lot of days on which he'd wake up in the morning, think of something in the past or future, and feel a miserable "Oh, no. . . ." Even if he didn't have a test or paper due, or coming back, even if he didn't say or do some idiotic thing that he'd get mocked for—there was *still* McCorker. Always with a smile, a punch, a "Hey, there, Artie-boy." And then that little wink. As if they had some secret, just the two of them. Which, in a way, they did.

Sully really never knew exactly what went on between his mother and McCorker. ("He *wouldn't* . . . ," people in his class would say.) Since his father'd split for Portugal, the day right after Sully's birthday party—he'd turned four—there'd been a lot of different men around his fourteenth floor apartment, just off Third. That was all for his sake, so his mother said: a boy should have a lot of men around. All his babysitters had been male, for instance, most of them in grad school at Columbia. Often they lived "out of town," and often by the time his mother came back home, the trains to where they lived had all stopped running. And so they'd stay the night, and still be "sitting" when he had his breakfast, wearing mid-sleeve robes with monograms, and thin gold chains around their necks, and calling Sully's mother "Ronni." Mr. McCorker got on board the year that Sully went into the Middle School, at twelve. Ronni came to Mother's Day and met McCorker, Sully's social studies teacher. The social study of that year was European history; McCorker told them lots of facts that weren't in the book

45

("Would you believe it? Louis Philippe had the longest penis in France, in his time!"), though not the day the mothers were in class. He and Sully's mother hit it off at once; he was six foot three and wore a double-breasted blazer with a Royal Norwegian Yacht Club emblem on it. Soon he was a semi-regular; squiring Sully's mother to the theater and the opera and often staying over, too, even though he lived six blocks away. When Sully's mother "had to see the sun" in Italy, three winters later, Mr. Mc-Corker volunteered to move right in for those two weeks "and batch it with the lad." Sully's mother said that that would be just wonderful.

Sully hated having him around. He drank a lot and smelled as if he took his bath in after-shave, or something. Most of what he talked about would have to do with sex—stories meant to be the truth about some movie stars, or other famous people, and the things they liked to do, supposedly. A lot of times he'd use some words that sounded really stupid (Sully thought) coming from a face the age of his, that smelled and looked the way that his did, and had that sort of almost-English accent. The first night he was there, he'd asked Sully to call him "Ian"—not in school, of course—"at home, when we're the two of us," but Sully told him that he wouldn't feel right doing that. He also didn't feel right having McCorker wander into his part of the apartment whenever he felt like it. Once he'd gotten out of the shower and walked into his room and found McCorker stretched out on his bed, looking at a magazine. So he started locking doors behind him, which he never used to do.

Things got worse between him and his mother after she got back. She said that he was "all closed off" and "secretive" with her, that she never knew what he was thinking anymore. When he came home, he went right to his room and locked the door; his grades got worse. "It's obvious he isn't *studying* in there," Sully's mother said, and rolled her eyes; she said she thought a little tutoring was called for. McCorker said he'd take the project on, and the two of them agreed on days and times. When Sully got the word, he just said no, he wasn't going to do it. She asked him what he meant by that, of course, and he said surely she must understand such plain and simple English. He added that McCorker was the biggest fag he'd ever met, and that he hated him. When she protested, he went on to say he hated *all* her friends, and school, and everything, in fact, about "this shitty city." He told her that her life was nothing but a fake and stupid (he was crying, then) and that he couldn't see how she could stand it, either. She said he couldn't speak to her that way, and he said if she didn't want to hear the truth, then he'd just cut out talking altogether. Slam. And so he did.

Weeks later, he found a fat envelope on his pillow. In it was an application to the Coldbrook Country School, as well as lots of literature about it. And a letter from his mother, hand-written on her heavy brown stationery, with a wide red felt-tipped pen.

The letter wasn't like his mother, really, but Sully was much too immature to know that kind of thing. It said that she'd been foolish and mistaken, too wrapped up in her own "problems" to see what she'd been doing to her son. She didn't blame him in the least, she said, for all the feelings that he had: about her friends, his school, New York, his life. *She* was the one who needed "tutoring," and she was going to seek it, soon, by joining in a Mother's Therapy Encounter Group. She knew she couldn't cancel out the past, she said, but maybe she could offer him a different kind of future. A service that she'd got in touch with had told her that the Coldbrook Country School would be "the perfect place" for someone with her son's potential. She could only hope that he'd forgive

47

her just enough to take a look at what the school was "all about" and, if he liked it, take a year there as a present from his "always loving Mom."

When she wrote the letter, she'd decided that calling Ian McCorker "a service" wasn't even a little white lie. As a matter of fact, she'd giggled when she wrote it.

Sully was so disarmed by her contrition and her offer that he not only agreed to go to Coldbrook, but also even spoke to her on Thursdays (when the cook did not come in) and did a little better in his school work.

But still he woke up with a groan on lots of days, and thought, "Oh, no. . . ." His mother's letter, and the fact that he would go to Coldbrook Country School, didn't mean the end of daily dread. Even when he *got* to Coldbrook, he was not exactly overconfident. In fact, it wasn't till the second morning, up at Spring Lake Lodge, that Sully, waking up, just felt plain good about the day ahead of him. It seemed as if his life was working out, at last; he felt he didn't have a thing to be afraid of.

The first thing Sully noticed, when he woke up Monday morning, was that Nat had gotten up already. His sleeping bag lay zipped a small ways down, as if he'd just snaked out of it. That Nat—he was a real outdoorsman, Sully thought: always getting up with the birds, rustling up some breakfast, starting on the chores.

Thinking simple thoughts like that made Sully feel just great. He looked around and saw that Coke was still asleep, and so he moved real carefully—you could say *stealthily,* almost—and carried clothes and boots so he could dress outside.

He put his stuff down by the outdoor fireplace. It was a great September day—sunshine with a little chill, a tiny taste of autumn in the air. Sully thought about a morning dip; maybe better not, the girls might wake up any time, and you could never tell what Marigold might say. It wasn't that he didn't like her—shoot, he really did, a lot, in fact. It was just that she was so . . . kind of *uninhibited* about everything. You could never tell what she might say, like, if she saw him naked. He'd never met a girl like Marigold. She was terrific. Sara, too. And Ludi. He'd never realized girls could be so easy.

Sully looked around for Nat and didn't see him. Maybe at the outhouse—with that neato rubber seat. Sully got his shorts on, sat down on a log to tie his boots. He'd wait for Nat to come on back before he hit the outhouse. He still could not get over Nat. It was hard to think he was a teacher, the same as "Ian" McCorker was a teacher. Sully couldn't imagine calling Nat "Mr. Rittenhouse," but he really respected him a lot; he didn't respect Mr. McCorker at all, but he'd never call him "Ian" in a million years. That seemed like a pretty fascinating and perceptive thought, to Sully.

Ten minutes later there was still no Nat. Sully got impatient and strolled down toward the outhouse. When he got quite close, he started in to whistle, and then, when he was almost there, he called "Yo, Nat!" Mr. O'Connell, a phys. ed. teacher at his former school—he'd say "Yo" before a person's name a lot, and he'd been a Marine.

He got no answer, though. Nat wasn't there. Sully took his time and used the outhouse; yessir, it had quite the view. When he got back, Nat still had not returned. He sat down on a log and hoped that someone else would wake up soon.

Sully had that "Oh, no . . . ." feeling once again.

When Nat got into bed the night before, he knew what he would have to do. He'd have to find out what was going on for sure, once and for all, if possible.

49

As soon as he thought that, he knew it *wasn't* possible. Things were much too bollixed up, unreal. It was the longest, widest, deepest mess he'd ever heard of, or imagined. He couldn't think what he was doing in a mess like this, although he also had to say he'd sort of seen it coming. Brought it on himself? Well, yes, you might say that. Parts of it, at least. But still. He still did not belong in stuff like this. He was simply *not at all* the type. He wasn't ready for this kind of thing, and probably he never would be. Face it: money, contracts, coming down on kids, weirdo little boarding schools—none of those would ever be his bag. And as far as being targeted himself . . . unthinkable! Right? Right. And to make sure of that (at least) all he had to do was be there at a certain place and keep his wits about him. Six o'clock should do it, which meant he'd have to wake up (no alarm) by one A.M. He set his mind for that and went to sleep.

He woke up more or less on schedule—a shade before, as it turned out. With his flashlight in his fist, he found his clothes and boots, some food, and his binoculars. He padded to the door, listening to Coke and Sully breathe, and quickly opened it and went outside. Of course there was no moon; there never is, except when you don't need it. When he'd tiptoed past the Lake and through the spruces for a little ways, he stopped to put his boots on.

"This is kind of fun," Nat thought. After that, he used his flashlight and made time. He was halfway there before he thought he should have left a note.

When Nat arrived at North Egg Mountain, it was close to six and daylight; the sun would soon be rising on a clear and lovely day. He found himself a spot below the knobby summit, looking down toward the boulders by the brook where Doctor thought he'd be attending to Group 6. At just about that time, in fact.

From where he sat and munched some fruit and nuts, with pocket lint, he could see both up and down the brook for quite a ways. It was a good fast trout brook; not wide, but it had some pockets that would hold good fish. He nodded to himself. A lovely brook, a lovely day. A guy felt lucky to be alive on a day like this, Nat thought.

Jesus Christ! Nat thought. No fucking *kidding*, Nat thought. He took out his binoculars.

Nat didn't know what he was looking for, but he was sure he hadn't seen it yet. Maybe he never would, which might be good. It was, well, *remotely* possible that all of this was an extraordinarily complicated and shamelessly expensive joke of . . . of his father's, say. A bit unlikely, since his father had never told him so much as an amusing limerick in twenty-two full years. More likely it was people he had known at college, that bunch that majored in . . . Experimental Living Theater, it was called. They could get, like, twenty credits, if they worked out something grand like this—"creating alternate realities," they called it. Avant-avant-*avant* stuff. Maybe what he had inside the bottle in his jacket pocket—not the pocket he had trail-mix in—was Southern Comfort, say, or Nyquil. Doctor'd said to put it in the breakfast drink, which was some tropi-flavored fruit punch stuff that Doctor said would mask the taste of anything. "Even Kool-Aid," Doctor said, and chuckled.

About an hour later, Nat saw something that looked very much like It. A good ways down the rocky slope, and to the left of where he was, three figures slithered, waddled, stumbled into view (respectively). They'd come around the shoulder of the mountain below a fairly steep rock face, and settled in amongst some scrubby little spruces there. The first of them was camouflaged from head to foot: jacket, pants, and hat; the second one was female,

51

and familiar; the third one was a second man, who wore a tweedy checkered driving cap atop a big round head.

All of them had deer rifles. The deer season didn't start for seventy-three more days, but they didn't have the look of people shooting out-of-season meat. And they didn't look like actors, either.

Nat sat and listened to his heart beat. There it was: the way that Coldbrook School took care of its loose ends. How they "fired" the "advisor" of Group Six.

He decided that he wouldn't call attention to himself.

If Nat had looked at things the way that Coke did, he might have come to think the reason he was sitting where he was was that he'd had lots of colds when he was little. You could really make a case for it.

Here's the way it went. When Nat was little, he had lots of colds, which meant he had to stay in bed a lot, which meant he learned to play a lot of different quiet games quite well, at quite an early age. Checkers, for example (English and Chinese), cribbage, and gin rummy; also backgammon, Parcheesi and Go Fish. He got better at throwing cards in a hat than anyone his age in the entire western world, possibly. On the days he went to school, and got to go to other children's houses, he'd play these games with them. And win and win and win.

He got to think that he was great at games. Games of so-called chance, and any game that you could play with cards. Nowadays, when someone gets a fixed idea like that, planted deep inside his head at quite an early age, it's known (among psychologists) as "imprinting." Once upon a time, it used to be "an awful dumb mistake."

For Nat was never all that good a gambler. So he

beat his mother, who played scatterbrained-maternal. The children in his grammar school were really pretty healthy, by and large, and never got to practice; by junior high, he had a reputation, and other children's interests turned to other adult games.

But when he got to boarding school, things became a great deal tougher. There were other kids around who must have had as many colds as he, or even more, and they played lots of other games—like bridge and many kinds of poker—that Nat had never learned before. He lost as well as won (money all the time, not jelly beans or gum), diversified still further, and pretty soon he noticed that he seldom went a day without some action of some sort. If there wasn't time to play a sit-down game, there always was a coin to flip, a deck of cards to cut, a next car to come by that had to be some kind or color you could bet on.

By the time that he enrolled at UVM, he'd become a bettor, rather than a player: football games and baseball games and basketball and hockey—mostly pro, but sometimes college. Nat did worse than ever, always struggled to get even. The problem was that he was really not a natural at gambling. No way, no how, and no sirree. What he was was what he looked like: a normal, friendly sort of guy, who liked the out-of-doors and hideouts, thought that happiness was possible for people, and felt the values of his father's world were pretty well messed up. But he also had this habit that he thought of as a part of him: "just the way I am." Some folks snored or skied or went to Ben and Jerry's every night or got the clap; he bet. And so he mostly owed a lot of twenty dollars here and fifty there.

Every year at college, till his last, his luck held out and somehow he'd escape before his creditors got ugly. Early on, his father used to help.

Twice a year, his father liked to give him one big

monstro check. Nat was meant to use those bucks to pay for everything in that semester: room and board, tuition, books, and all the other things a college person needed. His father thought that Nat would learn to "manage money" in this way, although, in fact, it never did work out. Nat always came to Dear Old Dad in pressing need of funds: unexpected car repairs, a little horror of a root canal, an overwhelming laundry and dry-cleaning crisis—even, once, the old lost-wallet-at-the-concert number. Mr. Rittenhouse was not amused or sympathetic; boys would *not* be boys, if he could help it. Finally, junior year, he said "the end."

"Your credit rating's down the tubes now, Junior," he explained. "And you are on your own. One check, twice a year, is absolutely it." The boy had bankers in his blood on both sides of the family; it couldn't be genetic.

So, spring of junior year, owing more or less a ton, he had to find a way out by himself. He didn't, as it happened; it found him.

No one, other than the players and their girl friends, ever went to college baseball games, including Nat. People who played baseball really well did not head north to college. Mostly, it was much too cold to play the game in any sort of comfort, not to mention watch it—and even if the day was warm, the watching could be painful. But on this Saturday in May, the sun was downright hot and the sky was absolutely cloudless, so a lot of people got the same idea at once: to go and get a tan out at the ball game. Nat, by merest chance, had parked himself beside one Stefan (Stuffy) Kinderhof, the grandson of a man who bought up most of Stowe in 1932, thinking he would raise some goats and maybe teach a little yodeling. The game dragged through eight boring innings. In the ninth, the Colgates scored six runs without a hit, to take a lead of seventeen to twelve.

Vermont at bat, one out; the Colgate pitcher bounced a curve ball in the dirt.

"Betcha a buck the next one is a strike," said Stefan.

"I'll take it," Nat replied. The pitcher put one in the backstop.

"Double or nothing on a ball," said Stefan, learning fast. The pitcher came back squarely down the middle.

Twelve times, Stuffy Kinderhof, the fat young millionaire from Stowe, had called the pitch; twelve times he was wrong. And then the game was over; called strike three. Nat had won $2048. That cleared his debts and got him halfway through his senior year.

And then disaster struck.

He'd gotten what would be his father's final check ("forever," Mr. Rittenhouse had said) and gone to pay his last tuition bill, a little nineteen-hundred-dollar item. When he reached the Bursar's window, he found he was acquainted with the clerk: a giant of a fellow who, he knew from escapades in town, was not opposed to making little wagers now and then. Nat put down his bill and, clipped to it, his nineteen-hundred-dollar check. In the other hand, he held a twenty-five-cent piece, his thumb beneath it in the "flip" position.

"How about it, Arnold?" he inquired. "Flip you for the whole half year, double-dip or nada."

"Why not?" said Arnold (Arn-the-Barn) Emfatico, the Bursar's clerk. "The state has got you covered."

"O.K., then. Call it for Montpelier," Nat replied.

"That's easy," Arnold said. "The Governor goes for tail."

Nat flipped the quarter in the air and caught it, then reversed it on the bill. The Governor was right.

"Lucky bastard," Arnold said. "I always go for head, myself. If I'd been betting, you'da won."

Nat sighed and pushed his bill and check across to Arnold. Then he started writing on a pad.

"What's that?" said Arn-the-Barn. "An IOU? Look, that won't work, Nathaniel. The state don't take no promises, just cash. This isn't me—but if you can't pay up, you'll go to work for all of us up here, like, making license plates at sixteen cents an hour."

"How much time can you give me?" mumbled Nat. He could see himself already, dressed in prison denim, turning out such highway ha-ha's as ICU2 and 4PLAY.

"It isn't me," said Arnold, once again. "It's the people of Vermont. They'll let you have a week. No, wait; that's bush." He put a finger to his temple, closed his eyes. "Make that the first of June, all right? I'll fix it up with them." He paused and dropped his eyes; he seemed to chew the inside of his mouth. "Say, by the way," he said, as if it just occurred to him. "It just occurred to me. . . . Do you know how to sail a boat? My uncle, see, he needs a guy. . . ."

Before Nat knew what he was doing, really, he'd said that he would fly to Lauderdale the first day of spring break. There he'd rent a sloop named Lucka-Lee and sail down to the Keys and pick up something—like, a present—that some people had for Arnold's uncle. All Nat had to do was anchor at this certain bay and then go fast asleep; the people then could come on board and hide the present on the boat some place. Then Nat would sail the boat on back to Lauderdale, hop a plane, and fly back up to Burlington, or home, or anywhere, for all that Arnold's uncle cared. Uncle, meanwhile—he would go and rent this boat, the Lucka-Lee, and have himself the fun of looking for the present. When he found it, he would be so happy that he'd probably tell Arn to give this nice guy Nat a present of his own—say, oh, three thousand bucks, less what Nat owed him for the air fare and the charter fee. Like nineteen hundred boffos, cash.

It sounded oh-so-simple, and it was. Everything worked perfectly, except that Arnold's uncle didn't find the present he expected. Instead, he found some pieces of a person who was shaped a lot like Cora's (Arnold's uncle's wife) first cousin, Harry. Harry had been Arnold's uncle's agent in the Keys.

All this put Arnold's uncle in so bad a mood that he told Arnold there would be "no presents for no Nats," and furthermore that he expected Nat to pay him back the plane fares and the charter fee. "He said he wasn't sending no Joe College on no holiday," said Arn. Which meant another thousand Nat now owed.

He went to see his father. It seemed as if it should have been a cinch. In less than eight short weeks was graduation; Nat would then become a Person, not a student anymore. As a Person, and an Adult, he would soon pick up a Job and start to make a lot of Money. He'd even offer an indenture to his father: bind himself to work for six months, say, at anything his father chose. His father'd get his money back with interest.

Mr. Rittenhouse said no-No-NO, quietly and firmly for a while, then ever louder as he heard the story A to Z. Nat was nothing but a ne'er-do-well, said Mr. R., a blot on the escutcheon and a dunderheaded twit. Let him find his own way out of this one, if he could. Mr. R. had had it up to here; he put his hand a foot above his smooth gray razor-cut.

Nat was hurt, and more than hurt: enraged. And more than angry: scared right down to the lug soles on his Dunhams.

He went on back to Arnold. Arnold, in a way, had got him into this (it seemed to him), or, anyway, the worst of it. Nat felt that with a little luck he could

57

have dodged Vermont, or maybe made a deal with it, whereby he'd send the state, like, three new tourists every year for, say, five years: people who would swear that Nat had talked them into going there instead of to the Catskills or the shore. But Arnold's uncle was a different matter. Arnold's uncle wasn't into cheese or maple syrup. "Do process" was his method, Arnold said: if a person didn't pay up, Arnold's uncle would proceed to do some things to him.

Nat got Arnold to agree to see his uncle, talk to him. He came back smiling.

"Uncle knows a job that you can get. He's gotten help for this same guy before. It pays a lot for hardly any work at all; when you get paid, you pay back uncle, *and* the state. What you gotta do is call this number, see?" Arnold handed Nat a slip of paper. "And tell the guy that you can help him ground Group Six. You got that? That you can help him ground Group Six."

"That I can help him ground Group Six," said Nat. "You sure that isn't 'grind'? Well, it sounds easy, anyway. But what does it mean?"

Arnold cleared his throat. "I'm not entirely certain as to all the details," he began, "but what I know is this guy is head of this . . . I guess they call it *boarding* school, out in the sticks somewhere. Where people send their kids that aren't shaping up so good, to get 'em to shape up? And they get rid of the kids for a while, in the bargain. Well, I guess it works out that some people would more or less like to get rid of their kid for good, if you know what I mean. You've heard they're working on this morning-after pill, for birth control? Well, this works just like that, except instead of *morning*-after, it's, like, sixteen years or so. And that's where you come in. Don't even take a week. And you won't—I promise—even have to teach a class, or any shit like that."

Nat was horrified. "You mean to say they *kill*

58

these kids? I can't believe it. That's grotesque! I couldn't do a thing like that."

Arnold shrugged. "If it isn't you, they'll just get someone else. From what my uncle tells me, stuff like that's been going on for years in different places. The good ones do a nice, quick painless job, he says, but some of them are terrible. They got these military ones, down South—like little West Points, or whatever; even kids that just go there for school are pretty well messed-up, my uncle says."

Nat shook his head. "I still don't know," he said.

"Three thousand bucks for one week's work," said Arn-the-Barn Emfatico. "Plus getting all my uncle off your back. Seems like a deal to me. When it comes to messin' up, my uncle *gives* the lessons."

Two days later, Nat sat down with Doctor in a restaurant near Keene.

"It helps to think of them as cars." Doctor pursed his lips and turned the knife upon his place mat, so that the sharp edge faced his plate. "Sometimes, a person gets a lemon, even if the name is Cadillac, or Rolls. And if you do, it doesn't seem to do a bit of good to take it back and back and . . . 'Back in the saddle again,' " sang Doctor softly. " 'Back where a friend is a friend . . .' It simply can't be fixed. No matter how many mechanics you hire, you've still got a lemon on your hands. The only thing to do is just get rid of it." Doctor nodded, speared a shrimp. "We take them off their hands, those lemons. Once and for all. Quick and neat and clean and utterly untraceable. We have these limestone faults quite near the school—these fissures on the surface of the planet. Some of them seem almost bottomless. Drop a lemon into one . . . we never hear it hit. We call that 'grounding,' Mr. Rittenhouse. A natural and wholesome term, I hope you will agree. At Coldbrook, we are definitely . . . organic." Doctor smiled. "You needn't be involved directly with the grounding part of the . . . curriculum. You'll offer the . . . prerequisite, let's say."

Nat didn't have much appetite for lunch, but he agreed, and folded Doctor's check inside his wallet. He'd be available on August thirtieth, he promised. Doctor said they'd iron out the details then. "We limit our Group Six to five," he said. "Some years there's a waiting list."

Nat didn't tell his father until Graduation Day; Nat's mother'd made him come to that. Of course his father'd hated all the costumes that the graduates put on—*some* graduates, that was, a fraction of the class. If there was any jackassery afoot, Nat would always be a part of it, it seemed to Mr. Rittenhouse.

"But dear, he's such a *sweet* boy," Mother Rittenhouse insisted (she who'd always knock for nine when gin was just a card away). Her husband made a sour face, and Nat, to try and cheer him up, told him that he had a job, at Coldbrook Country School.

Two days later, Nat was in a panic. He knew he couldn't kill a bunch of kids—or didn't *think* he could. He'd have to wait and see. Maybe he'd be doing them a kindness; maybe they were really, truly evil. (Yeah, just like Arnold's uncle might be, he remembered.) What he ought to do, he finally figured out, was sort of disappear till it was time. Stay away from places where a state (Vermont) might go, or where an uncle (Arnold's) might bump into you. He looked up Coldbrook on a map and saw how distant and remote it was: perfect for his purposes, uncle-less and state-free. Within a week he'd gone to work on building Spring Lake Lodge. He was lucky there was such a thing as aunts, and birthdays.

By seven in the morning (just when Levi Welch and Homer Cone and Mrs. Ripple took their places in the scrubby spruces) Sully couldn't stand it any more. Nat had not come back and no one else was up to talk to. Besides that, he was hungry. Whistling, he stomped into the woods, carrying a little axe of Nat's, a Hudson's Bay. He found a nice dead cherry tree that he could practice chopping on, not far from Spring Lake Lodge; that made some good loud chunking noises. When he brought an armload back to camp, he kept on standing straight and dropped it by the fireplace; one stick bounced up and hit the coffee pot and knocked it over. Perfect: good loud metal clanging sounds.

Within a minute, Sara staggered out, with Ludi close behind her, both still running fingers through their hair, and stretching. They smiled at Sully and the day and both of them looked beautiful, to him. He could see their nipples up against their t-shirts.

"Nat down at the outhouse?" Ludi asked. She must have done a bed check, going through the cabin.

"No," said Sully, "and I don't know where he is, exactly. When I woke up at six, he wasn't in his bunk. He's gone. Some place," he added.

Sara wrinkled up her brow. "That's kind of odd," she said. "You didn't hear him getting up, or anything?"

Sully shook his head.

Ludi shrugged and went down to the Lake. She knelt and cupped some water, put her face in it and rubbed, and made the sort of noise that seemed to her to go with mountain springs. She felt at home and not deserted, not at all.

"You think that I should wake up Coke?" asked Sully. Ludi heard the worry in his voice.

"Sure, I guess so," Sara said. "What do you think, Lu? You want to wake up Marigold? We better use the stove inside for breakfast, right?"

With Nat not there, the Group seemed slightly out of synch, but still the members managed nicely. Coke watched with great intensity while Sara scrambled eggs; he was amazed that such a complicated-looking bunch of food just happened, sort of, by itself. "There isn't anything but eggs in there?" he dared to ask.

Marigold began to set the floor. "Or shall we eat *al fresco*?" she inquired. Then she saw Coke's face and added, "No, don't say it, Coke." She took the plates and cups and flatware all outside. "You are *so* grotesque," she said, but smiled. Ludi mixed up breakfast drink; it was that tropi-fruit creation.

Once they'd all sat down to eat, they tried to work out what was going on.

"My guess is this is part of all the rest of it," said Coke. "I think it's kind of babyish. Step one, we walk our asses off, to prove that we can take it, I suppose. Step two, we show that we can get along, and even work together. Now we get step three: a crisis. How do we react without our leader? The thing that I resent is that they're playing games with me."

"Nat doesn't seem like he's the type for that," said Sara. "Though I agree it's just the sort of thing a school would think of doing."

"Well, if it is a test," said Sully, "what I think we ought to do is figure out the answer—what they'd want for us to do—and then do that. I mean, we might as well get off on the right foot with them, if we can."

Coke looked at Marigold and made a minor face. A kid was always meant to do exactly as "they" wanted. Another school, another "they" to tell him what was best for him. Fuck them.

Ludi said, "I doubt that it's a test. First of all, it *wouldn't* be like Nat to go along with that; I agree with Sara. And second of all, he didn't take his stuff. That means he's coming back." She looked around the Group. "I'm also pretty sure he's not up in a tree somewhere, just watching what we're doing."

Coke considered that. "I think you're right, but

still, it isn't Nat who makes the rules down there. He's just a teacher—and don't forget, he's new. I mean, if the school has this routine . . . this *game* they play with us, he has to go along with it, like anybody else. You got to admit—if he's not a part of this, it's pretty weird he didn't leave a note."

The more the situation sat on Coke, the more that he resented it. What made it worse was that the setup hadn't seemed so bad at first: the kids were sort of neat, and so was Nat. Everything was pretty cool. But now they'd started in again, trying to make it possible for him to be at fault.

"Yeah, that's true about the note," said Marigold, sounding more disgruntled than she felt. Marigold liked mystery, and complicated plots. As Coke had guessed, she mostly *didn't* give a shit, and so she didn't have a lot of expectations or involvement. Whatever happens, happens; no skin off her pantyhose. Life was like a movie with yourself in it, instead of Brooke Shields or someone, she thought. She loved to watch and see what she might do.

"But maybe," she went on, "he didn't think he'd be away this long. Maybe he's been, like, held up somewhere. Or maybe, God forbid, he's had an accident." She rolled her eyes: a woman close to terror.

"Well, anything *could* happen," Sara said, "but somehow I don't think . . ." She wanted to get down to cases, plan out their next move. There didn't seem to be a lot of sense in trying to guess what other people wanted them to do. They should just decide on what was right and do it. "Let's see," she said, "suppose we stayed up here today . . . ?"

When Nat's watch read just nine o'clock, there was a movement in the spruces down below; the person dressed in camouflage was standing up and moving. Very quietly.

He stayed up on the hillside, well above the brook,

63

and sidled noiselessly from left to right (seen from above) downstream. When he got above the place the boulders were, he started down the hill, staying well bent over, using trees and rocks for cover. Finally he reached the boulders, and he disappeared among them.

Three-four minutes later, there he was again, now walking tall and noisily along the stream bank, upstream from the boulders, coming back. When he got below the place the other two were hidden, he turned and shouted up the slope.

"There ain't no body there at all," yelled Levi Welch. "And there ain't no body *been* there, neither."

Homer Cone and Mrs. Ripple both stood up at that bad news, and looked on down at Levi.

"That just can't be," said Homer Cone. "Doctor *said* they'd be here. Are you sure there's no one there?"

"Jesus Christ," said Levi Welch. "Don't you think I know a dead kid when I see one?"

Mrs. Ripple shook her head in tiny shakes, just back and forth about ten times, as if she had a horse-fly on her nose and both hands full. She took a deep inhale. "Please!" she said. "I see no reason to be tasteless, Levi. There must be some mistake. Perhaps young Rittenhouse confused one mountain with another."

"But Doctor said *North* Egg, I know he did," said Cone, who sounded close to tears. "The boulders back of North Egg Mountain. He just as good as *promised* us." He pulled his rifle up and squeezed off five aimed shots across the brook, near where the boulders were. There'd been a muskrat basking in the sun back there, and Homer Cone's five bullets killed it lots more thoroughly than even its worst enemy would want it killed, you might say. Except that Homer Cone *was* its worst enemy, by far.

"Please! Mr. Cone! It isn't *Doctor's* fault," said Mrs. Ripple. All their voices carried clearly up the slope. "It's that young pip-squeak"—pecker-snicker, she thought—"Rittenhouse who's probably to blame. People of his sort are . . . careless in their speech. They don't give good directions. Levi. Search your mind. Do you know of any other boulders by a brook that would be near the base of any other mountain?"

"No, I don't," said Levi instantly. "And that's because there ain't none. Ask me what I think, I'd say that hippie just bamboozled you, but good." In times of stress and failure, Levi Welch fell back on us-and-them: them dang-fool city people.

"Well, I, for one, have better things to do than stand around this godforsaken mountain all day long," said Homer Cone. "Levy, you just zip on back to school like Doctor said, and get that Rover. Meanwhile, Mrs. Ripple and myself will start on down that road we spoke about, and you can come around and pick us up."

"Yes, *sir,*" said Levi, snapping hand to hat brim, regulation. "I'll do that right away, sir. Unless that dang transmission's acting up again. . . . " He quickly disappeared from view as he said that, so no one up the hill could see his wily smile. Homer Cone could use a little exercise, that big-mouthed, round-head lard-ass. Oh, he'd teach him a lesson, sure as Bob's your uncle.

Nat didn't move a muscle. Slowly, Homer Cone and Mrs. Ripple clambered down the slope and disappeared upstream. He figured that the road that Cone had mentioned was certainly the one that went across the stream where that old bridge had been, and then continued through a sugar bush. That's the way that he'd have gone, if he were going back to school by road. Levi Welch—Nat didn't know his name *or* Cone's *or* care—would cut back through the woods, the way they must have come. Nat figured he would wait till ten o'clock before *he* moved—another forty minutes. By then, he figured, he could loop around the school and scoot on back to Spring Lake Lodge, and never be in range of any of those rifles. The execution of the muskrat, more than anything, had made him see (once and for all) that this . . . this "happening" was not a joke, some play, but deadly serious. People who were not Viet Cong or Nazis or Iranians—or even Arnold's uncle—were not just out to kill him, they were *anxious* to. And the same thing with Group Six. He'd talked to Mrs. Ripple at the school. He could see she was a lady, a woman who had standards. Sure. A woman who would never shoot a person without reason. A woman who, if she were just to wound her prey, would track it for as long as need be, so she could make the kill. So as to end its suffering, of course.

Coldbrook was some kind of little school, Nat thought. But Arn had said that there'd been lots of Coldbrook-sorts-of-schools, for years and years and years. "Whatever happened to so-and-so?" How many times had someone said that to a friend? And gotten back the answer, "Oh, she or he just went away to school and I lost track of her or him." Oh, yeah. Mmm-hmmm. You bet.

The world was getting scarier by leaps and bounds. At ten A.M., he leaped and bounded off toward Spring Lake Lodge. He'd get there easily by two; he hoped the kids had kept their cool.

At more or less eleven-thirty in the morning, Coke got out his bottle of white rum. Group Six had finished breakfast long before, and talked about what was or was not happening to them till everyone was fed up with the subject. What they'd come to, in the end, was that they'd wait for Nat till noon, and if he wasn't back by then, they'd get together and decide on something. As noon approached, and Nat had not appeared, Coke decided it was party time.

He hadn't had a lot to do all morning. Sara and Sully spent the time by getting wood: smaller pieces that they sawed to stove length and stacked back in the corner of the Lodge. Marigold was putting up her hair in lots of skinny braids, sitting by the pond in just a halter, with her shorts rolled up and down for maximum exposure. Ludi, leaning on a tree nearby, was playing music on a penny-whistle: clear notes and liquid melodies that seemed to match the morning. Every other tune or so, Marigold would sing along, not words, just singing; she had a light and childlike high soprano, a surprise.

Coke lit up a Camel in the Lodge and came out with the bottle swinging in one hand: Cruzan Light, the Virgin Islands' best. He brought some tropi-fruit drink mix, as well, to take the curse off of the rum; he had no cubes, but there was lots of ice-cold water.

Marigold twitched her nose and turned. "Well, well," she said, "what have we here? Vice time in the Rockies? Adirondack high?" She switched into a city accent. "I'm sorry, sir. I'll have to ask you for some proof."

Coke grinned and lifted up the bottle, peered down at the label. "Eighty?" he replied. "That proof enough? P'raps mamselle will join me? An aperitif?" He ogled her long legs. "Heh-heh. I think I'll have a panter's punch."

"What have you got to mix it with?" she asked. "Oh—tropi-fruit. Of course. That'll cover anything. O.K., big boy. But not too strong now, heah?"

"Ludi?" Coke inquired, holding up the bottle. "Name your poison. Just so long as it's rum punch."

She smiled. "No, thanks. Liquor puts me to sleep, and I'm not ready yet." Coke rolled his eyes; she laughed. "Or maybe you're just trying to shut me up.

Is it time for me to stop?" She raised her eyebrows, holding up the little flute.

"Hell, no," said Marigold. "It's really neat. You're the entertainment, Lu." She took the tin cup Coke held out to her. "What a blast." She lighted up a Camel, made a face. "God, these are strong," she said.

Sully and Sara joined them.

"Be my guest," said Coke, with a wave toward his little bar. He thought he sounded like his father. Sara poured some punch into a cup. Sully did the same, then poured a little rum on top of it; he was relieved to see he wasn't being watched by anyone.

"Now this," said Coke, "is camping. Prosit." He held his cup toward each one of the others and smiled his foxy smile. Having a drink—having people for a drink—was making him feel powerful, in charge of life again. Ludi'd stopped the music and sat listening.

"Hoo-wee," said Marigold, through purple lips. "I'm getting bombed already." She put her cup up to her ear and crossed her eyes.

"Well, what say you?" Coke began. It was a joke, a mock, to use his father's lines, but also they were easy, had a certain ring to them. "It's almost noon and still no Nat. Tennis, anyone? Who would like the floor, or should I say the dirt, the ground, the surface of the earth?"

"*I* vote we should stay," said Ludi right away. "I think it's beautiful up here, and we have food for two more days at least. And besides, I'm sure that Nat is coming back. Did I say that before?"

"Well," said Sully. "Nothing against Nat, but I think we ought to go back." Drinking a drink was making him feel very responsible. "The way I look at it is—we have to be at school sooner or later anyway. And if it is part of our orientation, we'll certainly look good for being so totally self-sufficient and all.

68

That's thanks to Sara, of course, who can find the way back, she says. She *thinks*." He made a little smile in her direction; everyone was listening. "And if it isn't what we're meant to do, we can always come back here. Either way, we're in good shape. That way." He gave a small, self-conscious laugh.

"O.K.," said Coke. He took a stick and made two scratches on the ground—one on either side of the bottle. "That's one for staying, one for going." He looked at Marigold. "What do you say, legs?"

"*Moi?*" said Marigold. She put a finger to her breastbone. "I guess that *je* don't give a truffle either way. I like it fine up here, but just like Sully says, we can't stay here forever." Sully smiled. It was the first time he'd ever heard anyone say "just like Sully says" in his entire life. But Marigold then shook her head and scowled and waved a hand at all decisions. "Anything the rest of you decide is . . . okey-doke with me." She giggled. "What do you think, Sare?"

"Oh, gosh," said Sara. "I can see what Ludi's saying. I hate the thought of going down before we have to—just when we're getting used to it up here. And we've got the Lodge . . . I don't know, so *nice* and everything. I'm pretty sure that Nat is coming back, all right, but I also have the feeling that he's been . . . I don't know, *held up* somehow. His not leaving a note kind of makes me positive he meant to come straight back, you know? From wherever he went to. Before we'd get upset, or anything. I guess I'm pretty much for going back and seeing what the story is, at least."

"And I say make them come and get us," snickered Coke. "To hell with them. And that"—he made two other scratch marks on the ground, then raised and drained his cup—"means that we're deadlocked still: two to two, and one 'don't care.' I guess it's up to you, Godzilla," he said to Marigold.

"Poo," she said. "To hell with that. I told you I

69

don't give a shit. I don't. I won't play Miz Almighty Mothuh, Coke."

"Well, in that case," Sara said, "I guess *I'm* going to go. It doesn't mean that other people have to, though I'd love it if we stuck together. It seems to me it's worth it to find out."

"Hmmm," said Coke. "But if any of us stayed here, we'd be . . . let's face it, *lost.* I don't know where the fuck we are." He turned to Ludi. "Do you?"

"No," she said. "But I'm pretty sure I could find my way to *somewhere.*" She laughed. "I mean, some place with a name—like a road or someone's house or something. But if Sara and Sully are going for sure, then I will, too. I think Sara's right—we ought to stick together. The other thing I think we ought to do is leave a note for Nat."

"That's a *good* idea," said Marigold. She made adjustments in her shorts. "I'm going, too. 'Naughty Nora nibbed a note to Nat on nutty Nina's natty napery.' Say that three times fast and you can stay here by yourself," she said to Coke.

"Fuck that," said Coke. "You think I'd leave you three girls in the hands of a sex maniac like Sully?" Sully grinned delightedly. "One for all and all for one, and won't a ten-mile hike be fun?" He turned his tin cup upside down, meaning he had finished drinking. What he felt was just a little buzzed and very fond of all the people in his group. Especially Marigold. "Wherever she goest-eth, I goeth, too." He said that to himself.

Ludi wrote the note they left, and nailed it on the cabin door:

Monday, 1 P.M.

Dear Nat,

We couldn't figure why you left or where you went to, so we've headed back to school to try to solve the mystery. Sara knows the way all right; we promise not to get lost.

Hope to see you soon. Wish you were here.

Love,
Group 6

When Nat huffed up to the Lodge and saw the note, and read it, his watch said 2:19.

"Oh, Jeezum," he said loudly. He closed his eyes and straightened up, his fists clenched by his sides. He opened his eyes and blinked, and swallowed hard. He read the note a second time.

"Oh, *Jeez*um," he repeated, and turned and trotted through the spruces, heading back toward Coldbrook Country School.

Chapter Four

THE HIKE from Spring Lake Lodge to Coldbrook Country School should take about four hours. That's if you know the way, and if you don't stop now and then for this and that, and if you aren't acting slightly looped, and if you really want to get there in the first place. Or if, in other words, you aren't going with Group 6.

Sara saw, before they'd gone a quarter of a mile, that even though she was presumed to know the way to Coldbrook Country School, and meant to lead them to it, she was not in any other way to be the "leader." Marigold took charge of rests, for instance.

She'd learned somewhere—perhaps from calling cabs in New York City—to whistle with two fingers in her mouth: a piercing, sharp, authoritative sound. "O.K.," she'd say, having gotten their attention, "this is a mandatory rest stop. Everybody just relax, and nobody gets hurt; comfort stations left and right; smoke 'em if you got 'em." Rests would last from five to fifteen minutes, depending on the type and urgency of nature's calls, and whether anyone had taken off her boots (perchance) to paddle in a nearby stream.

Sully liked to play the mountain goat, galumphing down a slope full-tilt, grabbing little trees to slow himself sometimes, but mostly giving in to gravity. That meant he'd get ahead of them, and maybe angle off the line that Sara knew—or thought she knew—was best for them to take. If that happened, then the rest of them would have to stop and call for him and wait while he toiled back to where they were. After three such episodes, he read their eyes and cut it out.

Once, when they were halfway there, they came upon a house. It was the sort of posh, remote vacation home that's headed by the words "Executive Retreat" in real estate advertisements. The place was locked and vacant, the one house on a private road they later followed for a mile before it curved off in a way they didn't want to go. All of them looked in the windows. It was a huge, chalet-type building, with three different sundecks and a lot of sliding doors by Thermopane. It was the sort of place their parents would have felt at home in right away, and also their parents' children. Except for the fact that it didn't have connections to the outside world. Ludi noticed that: no wires running out of it; and Sara pointed out the row of gas tanks in the back.

"They probably use gas for cooking and hot water and the fridge," she said. "There's probably a gasoline generator in that little addition there. They can be real noisy, if they aren't soundproofed right; we used to have one up in Maine. And, wow, look at that woodshed. They must heat the whole place with those Jotuls we saw."

"Yodels?" said Sully. "What do you mean?" And Sara smiled and gave him more or less what every boy should know, foreign-airtight-woodstove-wise.

By the time they reached the school, then, it was after six o'clock. They'd come in from the back, instead of from the road side, and when they saw that they were really there, at last, some of them discovered they felt . . . strange. A funny kind of shy.

"You think we ought to march right in?" asked Marigold. She'd taken off her pack and then unzipped it on the side. She was looking for her hair-brush, but not in any great big tearing hurry.

"Yeah, I can just see it," said Coke sourly. "I go, 'Hi! I'm Coke DeCoursey. Hope you're glad to see me back.' And they go, 'Coke DeCoursey? From Group Six? Oh, man, you're meant to still be in the hills the next two days. What's the matter with you anyway? Leader leave you by your lonesome, Cokie-Wokie? Oh, brother, where do they get you kids from anyway?' I can just see it. They always ask you what's the matter with you, but just try to tell them and see what happens: you're a wise guy. That'd be strike one on us. And another school sinks slowly in the west." The rum he'd drunk had left Coke feeling slightly headachy, and now, on top of that, he felt the rumble-worms of nervousness go curling through his stomach.

Sara laughed. "Oh, *Coke!*" she said, and took a huge, slow-motion, roundhouse swing at him, which ended with a gentle fist-pat on his upper arm. "You're such a *pessimist.* I swear. Look. If it'll make you feel any better, I'll go in first and just sort of check it out. They've got enough new kids floating around so that no one'll know who's who or what's what, yet. I'll find out where we're supposed to be, and then come back and tell the rest of you, O.K.? If the worse comes to the absolute worst, and we're not supposed to be here, we can just go part-way back tonight, and camp."

Sully nodded. That seemed good to him. Sara looked completely loose. And smart, and strong, and real good-looking. He still remembered how she'd looked that morning, with her fingers raking back her hair, and her smooth brown arms, and her nipples showing up against her t-shirt. She was just one of those people, it seemed to him, who always knew both what to do and how to do it. In some ways, that was more like a guy than a girl, he thought. His mother, for instance, had a lot of opinions on everything and a lot of dumb ideas, but she didn't know how to do that much. Sara didn't act like a dumb, bossy woman. But she sure had a girl's body, and a girl's eyes, the way she looked at you. It was different than any way a guy ever looked at you. Her look kind of hit you in a different place, so that you felt a little neat . . . "connection" with her. Not anything exactly physical, like touching or feeling would be, but just a sort of nice awareness, you might say. It was nice to look back and forth with a girl like Sara.

Ludi didn't nod. She was feeling really funny, and had no idea just what the feeling meant, except that it was rotten. "I'll walk with you a little ways," she said to Sara, when she saw that everyone agreed with Sara's plan. They left the other three, and both their packs, inside the woods, and started out across the Coldbrook fields.

"I know that this is going to sound ridiculous," said Ludi, "but I want you to promise me you'll be real careful, Sare. Like, if anybody's asks you who you are, make up a name, all right? Tell them you're Mary Mason, or something. And if anything seems the least bit strange—just not the way it should be— you get out of there toot sweet, O.K.? You promise?"

Sara stopped and turned toward Ludi, and she saw that Ludi's huge dark eyes were full of tears. "Hey, what's the matter, Lu?" she said. "I'm just going into our school."

Ludi shook her head, and put a hand on Sara's arm, and twitched her lips into a smile. "I know," she said. "I'm being silly. I get these feelings sometimes, I don't know. Just promise me, O.K.? Then I'll feel better, anyway. And it never hurts to be careful."

"Sure," said Sara, and she put her hand on Ludi's hand, but she didn't pat it, the way she would a kid's. Ludi was short and slender and looked young, but she seemed mature to Sara. Like a woman friend might be. "Sure," she said again. "And I'll be back inside half an hour, I imagine. I'll be O.K., Lu."

And she smiled and turned away and walked off quickly toward the school. She thought she'd managed to conceal the fears *she* felt, just the way her father always wanted her to do.

A bunch of things that Sara did were what her father wanted her to do. And certain of her tendencies and talents seemed, to other people, lots like his. "You get that from your father," was her mother's line, delivered with a smile, as if it was a compliment. Sara'd thought it *was* a compliment, the ultimate, for years. She was, at least, her father's girl—if not her father's boy that he'd expected her to be.

Dr. Warren Worcester Winfrey never thought he'd have a girl; he had planned to name his first boy Samuel, after his father-in-law, a magnanimous tip of the hat to an old two-aspirin country doctor who made house calls, for God's sake. He figured Sara was an accident. Also Martha, Ruth, and Stephanie, his next three children. When the fifth one was a boy, he took no chances: Warren Worcester Winfrey, II. The lad was eight years old and stuttered—the second condition as temporary as the first, Dr. Winfrey told his wife, Natalie. "The boy will grow out of it," he said. Which was all there was to it, as far as he was concerned.

Dr. Winfrey was a surgeon, and he charged a lot of money for his operations. He was a moderately dexterous mechanic who thought of himself as a genius, and more than a genius, a saint. Sort of an athletic and suburban Albert Schweitzer, with a decent haircut. He encouraged his patients, and their families, and *his* family to think the same of him.

"I took your [your husband's, Mr. Rothman's] heart in my left hand, and shut my eyes for just a millisecond. And then I opened them and *knew what I would have to try to do.*"

So did the first-year surgical resident, standing just behind him, slightly to the left (who never closed her eyes at all), but Dr. Winfrey never mentioned that. He never talked to the resident, either, after the first day when he told her to be sure to step well back and to one side, whenever it seemed likely she would faint.

"The surgeon is the captain of the team," he'd said to Sara once. "He has to be a leader and be instantly obeyed. I'm just not sure that a woman can command that kind of respect. Or should want it, for that matter. Other kinds of respect, certainly. Of course. Unquestionably. But these are *life and death* decisions." He'd nodded; Sara'd nodded. She was going to be a pediatrician, and her father could operate on any of her patients who needed an operation. She wouldn't care. Actually, it would be a sort of a relief. That's what she'd thought when she was twelve, at least.

Her father *was* an athlete. "They get all that from him," her mother said, when speaking of her children's skiing trophies, or their tennis skills, or the way that they could do the butterfly. Dr. Winfrey knew the girls were accidents—but just their girlness, their sex, not their existence or their tastes. He was meant to have a lot of children; he had known that all along. And children who took after him, by being strong and smart and skillful. And revered, of course, in time. Sara was his oldest, so he'd really learned the father part while practicing on her and having her respond to him. He loved it when they'd whiz on down a mountain and people at the bottom would mistake her for a boy. He also liked to hear his friends insist that "she's a Winfrey, that's for sure," and he made sure she knew exactly what that meant and took a lot of pride in it herself.

"We Winfreys don't expect to win for free," he told her. "You have to pay the price." And then he laughed, for he had made a little joke.

Dr. Winfrey's life ran on a schedule. Every day, and every week, and every month was sectioned into blocks of time in which specific worthwhile things were done, and certain goals were aimed at and attained. So other, higher goals could then be set. Of course his children had the same *modus vivendi,* as Sara quickly came to understand. Being on the safety patrol was all right for now, but elections in the homeroom are next month, eh, what? Can a person get elected captain of a Color Team and also be class president? Had anyone ever been? How many years in a row? He had always liked the maths and sciences the most, but English had been one of his best subjects, too. He was sure that Sara, if she really worked, could get her English up there with the rest of her grades. How about some book reports for extra credit? Maybe they'd still be glad to do that, if she asked.

He never missed a swim meet or a tennis match. When he learned that weights are used for training swimmers nowadays, he'd bought her school a Universal Gym, and when he'd read about the light-weight racing suits that German swimmers wore, he'd sent her swim-club coach a set. The coach, a woman, wouldn't put them on her girls; you could see right through them, she maintained. "For gosh sakes," Dr. Winfrey said to Sara. "Can't you swimmers make her change her mind? Everybody's got a body, what's the big deal? And we're talking maybe half a second every fifty meters, after all. . . ."

Sara's father had once written a book about being a surgeon, and about the various duels he'd fought with the Grim Reaper over the very nearly lifeless bodies of a lot of very famous people ("I always called him 'Corky.' "), and their cooks and cleaning women, too. "Disease does not discriminate," he'd written, "but neither does my steel. It speaks the same sharp words to everyone: cut, slice, excise, section, scarify. Rotarians or Rastafarians," he wrote, "morbid tissue always smells the same." Dr. Winfrey had once rented a villa near Montego Bay.

In spite of Dr. Winfrey, or because of him, Sara always had done well at school: in sports, in grades, in popularity. She'd been made to eat (and like) nutritious foods since infancy and, too, she exercised a lot, and both her parents had good features and straight spines. She was used to doing just exactly what "they" told her, and not sulking about it either. Learning wasn't hard for her to do, especially in math and science. Successful, she was happy, friendly; smooth of skin, bright of eye, wide of mouth, and round of hip and breast, if *never* heavy. Though every now and then she wished she were a boy, she'd come to womanhood with no regrets, knowing she was near the top of what she had been born, so far. It never struck her that she didn't have close friends, or crushes; everybody seemed to like her fine—as you could tell from all the presidents and captains she'd been. Her only major weakness was: she wasn't any good at writing.

Oh, she could write reports, all right—like on "The Economy of Brazil" or "The Voyages of Discovery." And she could also do a decent job on "Conservative Elements in the U.S. Constitution," or "Good Vs. Evil in the *Red Badge of Courage*." The writing that she couldn't do was what they called "free writing" at her school: stories and poems. "Journeys to the worlds inside yourselves," as Mrs. Martin (English 10) would put it.

She dreaded those assignments all through seventh, eighth, and ninth; the very words "free writing" drenched her palms. She couldn't think of anything, and if she did, she couldn't make it come out sounding any good. Everything she did, no matter what her subject, came out seeming like her sister Ruth had written it, or someone stupider than Ruth, in her same grade.

But in the summer just before her tenth-grade year, she'd stumbled on her savior, one Terence Arthur Updike. Not that she ever met the guy. She'd like to meet him now, and *kill* him. But where she found his work was in the college library, in her hometown. She liked to go there when she felt like being by herself, away from all the other kids at home, away from all the items on her schedule. All she'd do was poke around and look at things: old magazines and picture books of different kinds; there were just rows and rows and rows of open stacks.

On this one day, the twenty-eighth of August, she wandered into one big section where she'd never been before. In it there were hundreds, even thousands, of slim bound volumes, all nine-by-twelve in size, all typewritten instead of printed, and almost all of them by writers never to be known as writers, other than this once. What she'd found were stacks of senior theses, written by whoever'd been an English major at the college, lo these past one hundred years.

Terence Arthur Updike '54 had *loved* free writing. He wasn't awfully good at it; in fact, the only story that he ever sold (he kept on "writing" five years after college) was a "little thing" he'd sent to *Peek* (that was the porno mag, and not the self-awareness monthly by the name of *Peak*, but if a friend of Terence Arthur's just assumed the opposite, he didn't get corrected). The piece, for which he got a fifty-dollar check, was actually a dream he'd had about a college guy whose Saab broke down on some back road in Georgia. . . . His senior thesis wasn't much like that, though. It was called *Ten Stories,* which is what it sort of was: ten odd, uneven stories he had (mostly) written, most of them about the pressures on young people, poor and black included.

Sara found she could take parts of Updike's stories and, changing just a word or two (like "fuchsia" into "purple"), make them quite presentable as her "free writing." Mrs. Martin mostly gave them 83, or 86, or sometimes 92, and often added words like "Nice," "Perceptive," "Taut," or even "Stunning!" So everything went well until the day in May when Sara handed in a story fragment that began, "Imagine, if you will, the letter 'A,' of which the right-hand leg becomes the road from Littleton to Crawford's Corners. . . ." The place names were her own, the rest was as she'd found it. How was she to know that Terence Arthur Updike was a lousy plagiarist—and that Mrs. Martin was a Victor Hugo freak?

Sara's world came down around her ears that May. At school, the operative words were "heavy disappointment," though what a lot of teachers really felt was "hatred." Their best girl, the girl who'd always best personified the strengths and values of the school (so like their own!) had cheated; if they couldn't trust a Sara Slayman Winfrey, well then, who could they *ever* trust?

The Discipline Committee met and said she could not come back into school that year, although she could return to take her finals *after* school—a special set, of course, prepared by each department chairman and proctored by the Dean of Students, in the flesh. And if she really wanted to, she *could* (because—and just because—she'd always been so good before) return the following September. On probation, naturally. For all the first semester. A person on probation couldn't represent the school in sports, or hold an office on the Student Council. And she would certainly be watched, for reasons she could surely understand. A hawk could take a watching lesson from a teacher who'd been personally (and professionally) "let down."

But anything her teachers may have felt, Sara's father felt as well, and multiplied by fifty thousand, say. The family had been disgraced ("*La famille, c'est moi,*" the doctor might have said). He'd been repaid for all those skiing trips, and Universal Gyms, and unworn racing suits—by One Unconscionable Crime.

Forgiveness? Forget it!

Forget it? Never in this life!

There could be no question of Sara returning to her old school. Her life was ruined. Coldbrook was the only answer, Dr. Winfrey realized. Perhaps, he told his wife, they'd have another child. Another boy, he thought.

When Sara grabbed the door of Foote Hall and opened it, everyone at Coldbrook Country School was eating supper. Except, that is, for the kitchen staff (who ate early), one or two girls (on diets), and Homer Cone and Mrs. Ripple, who weren't anywhere around.

Levi Welch had found, as he had feared, that the Land Rover's transmission *was* "actin' up just turrible." And he had had to work on it all day, right up to six o'clock. *Then* he'd gotten in and started it right up and sailed along the indicated roads till he met Homer Cone and Mrs. Ripple, who had walked and stopped and stamped and stopped and limped and stopped for fifteen miles, since nine o'clock that morning—but still had eight more miles to go before they'd get to school. To say that they were out-of-sorts would be ridiculous—"killing mad" was closer, but still mild. Levi gave them lots of earnest shakings of the head—his country-stupid act; "just tryin' to do what Doctor said"—and short of giving him the SAT's, they couldn't prove that he was smarter than he seemed. Knowing they were late for supper, they made him drive them all the way to Boynton Falls, where they had three Manhattans each and Brook Trout Amandine at a restaurant where Levi's sister Patsy was a waitress, so he wouldn't eat there. They made a lot of substitutions in their orders and, after much discussion, stuffed the tip inside the slender tulip glass that Homer's Neapolitan had come in. "That'll fix him," Homer Cone opined.

Foote Hall, the building Sara entered, was where the offices and classrooms were and so, right there in front of her when she came in, was one whole huge official wall of notices, thumbtacked where the students learned to find them.

"Check your locker number" said a printed sign, in big red magic-markered letters. Sara went and did so, without thinking: "Westwood, Madie; White, Armitage; Wolsey, Caitlin; Woodson, Jeffrey," she read. That was odd; somebody goofed. They didn't have her name. So, just for fun, she looked for "Sullivan" (she didn't know his real first name) and then "DeCoursey, Coke" (or something). No Sullivans and no DeCourseys. And no "Locke, Louise," either. She couldn't look up Marigold, because Marigold had flatly said she wasn't going to use that other name of hers and so there wasn't any point in telling it to them. But still . . . She scratched her head, and then she had a thought. Probably the new kids weren't even given lockers yet. Let's see, she thought, that girl she'd sat with on the bus coming up—what was *her* name? Everybody on the bus was new. Heron, was it? Guerin? No, Ferron, that was it. Molly Ferron. She ran her finger down the names: Farley, Fellows, Fields . . . ah ha. No Ferron either. But then her eyes strayed *up* the list a little ways, and there was "Fairen, Mary." Was Molly short for Mary? She really wasn't sure. She didn't know the name of anybody else.

Well, she thought, what else is there up here? Yay, look: a list of all the teachers at the school, and where they lived (with phone numbers), and subjects they might teach. But . . . this was *really* funny: no Nat Rittenhouse at all.

Well, hmmm, she thought. Another heading: "Room assignments." And another list. Once again, she couldn't find her name, or Sully's, or Ludi's, or Coke's. This is really getting weird, she thought.

"Hi!" A woman's voice from down the hall.

Sara turned and stared. It was a rather heavy girl in tailored jeans, with long red hair, a girl who looked to be a little older, but a student anyway.

"You look freaked out," the girl was saying. She had a lot of bracelets on one wrist, and now she shook them up her arm. You could tell she was the friendly type. "Is there anything that I can help you with?" she asked. "I know it all seems really different for a while. When I was new," she rattled on, "I kept on calling home and crying for the first three weeks, I swear. The way we organize the classes is the strangest part, if that's what's bugging you. You see, what happens is, tomorrow, in the morning, everyone convenes at . . ."

The girl was clearly in the mood to tell her lots of things that Sara didn't want to know right then, but at least this chatter gave her time to think. The thing that she had come to find out first was where Group 6 was meant to be right then.

So when the redhead paused for breath, she said, "Oh, boy, that helps a lot. And just one other thing. There was this girl who came up on the bus with me who seemed real nice. I think she's in Group Four. Is there any place it says when different groups get back?"

The heavy girl smiled at Sara. "All the groups *are* back," she said. "You didn't go to supper, did you? Well, that's O.K., if you're not feeling well, or just want to go without a meal from time to time. I'm dieting myself. But if you're smart, you'll stick your nose in for Announcements. That's what I did. Everybody's back. If you hurry, you can catch your friend before she's finished eating maybe."

Sara said, "You're *sure* that all the groups are back?"

"Absolutely," said the girl. "One through Five, inclusive. Two nights out is all that anybody spends; tomorrow is for organizing classes, like I said—and then the next day they get started. And anyway, I heard it all with my own two ears. Doctor *said,*" the redhead smiled, "and Doctor *never* lies."

Sara did her best to match the smile. "You've really been a help," she said. "I hate to ask, but one last thing . . . is there a phone around? A sort of private one? I have to make a call—collect. My parents are expecting . . . ," Sara lied.

"Sure. Of course." The heavy girl was serious-maternal now. "I understand. Just down the hall and to the left. The second door's a phone booth. Nice and private. Believe me, I know."

"Thanks," said Sara as she moved in that direction.

"Sure," the girl replied. "Say, what's your name? I'm Sandy Salton—fourth year class."

"Molly," Sara said, and fled. "Molly . . . Mason, third year class. And thanks a lot now. 'Bye." And she had turned the corner.

The phone booth was a little room, with just a phone on a shelf, and a straight-backed wooden chair. There was a bare light bulb screwed into a fixture on the wall, and a hand-painted sign that said "Collect Calls Only." Somebody had inked a diagonal between the two *l*'s in "call" to make the sign read "Collect Cans Only." The yellow wall in back of the phone had been washed fairly recently, it looked like, but you could still see a lot of faint writing on it, from the year before, she supposed. "There once was a girl from Peoria," she could barely read, but they'd done a better job of washing on the next three lines of the limerick. The last line was "And the band at the Waldorf-Astoria." Sara picked up the phone and started to dial.

And then she stopped.

What did she think she was doing? It had been a kind of reflex, really. When in doubt, punt. When confused, call home. But what would they know, really? It'd sound like crazy talk: my teacher's disappeared; my name's not up there on the locker or the room-assignment lists, and neither are my friends'; and Doctor said that all the groups are back, but *we're* not. She could imagine how her father would respond to that: "Well, *go* to Doctor. *Tell* him that your group has not come back, and *ask* him for a locker and a room. Some secretary's bungled up her job, that's all. I'd think that even *you* could handle that, at sixteen years of age. . . ."

But if she got her mother, they could talk a little, anyway. And that'd feel good. Here's what she'd do: if her father answered, she'd say hi, and everything is fine, and then she'd ask to talk to Mom.

She dialed the operator, gave the number, said "collect."

"Who shall I say is calling?" said the operator.

"Sara," Sara said, "their daughter Sara."

She heard the call go through. Two rings. Her father: "Yes?"

The operator: "I have a collect call for anyone from your daughter Sara."

Pause. Her father's voice: "I don't think this is very funny, Doctor." Pause. "I'm sorry, operator. I have no daughter by the name of Sara." Click.

She hung up, too, with the operator's question in her ear.

* * *

When Ludi first saw Sara coming back across the field, she felt a little happy bounce inside her chest, as if her heart was jumping rope while all the rest of her stayed still. But when she kept on looking, she had another feeling, too: that sense of something being very, very wrong again—and now attached to Sara. She started out into the field.

Sara raised a hand and brought it down in one strong gesture, palm to Ludi: *Go back now.* Ludi hesitated, then stepped back into the shadows. Sara knew she had to get the others out of there. The others. Right away. She put her hand inside her jacket pocket, touched her compass: there where it belonged. Knowing she knew how to use the thing made her feel a little better, though she also knew she'd never find Spring Lake Lodge at night. She'd get them moving fast, and cover all the ground they could before it got too dark, and then they'd camp, just like they said they would, and then, at dawn, they'd start right up again and make the Lodge for breakfast. The kids would be some kind of hungry, but they'd make it; they'd survive.

It was, like, sometimes with her sisters and her brother, when she had to be the grown-up—not let on that she was worried in the slightest ("I *know* it isn't broken, Ruth"). She had to just be cool, and not discuss it right away, until she'd made some better sense of it. Right now, it still seemed almost like a joke. Or a *game,* as Coke would say. Like when you were a kid and you and some friends got together and agreed to pretend that another of your friends was, like, invisible. So no matter what she said or did, everyone pretended there was no one there. ("Did you hear something, Elsie? Did you hear someone saying something?" "No, I didn't hear *anything,* Sare. Did *you* hear something?" And so on, and on and on.) But grown-ups weren't into jokes like that. It wasn't their style. It really *couldn't* be that her parents, and Sully's parents, and Coke's parents, and Ludi's parents, and Marigold's parents had cooked up this deal with the school, as part of their orientation—some sort of survival training, or what have you. It couldn't be that. But what else could it be? It was hard to explain her father's voice; he'd sounded furious. "I don't think this is very funny, Doctor," he had said. What on earth did that mean? If there was a joke of any sort in progress, her father wasn't part of it, for sure.

She reached the tree line, and at once the Group surrounded her, everyone just one big grin, except for Ludi. And a million questions, all at once.

"O.K., what's the story? *Are* we where we're meant to be? Did you see Nat? Well, is it just a game, or what?" And then Marigold said, "I hope you remembered to pick up my mail." She was all right until Marigold said that; everything was under control. But for some reason . . . Had Marigold actually asked her to do that, or was she just kidding around? She couldn't remember. She looked at each of them. She knew that they were very good people. Naturally good. No one moved; everyone was looking at her; her eyes got very big. And Ludi opened up her arms to her, and Sara stepped straight forward into them, and made an awful moaning sound as she began to cry.

"I know, I know," and Ludi stroked her hair. "You've found out something terrible. . . ."

When Nat arrived at Coldbrook Country School, he didn't know if he had gotten there before Group 6 or after. He also didn't know if Mrs. Ripple and the man in the tweed cap had been collected by the man in the camouflage suit, or whether anyone had told Doctor that there hadn't been a grounding after all.

The expression "game called off on account of wet grounds" popped into his mind, and he imagined huge piles of steaming coffee grounds all over a base-ball field, with a lot of groundskeepers with brooms standing around them shaking their heads. He hoped that all the Coldbrook Country grounds-keepers were shaking *their* heads, too; their game (himself and Group 6) hadn't been called off, it just didn't show up to get played.

He decided to continue with the no-show strategy. Better, first, to try to figure out—if possible—just who was where and knowing what. He climbed up in a tree that offered him a view of most of Coldbrook's campus but also let him see the road and fields. That way, supposing that Group 6 had gotten slightly lost and hadn't made it yet, he'd possibly (most likely) see them coming. He got out his binoculars and slowly panned the area: no sign of them. He focused on the school.

It appeared that supper had just ended. Kids and staff were exiting the dining hall, in little groups and solo. Nat could see each person perfectly; he even counted them, for no good reason, really, seeing that he didn't know how many on the staff or in the student body. But it was something to do, and he sort of thought that if he got to a hundred and twen-ty-five, say, that that'd be everyone. Alternative schools just had to be small, if they were going to do the job they claimed to do.

He only got to ninety-eight before the door stopped opening and no one else came out. That was good; Coldbrook might be a better school than he'd thought. At least fifteen or twenty of the people looked as if they could be staff, which meant a student-teacher ratio of maybe 4.5 to 1, or there-abouts.

Nat gave his head a little shake. The really good thing was that he hadn't seen anyone he knew come out, except Doctor and Luke Lemaster and one other guy with a beard whose name was Barry Mustinghouse, or something like that, who taught mostly stuff like Social Ecology. And some of the kids on the bus from New York, of course. But no Mrs. Ripple and no camouflage suit and no tweed cap. And no members of Group 6.

Of course that didn't mean for certain-sure they weren't there, he realized. They could be locked in the Infirmary, with Mrs. Ripple (he could see her in a nurse's uniform) getting, like, their "medication" ready, while the other two leaned back in chairs outside the door, with rifles in their laps. Nat shuddered. "Please." He said this to the treetop. "Please. Not so." He decided what he'd do would be to scout around some more: circle through the woods on the north side of the school, where they'd most likely come from. Sara'd said she wasn't very good at compass work; it really was quite likely that he'd gotten down ahead of them.

As it turned out, he heard them just before he saw them. All of them were shushing one another, as they got their packs back on their backs and argued whether they could get to Spring Lake Lodge by nightfall. They also said such things as "This is crazy" and "I can't believe what's happening" and "Look, there's got to be a simple explanation" quite a lot.

When Nat came bolting through the woods, fullspeed, they turned and looked at him, at first in terror, then relief.

"One, two, three, four, five," he counted them. "Thank God."

Of course they started in at once, telling him what Sara saw and heard and said, and asking where he'd been and what (the fuck) it meant.

He just said, "Look. This all just has to wait. The thing we've got to do is walk. Back up to Spring Lake Lodge. As quickly as we can, O.K.? I'll tell you what I know when we get up there, but now we really

90

ought to move. Let's stick together and try to keep a nice even pace, but if anyone absolutely has to stop or slow it down, we can. The important thing now is just to get going. Is everybody O.K.?"

Everybody nodded, but some of them were looking at the ground and not at him: Sara, Coke, Marigold. He asked another question: "Do you trust me?"

He looked at Ludi first, and she just rolled her eyes around; a hugely welcome insult, that, like: "What do you think, stupid?" Everybody else, they nodded hard, and if Coke had to add "It doesn't look as if we have much choice," he said it with his bitter, vulpine smile.

It was well after eleven by the time they reached the Lodge, and they'd done the trip nonstop. Nat had flat-out said that he would take each person's pack for a mile or so, by turns, and no one said he couldn't when their turn came. When it got dark, they just had Nat's one flashlight for the six of them, so there was stumbling, all right, and lots of muttered "Shit," but no one really fell completely down or got an injury beyond a little twist or scrape.

"O.K.," said Nat, when they arrived. "I'm going to get some goulash started on the stove inside. I am so *incredibly* hungry, I could eat"—he searched his memory—"a Brussels *sprout,* I'll bet. If someone'll start an outside fire, too, we can eat out there, and maybe have some coffee or hot chocolate on. . . ."

Coke said, "Hey, Nat. I brought some rum with me. Is it O.K. if maybe people had a little drink?"

"Sure, I guess," said Nat. He wasn't used to being asked questions like that. "Provided I'm part of 'people.' Just everyone remember we're real tired and real empty and that alcohol's a depressant and . . . shut *up,* Rittenhouse," he said. "Isn't everyone glad I brought my father?" he smiled and asked the floor.

"How come you asked permission *this* time,

91

Coke?" teased Marigold, putting on the voice of teacher's pet.

"Oh, just *fuck* you," he snapped at once, and for the first time sounded like he meant it. Marigold shrugged and turned away; Coke muttered "Sorry," and she shrugged a second time, not looking at him. But when he'd gotten water from the spring and mixed the tropi-fruit drink and set the pitcher and the bottle on the box beside the stove, she made herself a drink and showed the cup to Coke and told him "Thanks." Everyone had rum this time, and Sully even shook his head and said, "Hey, boy, I needed this."

While the food was heating, people milled around and sipped their drinks and talked about the tiredness they felt, and how good the goulash smelled. It was like their parents' cocktail parties; no one talked about important things at all. Sully did ask Nat if what was going on made sense to him, but Nat had said he thought they ought to eat first and talk after. Partly, he was stalling: trying to look for ways of saying things that didn't make them sound so terrible. And also, this way, they could get some food down, anyway.

And indeed they did; everyone agreed it was great goulash, and by the time that they were done with it, Ludi was feeling/looking sleepy, just as she'd predicted.

"Look, this can wait till morning . . . ," coward Nat suggested. There wasn't any way to tell people something like this, for Christ's sake. But no one wanted any rainchecks; they thought that he was kidding.

"O.K. Um, well," said Nat. "The first thing that I want to say is this. We're going to be all right. I really believe that, and, um, I think it's real important you do, too. I think you're . . . well, a terrific group. Of people, that is, not just as a *group*. You know what I mean. Every one of you is great. If I didn't think that, I'd be fifty miles from here by now, or more." He looked around the circle, hoping that everyone believed him, even if they weren't making a lot of sense out of it so far. This really *was* impossible, he thought. But he had to keep on going. "And from what I've seen," he said, "I think that all of you care for each other, too, in spite of the fact that you've just barely gotten to know everybody and all."

"Nat," said Coke. "What *is* this crap? Will you get to the point and stop babbling?"

"O.K.," said Nat. "But none of that was babble. I mean it. Every word. But"—he sighed—"O.K. Fasten your seat belts; this gets pretty rough. Your parents sent you to Coldbrook Country School to have you, um, killed. And the school paid me to do it. I was meant to poison you. And then—I didn't know this till today—they were going to kill me, too. And bury us together in some deep crevasse or something."

They looked at him. "Wait a minute," Coke said. "You were kind of looking at Sara when you said part of that. Sara's parents really paid to have her *killed?*"

"*All* of yours," said Nat. "Yours and Sully's and Marigold's and Ludi's and Sara's. For one reason or another, all your parents wanted to get rid of you. Cripes, I know that none of you *deserves* to be killed, or any, um, ridiculous thing like that." This was coming out absurdly badly. He groped: "Any more than *I* do, for God's sake!"

Everyone was just staring at him now, except for Sara who had dropped her head and was starting to cry. She'd tried so hard and been so good so long, and now she wasn't even going to get a second chance. Sure, she'd done an awful thing, but she'd been punished and been shamed, and she'd thought that it was over with and that, if she did great at Coldbrook

. . . She wanted to get furious, think up a plan, but all she felt was stunned and sorry for herself.

"I can't believe it," Sully said. "My mother'd never do . . ." And then he thought: McCorker. He'd do anything, that Louis Philippe's penis. "It's so *unfair,*" he blurted out, meaning just about everything that had happened in his life so far.

And Marigold said, " *I* believe it. Why not? Who said anything is fair? You want to know the truth? I'm not surprised at all. Grown-ups kill each other all the time. Everyone saw *The Godfather,* right? I mean, doesn't it make perfect sense that there'd be people who'd kill people's *kids,* for a price? What's so special about kids? In the old days, they'd leave a baby by the side of the road if they didn't want it. Especially girls. I could see my parents—my mother, anyway—wanting me out of the way. Couldn't the rest of you? My mother'd have her reasons." Marigold had dropped the jokes, the imitations. Nat thought she looked, like, ten years older, in the firelight.

"*Wanting,* maybe, yes," said Ludi softly. "But *doing* it? Going *that* far?" She turned to Nat. "What about . . . the rest of it? How did you get into this? You said the school paid you to kill us." She shook her head. "How come? I mean, why you? I know you're not"—she did the eyes again—"a 'hit man,' or whatever they call it. And where were you all day and all?"

Nat nodded. "It goes back to my last year at college," he began—and then he told them all of it. About his debts, his pickle with the state and Arnold's uncle, his father's attitude, and how, in desperation, he'd agreed to work for Doctor. And how (of course!) he'd realized right away he couldn't, and how he got to thinking he might be marked himself, and how, that day, he'd gotten proof of it. It was kind of a relief to tell it all, from top to bottom, as if by telling it he might begin to forgive himself.

When he was done, he looked around the group, and Coke said, "Bullshit."

Nat said, "What?"

And Coke said, "I said bullshit. I don't believe a word of it. I still think it's a game, a test, a gimmick of some sort. I mean, I admit you've done a great job of setting the whole thing up. You, and whoever else is involved. For all I know, all of you may be in on it. This whole thing may be all for my benefit. But the thing is: I don't believe it. Something like this couldn't happen. My father's an asshole and my mother's a moron, but they wouldn't do a thing like that. People in their . . . circle—or whatever you want to call it—just don't kill their kids!" Maybe if he called their bluff, they'd just admit it was a game, and they could all go down and start this stupid fucking school. Not listing your kid in the Social Register was one thing—but killing him?

"Coke," said Marigold quietly, "you think Sara's acting? Does Sully look like an actor? Does Ludi? I could see how you'd think *I* was—dahling—but the rest of them? And I'm telling you I'm not."

Coke looked a little flustered. "Well, maybe you're not. Maybe no one's in this but Nat and the school. I just sure as hell know my parents aren't going to pay to have me killed."

Marigold's voice got really sharp again. "And *I* know goddamn well my mother'd have me killed in a minute if she was sure that she could get away with it. You understand what I'm saying? Parents don't kill their kids for the same reason people don't do lots of other things: they're just afraid of getting caught. Proof? In the old days, when it was all right to do it, everybody did. Even kings and shit. Like Moses." Marigold shrugged.

"Look, Coke," said Nat. "I don't blame you at all

95

for feeling the way you do. And there's no way in the world you can know that I'm telling you the truth if you think that I'm not." He paused and scratched his head. "Does that make sense? But you know what I mean, right? So how do I convince you? Is there any way?"

"Take me down to the school tomorrow," Coke replied. "I'll bet you won't do that."

"Oh, Lord," said Nat. He dropped his head and rubbed his eyes. He looked around the Group again. His face was full of shadows and looked gaunt. "I just don't know," he said. "Maybe that *would* work. Maybe if we all went back they'd have to pretend there was some sort of clerical mistake, or whatever they call it, and get in touch with your parents and tell them the deal's off. And if I accused them of anything—well, they'd just prove I was crazy or something." He gave a little laugh. "That wouldn't be too hard, I guess. From what I heard from Doctor, there's no way in the world to find . . . well, um, the earlier Group Sixes."

"So what are you saying?" said Coke. "Will you do it?"

"Coke, please," said Ludi. "It's just too big a chance. Those people are *crazy;* I mean, they have to be. Suppose they didn't decide what Nat just said; suppose they were still out to kill us. We have no idea what they might do, nobody does."

Coke shook his head, but he didn't say anything.

Sully said, "But if we don't go to school, and we can't go home, what *are* we going to do?"

Everybody looked at him, and kept on looking.

"Well, don't look at me, for Christ's sake," said Sully loudly. "*I* don't know what to do. I was just asking."

"God damn them," Marigold said suddenly. "God damn them anyway. We're in a goddamn *trap.*" She laughed, not pleasantly. "Anyone see that rerun on

TV? *The Fugitive?* About a guy being chased all over the place for something he didn't do? Well, that's us. Except that there's six of us, instead of one, and nobody's *accused* us of doing anything, whether we did or not. And five of us are minors and have no legal rights at all, just about. We can't vote, or get a fulltime job, or buy a drink or probably even *fuck*, for Christ's sake." She turned to Nat. "What are we going to do for the next two years? That isn't illegal or unsafe, I mean?"

"I'm going to go home," Coke said. He was looking at the ground now. "I'm not going to let my parents get away with this. I know a kid who's got a gun. No shit. He'll let me have it if I ask him. And then I'll, like, discuss it with them face to face. My old man's such a big bullshitter. I just want to see what he says."

Marigold said, "You're crazy. Who's acting now? That sounds dramatic as hell, but what are you going to do? Have your parents arrested? Sure. Fat chance. Shoot them? Great. You know what happens to kids who shoot their parents?"

"Yeah, they put them in the hospital and give them psychiatric tests. I've had a lot of those," said Coke. "There's probably some shrink somewhere who's already put down that I'm crazy. I'm the sort of guy you always read about—where the courts put them back on the streets and they end up raping some eighty-five-year-old woman in Queens or something."

"Oh, shut *up*, will you?" Sara'd kept on crying, sitting huddled up, her arms around her knees, her forehead on her knees. She'd picked her head up now. "Maybe it doesn't matter to the rest of you, but I just can't stand being *hated* that much." And she started to cry harder, rocking her head back and forth. "'I don't have a daughter named Sara'—that's what he said! Oh, God—what am I meant to do *now?*"

Sara wailed the word, not even caring she was being such a baby (as her father'd say), feeling nothing but the pain. She dropped her head again.

Ludi put an arm around her shoulders, leaned, and whispered in her ear.

"Well, you're not going to give up," said Sully, talking loudly once again. "I won't let you." He wanted to say something important to Sara, something that would make her feel good right away, and he'd just opened his mouth and started talking, and that was the first thing that came out. "Don't you see we need you?" Sully said. "Other than Nat, you're the only one who knows how to *do* anything. I mean, a *lot* of things. So whatever we end up doing, you've got to help us," Sully said. His face looked white in the firelight, and his fists were clenched on his bare knees, and his weight was forward on his feet, as if he was going to spring up any second and do something quick and vital.

Marigold was looking at Nat. "All this other bullshit to one side," she said, "That *is* the bottom line—what both of them just said. What *are* we going to do?"

"Well, one thing that we ought to do real soon is get some sleep," said Nat. "Whatever any of us ends up doing, we've got to have some rest. Right now, everything looks impossible and crazy. But what I've been thinking is we—each of us—has got to have a short-range and a long-range plan. The second one may take some time—to plan it out, you know?—so what I'd like to do is put our heads together in the morning and talk about the next two weeks, or a month, or some period of time like that. *My* vote is to hole up in the hills, but of course I'm used to that. I'm comfortable up here—maybe other people wouldn't be. And I hope we can stick together. What I'm feeling right now is that I'm afraid but not petrified. It's really weird. The world seems about a million times

98

more fucked up to me than it's ever been, but for myself, I still feel O.K. Crazy as it may seem, I'm actually looking forward to a long and happy life, doing what I want and being who I want to be. Regardless of all this." And he smiled, the fire flicker lighting up his scraggly-bearded face and lightening his long blond hair.

Ludi smiled back at him, and everybody else looked—even Sara, who'd stopped crying as he talked. She couldn't think of this as a beginning yet, but maybe, just maybe, it wouldn't be The End.

Ludi felt completely sure that she was not about to die; when she was going to die, she'd know it. About her parents, she felt nothing special, nothing really new. She'd never liked her stepmother at all, and she'd long since realized her father and herself were like two different sorts of beings. So, while it was a shock to her—as Sara said—that anyone could hate her all that much, she felt (with no conceit involved) he had no reason to at all. When she'd come to Coldbrook—gone away from home—she'd felt that she was starting on a new phase of her life, and here it was. It didn't seem that things had changed so much. *She* hadn't changed. Her father had the power to kill her—so he'd thought—but not to change her, ever. She wished she had a way to get that feeling into Sara. And the rest of them, of course; but Sara first.

Nat stood up. "*Please* go to bed," he said. "I don't mean to sound like your camp counselor or something, but please go to bed. Even if you'd rather stay up and talk, and even if you're sure you'll never get to sleep. We've really got all sorts of time to talk; there isn't any rush to settle anything tonight." He had to laugh, just once. "I promise I'll never ask anyone to go to bed again, if you'll do it this one time."

"Now easy *does* it, Natty." Marigold laughed, too; it was her old voice, back again. "You just said you were planning on a long and *happy* life. . . ." She stood up. "Jesus, I'm stiff. Girls got dibbies on the outhouse." And she went up to get the flashlight.

Ludi stopped by Nat. "Are you O.K.?" she asked him. She came up to his chin and stood there, straight and serious.

"What?" he said. "How d' you mean?"

"About this whole enormous mess," she said. "About seeing those people who wanted to kill you. This must have been an incredible day for you."

"I'm really so tired," Nat said, "I don't know how I am. O.K., I think. I realized, a little while ago, my father'd like to kill me, too, I bet—but, well, I think I know he *shouldn't.*" And suddenly he found himself crying. "Listen, thanks for asking, Lu." The tears were coming down his cheeks and disappearing in his beard, but he was facing her. "I know it's hard to tell the way I'm acting"—he made a sort of barking sound—"but it really helps to have you ask."

He closed his fist and dropped it on her head, but gently; then he turned and walked up toward the Lodge.

Chapter Five

BY THE TIME that Homer Cone and Mrs. Ripple
made it back to Coldbrook Country School—
chauffeured still by Levi Welch—the clocks said
quarter after nine P.M. Levi'd passed the time in
Boynton Falls at Osgood's Perfect Pizza Place, where
he'd enjoyed a baked-bean-pepperoni pizza, accompanied by Genesee Cream Ale, two bottles' worth. He'd
also won two games of bumper pool from Henry
Dunham, Junior, age of seventy-two, who had a
wooden hand. Years before, a big old Pioneer had hit
a stone he hadn't seen was there, and jumped back
off it, heading for his face. He'd got his hand up just
in the nick, he liked to say, and caught that chain
saw right across the palm. "Lucky thing I did," he
often said. "Hardly ever seen a wooden head I liked."
"June" Dunham claimed his artificial hand made
just the perfect bridge for shooting pool, but Levi
beat him anyway, two games to none, and then he
and June Dunham each had a Genesee on June.
Them other two could cool their heels some more, for
all he cared.

During dinner, Homer Cone and Mrs. Ripple
finally finished their in-depth evaluations of Dr.
Scholl (pro) and Levi Welch (con) and came to focus
on the matter of Group 6.

"I suppose," said Homer Cone, "he won't be

pleased at all. I don't believe we've ever lost a group before."

"I imagine he'll be *furious,*" said Mrs. Ripple, shuddering with pleasure. "Doctor has a wild, ungovernable temper, I feel sure—even if I've never seen him lose it. You can tell by the shape of his fingernails." Mrs. Ripple checked for wisps above her collar in the back. "But let's not be defensive, Mr. Cone; none of this is *our* fault. *We* didn't misplace poor Group Six; we never had it to begin with. So Doctor can't blame *us,* not for a minute"—she pursed her lips and wiped them with her napkin—"if anyone's to blame, it's he himself."

"That's true," said Homer Cone, speaking somewhat louder than he needed to. "If anyone's to blame for this snafu, it's Doctor Simms himself!" Homer Cone liked people to believe that he was a veteran of World War II, and so he sometimes spiked his conversation with words like "snafu" and "fubar" and "Dunkirk" and "Anzio."

"Young Rittenhouse is *his* responsibility," said Mrs. Ripple. It would not do for Levi Welch to know that she'd been drinking, so she'd gotten a Clorets out of the package in her jacket pocket, and now she squeezed the little candy in her palm. It would not do for Homer Cone to know she sucked Clorets. "He must be made to see that. We must make that very clear to him, and not be in the least defensive. There's no reason for us to be the . . . autumn persons, as I think they're called." She gave a little cough, but when she'd covered up her mouth before she coughed, she'd popped the Clorets into it.

"Exactly," Homer Cone agreed. "Doctor bollixed this one up but good. You get what you pay for in this world, and that bird Rittenhouse looked about as tacky as they make 'em." Homer Cone had forgotten that he had never laid an eye on Nat. Three Manhat-

102

tans always knocked his memory a little bit askew, but sharpened his aggressiveness, as well.

And so, when Homer Cone and Mrs. Ripple rapped on Doctor's study door at nine-fifteen, both were feeling quite offensive.

Inside, Doctor had been practicing throwing a Nerf ball into a little orange plastic hoop that was held in place on his lavatory door by two big rubber suction cups. When he heard their knock, he caroled, "Just a *min*ute, please," and went and got the ball and hoop concealed up on a closet shelf. Then he opened wide the study door.

"Ah," said Doctor, happily, "Homer Cone and Mrs. Ripple! Mission accomplished, I presume?"

"Ha!" said Homer Cone.

"Sadly not," said Mrs. Ripple sharply.

Doctor made his eyebrows jump. "Come in, come in," he said, his face darkening. "Would you care for a liqueur?" he asked them—quite correctly, Mrs. Ripple thought.

She said a Cherry Heering might be very nice, and Homer Cone allowed as how he would enjoy a B&B, if Doctor would have one, too. Whenever anyone offered Homer Cone a drink, he'd always say, "If you'll have one with me." Usually they did, which made Homer Cone feel very much in charge of things.

Doctor poured Mrs. Ripple's and Homer Cone's liqueurs into highball glasses from his Titans of the Turf set. The set took up one whole shelf on the wall above the dry sink, where Doctor kept his bottles. Each glass had the name of a famous race horse on it, plus the names of the famous races that that horse had won. Every year or two, the Titans of the Turf people would send Doctor another glass, it seemed, and he would send them only $4.99 and add the new Titan of the Turf to his collection. He decided to give Mrs. Ripple Ruffian, and Homer Cone Foolish Pleasure. He poured himself a cognac in a large, round, crystal brandy snifter.

Mrs. Ripple knew that Doctor knew better than to put a Cherry Heering cordial in a highball glass, and she also knew that he knew she'd resent a glass named "Ruffian." Sometimes, she thought, she'd like to kick Doctor right in the A-double-Q.

The story of their uneventful day was quickly told. Doctor's pink cherubic face was furrowed with a scowl before it ended. Even knowing that the Brook Trout Amandine in Boynton Falls had been first-rate didn't do a lot to cheer him up. And Mrs. Ripple didn't help at all. If Doctor thought that she was a ruffian, why, then she'd act like one, and just let Homer Cone do all the story-telling, in that boring, nasal voice of his. At that point, she wanted nothing more than to get out of her Carharts and into a nice hot bath.

"Quite clearly," Doctor said, when Homer Cone was done, "I put my faith in a very leaky vessel. This Rittenhouse is nothing but a blackguard—*Rotten*-house I'll call him from now on. Obviously his word is not his bond; his handshake isn't worth the . . . fingers it's composed of. I don't know what the world's coming to. . . ." Doctor shook his head. "Am I just being old-fashioned when I expect a day's work for a day's pay? Maybe it's this country . . . ''tis of thee,' " sang Doctor. " 'Sweet land of liber-tee . . .' The other day," he said, "I read a piece that said the Japanese auto worker is forty-two percent more productive than his American counterpart. I probably should have hired a Japanese," he mused, "or maybe someone from Hong Kong."

"Or maybe just used local labor," said Homer Cone, offensively. "No," he nasaled on, "I'm afraid you got what you paid for, Doctor. A real Dunkirk. Rottenhouse—that's good—is nothing but a tenement, I'd say."

"Yes," said Mrs. Ripple spitefully. "Our clients aren't used to shoddy goods, poor people. This isn't any fun for them, you know."

"Yeah," said Homer Cone, the mathematics teacher. "What does it say in the Bible? Something about a toothache and a worthless child?" He realized he was rubbing it in on Doctor, using Bible quotes like that, but it was *his* fun that Doctor ruined.

"I know, I know," said Doctor, holding up a clean white hand. "I've learned a hard lesson, bird-and-stone-wise. All I can say, in my own defense, is that Ritten . . . *Rotten*house was sent to us originally by one of the leading authorities in that particular field, a man of absolutely impeccable credentials. And while there is no written guarantee, of course, there's still a certain understanding. Believe me, I shall be in touch with him, and I'm quite sure he'll help us . . . make adjustments. But meanwhile"— Doctor sat straight up—"where is our Group Six? Where's that rotten Rittenhouse? Are they together or apart? Near or far away? 'Long ago and far away,' " sang Doctor, " 'I dreamed a dream one day. . . .' "

"Well," said Homer Cone. "I doubt that they've gone home. I'll say that much."

"Brazil?" Mrs. Ripple thought she might provide a little humor. Homer Cone and Doctor were such serious old stick-in-the-septic-tanks. "Bet they headed straight for Brazil," she giggled, "fast as their little cariocas could carry them."

"No," said Homer Cone. He tried to spit the word at Mrs. Ripple. He leaned way forward in his chair and made his eyes two narrow slits. "I know they're out there somewhere." He gestured toward the window. He'd made his voice a nasal whisper, strewn with gravel. "Hiding. Holed up. Desperate. Dangerous." There were, after all, *six* of them, and three of them were teenaged girls.

"You may be right," said Doctor, "and I hope you are. I still have every intention of fulfilling our contracts with their parents. I am—we all are—honorable people . . . 'who need people,' " Doctor sang. "Quite *un*like young Rottenhouse."

"I intend to comb the woods," said Homer Cone, "until I find them," forgetting that he had once got "hopelessly lost" while driving south, through Baltimore. "They've got a date with Homer Cone, my friends."

"An' I sha' he'p," said Mrs. Ripple cheerfully and helpfully, her Cherry Heering having washed away her *l*'s.

Doctor rose and bowed them to the door. He couldn't blame Cone or Mrs. Ripple for the day's events, or non-events, but that didn't mean he had to like them, either.

"Good night, now, Mr. Cone," he said. "Goodnight, dear Mrs. Ripple."

With just one window in each room, Spring Lake Lodge stayed dark in the morning, but people might have slept late anyway. When Nat woke up, his watch said noon, and he didn't hear a sound from anybody else.

Tired as he was the night before, he couldn't get to sleep right off; he'd felt like he was speeding. His mind would run on rewind for a while, playing if-I'd-only with the past. Then, without a pause, or click, he'd find it on fast-forward, saying, "Maybe if we . . . such-and-such" or "Don't forget to . . . so-and-so tomorrow." It was a pain. He'd shifted in his sleeping bag, noticed Coke and Sully's breathing change, and envied them. His mind went raving on; the battery ran down at last; he fell asleep.

But when he woke at noon, he felt much better than he thought he would. He wasn't tempted to go back to sleep again, nor did he wish that he had just

. . . well, kept on going, after seeing what the situation was at North Egg Mountain. He'd been a bit afraid he might wish that. But, no. In fact—was this perverted?—he was having fun. Well, maybe not exactly *fun*, he told himself, but something in that neighborhood of feeling.

He smiled then, lying on his back inside his sleeping bag. He heard murmurs from The Ladies Room and smiled some more.

Nat's father, Robert Rittenhouse, did not believe a person should expect much fun from Sunday afternoon to Friday evening. Sunday night supper was always a terrible meal at his parents' house; his father seemed to like a really lousy meal, to sort of set the stage for Monday. Mr. Rittenhouse would always have a bowl of some cold cereal, like shredded wheat, with blue skimmed milk. Once, Nat convinced his Mom to split a pizza—"abbondanza" from Celeste. You'd think they both had stepped in dog shit, the way his father'd twitched his nose at them. They'd broken training for the game of Life: that heavy, cutthroat, no-fun race that started off again each Monday morning.

Nat could never understand why Life should not be fun. He'd really given quite a bit of thought to fun, for quite a space of time. Fun was not a beer blast at the Delta house—or getting rays or getting laid or getting off or getting even. Not that all of them were not enjoyable at times. Fun, the real big F, was something different: doing with your life what *you* were meant to do. Not "meant to" in the way your parents said it—"You were meant to clean your room today, as I recall"—but "meant to" in an almost cosmic sense. Fun is doing, working at, the stuff that makes you feel the most like you. So, in the case of N. P. Rittenhouse, figuring was fun, and building things was fun, and cooking-eating food was fun, and hiding out was fun, and helping someone else was fun, and playing the guitar was fun. And saving your own life, and other lives, was lots and lots of fun.

O.K., he thought—and now his mind was working as he liked it to, on normal cruising speed—they needed some supplies, a lot of them. So . . . money was a big concern. And space to store things in. Yeah, and transportation.

"Hey, knock-knock. You decent?" Ludi's voice, from near the door.

"Ask if they're awake first, stupid." That was Sara. " 'Decent' is subjective. What *you* call *real* indecent could be someone else's way of life."

Nat was glad to hear her laughing, being foolish. Kids were meant to snap back fast from things, but these kids weren't really *kids,* and knowing that your parents paid to have you killed seemed to qualify as something more than "things." Ludi'd seemed the least affected of the five, but you could never tell. He'd have to really keep an eye on all of them. That thought was so avuncular it made him smile. Dirty old uncle.

"Look, barge right in," said Marigold. "They won't mind. This is strictly an anything-goes type scene. D'you suppose his girl Friday worried about walking in on Robinson Caruso?" Marigold was a hard one to figure, thought Nat. She seemed extremely tough and cynical, but maybe that was all an act.

"Good after*noon,*" said Nat. "Yes, *do* come in. You must be the maids. Or is it room service? Orange juice, fresh squeezed, three eggs over easy with grilled ham, and English muffins. Coffee."

"Well," said Marigold, pretending to write, "we'll have to make a substitution here and there. We're out of orange juice and eggs and ham and muffins. May I suggest the tuna-noodle casserole?"

"Yuk!" said Sully, sitting up in bed. He smiled at

the girls; he smiled at Nat; Coke still lay there with his eyes closed. Sully looked as fresh as butter in the mornings; sleep never seemed to leave a mark on him: his eyes were wide and bright, his short hair flopped in place, he even smelled good, if you got that close. He had a yellow t-shirt on that he was growing out of, so there was skin between the bottom of the t-shirt and the sleeping bag that lay across his lap. Looking at him sitting there, Marigold decided he was worth at least an 8—still in the Prep department, maybe, but a really nice little bod. Odetta and herself had made a scorecard at the country club at home: 1 through 10 in four divisions, Boys, Prep, Men, and Seniors (yet!). Skinny guys like Coke were hard to rate, they found, but she had always scored them kind of high. O.D. would have a *snake* when she found out that Marigold was . . . well, marooned with guys who *averaged* an 8. If she ever did find out, that is.

". . . story with supplies?" Sully was saying.

"High priority," said Nat. He slid his legs out of his sleeping bag. He had on track shorts and a long-sleeved baseball undershirt: solid blue from cuffs to shoulders, white in the body, with long tails. "Spare me tuna-wiggle in the morning. Um, look. Let's make some . . . pancakes maybe? And then get down to business." Marigold nodded her agreement. Give those legs a 9, she thought.

For the next hour, people just did ordinary morning things, the way they might have anywhere. Already they could feel a different atmosphere, as if the space between them had been redefined, and softened. Before, they'd been a group of travelers—people on a trip to somewhere else. Their main thing wasn't journeying, and everybody knew it; the future was what mattered. Now, the present was the future, too, you might say—as far as anyone could see or tell. Most people didn't notice it in quite those terms, but living in the present felt a good deal better in a lot of ways. If only they could keep the past from messing up their minds. . . . Coke was very quiet, more laid back than ever.

They sat around the outdoor fireplace to talk; by now they did that automatically, even going back to the places that they'd had the night before. All three girls were barefoot, for the moment; they all had shorts on, too, and when they sat, they sprawled, and touched each other. Marigold restructured one of Sara's braids; Ludi, lying back, had propped her feet on Sara's knees. Ludi's legs were not the least bit skinny—they had been developed, worked on. Her thighs and fanny were the tip-offs: a skater's engine room, thought Nat. Or maybe she's a dancer. He realized she wasn't such a kid at all. Height and faces fooled you, lots of times.

Nat had a plan to offer. How about, he said, they just rest up that day—it being after noon already—but leave at next day's dawn for Boynton Falls? His thought was that he'd try to cash a check from Coldbrook Country School, an old one. If he could, then they'd be golden—at least in terms of money for supplies. He showed them those humungous checks ("Blood money," said Coke). They started in to make a list.

"Boy, this is going to be a lot to carry," Sully said. "How far is Boynton Falls from here?"

"It *is* a haul," said Nat. "And that's why I've been wondering about a car. Just some old junk. We could hide it off the road somewhere, I think. And even though we couldn't get stuff all the way to here, it sure as hell would mean a lot less packing on our backs."

"Hey," said Ludi, sitting up. She looked at Sara. "How about that house? The one from yesterday? With all the porches?"

Sara nodded, turned to Nat. "We found this

house—a really nice one—on the way to"—she shook her head—"school." She made a face. "It's got its own long private road, and tons and tons of space. Maybe—I don't know—five, six miles from here. Or more?" She looked around the Group. "I'm terrible at distances."

"My God," said Nat. "I think I know the place you mean. I'd forgotten all about it. Looks sort of Swiss? But lots of sundecks? Yeah. Hmm. That's really a thought. It sure is private, that's for sure."

"And it sure looks elegant," said Marigold. She held up a cautionary palm. "Not to knock the Lodge at all," she said. "It's just a different decorating scheme. For instance, they've got mattresses down there, and—how you say?—a toilet with ze floosh attachment. And an oven just the perfect size for quiche Lorraines and devil's foods and Key lime pies and pizzas! I, of course, would never touch fattening foods like that. . . ." Suddenly she bunched her fingers into fists and bounced up and down in her seat. "Oh, Natty! Can we? Can-we, can-we? Just *borrow* it a while? All the other kids have places in the country."

Sara said, "You mean, break *in?* And *live* in it? Boy, I'd feel pretty funny breaking into someone's house, I think. And anyway, don't you think they use it weekends all the time?"

"Either way, it looks like it'd be a great place to drop off supplies," Ludi said. "If we got a car, that is. We could probably put the stuff in one of their woodsheds, even, and then make as many trips as we have to, to get it all up here."

"Jeez—are we ever going to be in *shape,*" said Sully, rubbing up and down his thighs.

"Look," said Nat. "Um, well, I hadn't thought of anything like that before, but maybe Marigold has got a good idea. I don't like the thought of breaking into someone's house," he said to Sara. "And I'm

111

sure she doesn't, either." Marigold popped her eyes real wide and shook her head, her fingers on her breast. "But it just occurred to me—it wouldn't be too bad if we had lots of different . . . hideouts, sort of. This could be our major base, the main one. But if we stashed some food and stuff in lots of places, why then, we'd be a lot more mobile. And supposing someone stumbled into here, we'd still have other places we could go to." Nat's imagination shifted into high: he could see them finding caves and throwing up a lean-to here and there—and tree houses! My God, a tree house would be fun. And every place well stocked and cozy: cookies, hams, and cocoa—*YUM!* He knew he wasn't being "realistic," but . . .

"Shit," said Marigold, "I didn't mean we'd hurt the place at all." She touched Sara on the knee. "*Moi*? Marigoldilocks?" Sara smiled. "Seriously. I just meant to use it for a while. We could clean it every Friday morning—Coke could—and clear out." Coke didn't bat an eye. "And anything we broke, we'd leave some money in the sugar bowl or somewhere." She turned to Nat. "Right?"

"Yeah, sure," he said. "Provided we can get some money in the first place."

"O.K.," said Marigold, "let's take a vote. All those in favor of renting the Swiss family Robinson's place for a little while, raise your right hand." Five hands went up, Sara's with a little sigh, a shrug, a slightly painted smile. "All those opposed?" No one. "Hey, Coke, you didn't vote," she said.

"I didn't see the point," said Coke. "Chances are, I might not be there, ever. I'm going home, remember? I told you that last night."

Marigold made a mouth at him. "Come *on,*" she said. "You cut that out. You can't go home. It doesn't make any sense. Everybody tell him to cut *out* this shit, O.K.?"

And everybody did—all at once, at first. Coke

didn't look at them, but just sat staring at the ground between his feet and giving little head shakes. He kept curling a strand of his long black hair around a finger; curling it, releasing it, and curling it back up again.

Finally he said, "God damn it. Leave me alone, will you?" And he got up and started walking toward the Lodge. Then he stopped and turned to Nat. "Just get me to a road, all right? And tell me how to get to town from there. I've got money for the bus, or maybe I can hitch a ride."

"How about tomorrow?" Nat replied. "We'll all be going on to Boynton Falls. You could just come with us."

"No," said Coke, "today." He looked real close to crying.

And so it ended up that all of them hiked down to what they always called the Robinsons' (Swiss family variety), even after they found out some people named Novotny owned it. Nat opened up the kitchen door with ease, using his I.D. from UVM. The other five were going to spend the night on mattresses—they'd never get to Boynton Falls before the bank closed—but Coke was leaving right away. Walking down, they'd nagged him to the point that he agreed he'd come back up, once he'd seen his parents. Sully wondered if he really would, and Sara doubted it. Ludi hoped that he'd be able to. Nat said that if they weren't at the Robinsons', they'd leave a note—and map, if needed—tacked inside the woodshed. He showed Coke just exactly where he meant, and shook his hand out there.

"I wish I could talk you out of this," he said, for about the fifteenth time.

Coke stood there, saying nothing.

"Well, good luck," said Nat. "And hurry back, O.K.? It's hard to find good help up here." He laughed, then shrugged his shoulders, feeling foolish and incompetent. He wondered (for about the fifteenth time) if he should try to physically restrain him. He turned back toward the house.

Marigold was standing on the porch. "You going?" she called down to Coke.

"Yeah," he said. "I guess so."

"I'll walk you down a little ways," she said.

He didn't answer anything, but waited while she came on down the outside steps. They started walking in the road.

"I want to tell you something," Marigold began.

"Like what?" said Coke.

"You'd better come back quick," said Marigold.

"Why?" said Coke. He knew he'd never dare to say that if he wasn't going.

"Because I need you here," said Marigold. "God damn it." She'd turned her head away from him, and stopped walking.

Coke reached a hand out for her shoulder. He thought that she was crying, maybe, and he wouldn't want for her to cry. But before he could touch her, she swung around real fast and faced him, and she *was* crying, and her face was twisted up and kind of red.

"You selfish fucking *asshole*," she screamed out at him, and then she ran right by him, up the road, running sort of like she had a dress on, straight-legged, with her hands out to the sides.

Coke went slinking down the road, feeling worse than ever.

Because they started from the Robinsons', instead of Spring Lake Lodge, the trip to Boynton Falls was shortened by two hours, anyway. But still it was a hike, even taking shortcuts, as they did. By the time they reached a pasture, by a corn field that was on the edge of town, there was just an hour left for busi-

114

ness at the bank, and very little spring in anybody's legs.

"Christ," said Marigold. "Why don't we just all lie about our ages and enlist? United States Marines. Then at least we'd get *paid*. And it'd be an absolute vacation after this. Plus they could teach us forty ways to liquidate our parents, if we wanted. . . . Look, I'm only kidding, Sully. You don't have to look at me that way!"

Nat had brought a sport shirt, and some khaki pants that were permanent press, and moccasins. Before they'd left the Robinsons', he'd trimmed his hair and beard, to neaten them a little, and now he combed them both. Ludi thought he looked a little like the tennis player, Borg, except his cheekbones and his eyes were much more wide apart. He changed his clothes right there, with all of them around, seeming not the least self-conscious. He had on bright red briefs, the kind that's like a really skimpy bathing suit.

The plan was this. Nat, alone, would swagger into the bank and try to cash one check. Because he had I.D., and because it was the Coldbrook Country School's own bank, he thought that they would cash it. He guessed that Doctor'd think he'd cashed his checks already—long ago, in fact—and so he wouldn't have stopped payment when he got the news from Mrs. Ripple and her friends. He wouldn't mail the final check, of course, but what the hell, thought Nat.

Then, with pockets bulging, he would wander down to Ace A-1 Used Cars, a block away, and use the other check to purchase Ace's leading piece of citrus for their purposes. This he'd drive on up the road toward Suddington, and stop by . . . "See those pine woods right up there?" They did.

"I imagine that you'll hear me coming," Nat informed them, "but even if you don't, there should be smoke."

Before he headed off, he handed Ludi twenty-seven dollars, all that he had left of three aunts' birthday bounty. "Keep this for me, will you?" he besought her. "With my luck, I'll get mugged before I even get to Boynton Falls."

It turned out Nat predicted right in all particulars, except the mugging part. His check was cashed, in tens and twenties, and he was smiled upon and urged to have "a real nice day." Ace, whose other name was Wilmer T. Buchanan, also beamed approval of a Coldbrook Country check ("Good as goldmines, friend . . .") for which he gave—or let Nat steal, as he expressed it—a '69 bright orange bus, by Volkswagen. It was rather badly rusted here and there (riding shotgun, you could see the road between your feet), and the heater didn't work at all, but, as Nat said to Ace—not once, but many times— he was heading way down South before too long, and wouldn't need a heater anyway.

The car did not delight Group 6, exactly.

"I've heard of lemons," Ludi said, which caused a coughing fit by Nat, "but a *pumpkin?*"

"No, no," said Marigold, a hand on Ludi's elbow, "it'll turn into a *car* at midnight, don't you see?"

"Isn't it a bit conspicuous?" said Sully.

But everyone piled in, and there was lots of room, and Nat drove briskly, valves a-chatter, down the road to Suddington, some fifty miles away, the county seat. If anyone observed them heading south, that wouldn't matter anyway, said Nat. Driving back at night, the orange wouldn't look so orangey, he said, and once they were at the Robinsons' again, a transformation could take place. "Just as the brilliant butterfly becomes a caterpillar," Nat reminded them, "so shall the Pumpkin turn to . . . cantaloupe, perhaps. Or something equally discreet."

"But," Sully started, ". . . isn't it the other . . ." Sara dug him in the ribs and made a funny face, and Sully laughed.

In Suddington, they patronized a lot of different stores, and never more than two of them went anywhere together. "This may be hard for some of us," said Marigold, a hand behind her neck, "to not be *memorable*, you know. Me—pretend to be a local high school girl? Maybe if I got a polyester top . . . and curlers . . . and, say, three packs of Juicy Fruit. . . ."

What they bought were basics: food, some boards and tarps for storage boxes, extra nails and hardware, paint. Also clothes, in mostly greens and browns and olives ("Earth tones, don't you love them?" Marigold asked Ludi. "They bring out all the yellow in my skin"), boots for those who didn't have them, ditto running shoes. Nat bought clothes for Coke, estimating sizes; he didn't mention that he'd done that, though. No one mentioned Coke, and Marigold was cracking jokes, but Nat thought she, and everyone, was missing Coke a lot. It was more or less as if he'd died.

They also bought flashlights, whistles, compasses, and first-aid kits, and axes, knives, and bows and arrows.

"Who knows how to shoot these things?" asked Sully, handling this very ancient weapon, now made out of fiberglass and plastic.

Ludi'd taken archery at camp, and so had Sara. Nat admitted he had "fooled around" with bows a little. No one asked to know exactly what the bows were for.

For supper they got take-outs from a Burger King, and everybody got a little solemn at the thought of no more fast food for a while. Sully went and got a final round of fries, to pass around the Pumpkin on the way back "home," but when they got to Boynton Falls again, there was a last request from everyone. And so Nat stopped outside a little grocery, where Sara went and got just four half gallons of Coronet All-Natural Chocolate Chip. There *was* a freezer at the Robinsons', they said, and this was only Wednesday, after all.

Going up the gravel roads, they didn't see a single car, and half the houses that they passed were dark. The rest had maybe one room lighted, sometimes only by the silver of a TV screen. Once, they came upon two deer, standing squarely in the middle of the road, and Sara thought she saw some others in the fields they passed. Driving through the night, in such an empty, *country* sort of place, their whole predicament seemed more unreal than ever. And scarier, somehow—they felt exposed and vulnerable. Everyone was glad to reach the roadway to the Robinsons', and surprised when Nat turned off the lights and stopped, perhaps a quarter mile below the house.

"Until we get a system of some sort," he said, "like a lookout or a sentry—some darn thing—we'd better just be super-cautious. I stuck a piece of leaf in both the latches when we left—and of course we'll see the car, if anybody's parked. . . ." They started up the road in single file, not talking, trying to step as silently as possible.

Ludi whispered, "Nat. There's someone there."

And he said, "Where?"

And she said, "There." She pointed. "Up inside the house." Everyone looked back and forth, from her to that big house shape up ahead.

Nat said, "You can *see* somebody up there, Lu?"

And she said, "No, it's just a feeling. I can tell."

He nodded. Ludi just took tiny breaths. She knew that she was right in what she said; she also knew

118

she'd had to say it. What she didn't know was what they'd think and say—what *he'd* say, first of all. It seemed like a big moment in her life.

"Do you know who it is?" Nat said. There wasn't any doubting in his voice—no what's-this-crazy-talk?, no little-lilt-of-laughter.

"No," she said. "I can't even tell how many. There could be more than one."

Nat didn't hesitate at all. He hunkered down and started to unlace his boots. "I'm going to check it out," he said. The house appeared completely dark; it certainly was silent. He took his boots and socks off.

"Do any of you drive?" he asked.

Sara answered, "Yes, but not a stick."

Marigold: "Same here."

Ludi said, "I can." Nat handed her the car keys, and then, once more, his money. He smiled. "Dramatic precautions department, N. Rittenhouse, Director." He slipped off the khaki trousers. "It isn't that I'm expecting Bo Derek," he said to Marigold, "it's the noise factor. You've probably noticed in the frontier flicks how the Indians never wore corduroy pants . . . ?"

He faced them all. "Just wait right here," he said. "If anything that I promise you isn't going to happen happens, coast the Pumpkin down the hill till you get to the road, and then . . . I don't know, head for California or something. Maybe Dayton, Ohio; nobody looks for anyone in Dayton. You'll have to decide. But of course that isn't going to happen. It's probably just a pair of local lovers. Or Mrs. Robinson. Anyway. I should be back inside a half an hour."

And then, to everyone's surprise (and Sully's—face it—horror) he shook their hands in turn and gave them each a kiss. "For luck," he said, and winked, and started up the road, staying on the shoulder, bent way over. Sully wished he had another guy—

like Coke—to look at, so he'd know what he should feel, for sure. Maybe what he should have done was go with Nat, but what *good* would he have been? Sully sank to one knee, like the on-deck hitter in a baseball game; that was better than standing, waiting, and he thought it looked kind of ready-for-anything. Right away, the three girls all got down on the roadside beside him, which made him feel a great deal better.

As Nat got nearer to the house—feeling just a little bit absurd, but also more than mildly frightened—he veered away from it, staying in the shadows. The driveway widened out to make a larger space for parking all along the near side of the house. There were two ways of gaining access from that side. First, there were some rustic steps quite near the front, which went up to the biggest sundeck, on the second floor. The "front" door, if you will, was there; you entered in the living room. The second door was almost at the back, at ground level; it led into the kitchen. Actually, there were two doors there; an outside one that opened on a little hall where there was place for boots and coats, and then the kitchen door itself.

Nat circled all the way around the parking space, behind a woodshed, and so approached the house from its back side, walking toward the kitchen windows. It was a big country kitchen that ran the full width of the house.

There was a kerosene lamp burning on the kitchen table, with its wick set low.

Nat crept toward the house, setting down his feet heel-first and walking on their outside edges. He got close enough to see the room from end to end.

There was no one in the kitchen.

He turned and moved back from the house. Now he circled to the house's other side, staying at a distance. There were no other lights. Not in the two big

120

downstairs bunk rooms, or in the downstairs den, or bath; not in the two upstairs bedrooms, or the living room, or upstairs bath.

Nat considered. Could the person(s) be asleep? Might they just be sitting in the dark? Lying in the dark? Well, sure, why not?

Could they be *outside,* somewhere? Maybe even driving back, say, from the store, just the same as they had done. Which meant they'd see the Pumpkin in the road, and then the kids—and then what?

Thinking all those thoughts made Nat decide he'd have to see if there were people in the house, and if there were, how many. Their sex and size would be of interest, too.

He circled back behind the house again, and over to the woodshed. There he found about a two-foot piece of stove wood, round and hard as a rolling pin; it made him feel both better and ridiculous. His legs were getting kind of cold.

The outside kitchen door—the leaf no longer in the latch—was what is called a storm door: a plexiglass-aluminum affair with one of those good strong springs on the top that slam the door closed after you—or on you. So what Nat figured he could do was open up that door real wide, and then let go—and duck around the corner of the building as he did so. Whoever came to check the noise would have to pass the kitchen table and the lamp, and he, the perfect Peeping-Nat outside the window, would see him-her-them-someone, in terrifying, big-screen color.

He did it. The door, amazingly, was squeakless as it opened. He let it go and scooted.

Slam!

He waited. And pretty soon there *was* a person, tall and lean and walking in an awkward kind of glide, with an L-shaped poker held in front of him, as if it were a sword. His eyes were wide and staring.

"Jeezum. Coke!" said Nat-the-cotton-mouthed.

The words came out a mumble. He got saliva going, licked his lips, and went up to the window. Coke was now beside the door, flattened to the wall, and listening. Nat decided not to tap on the window; give the guy a break. Instead, he walked back to the door he'd slammed and opened it, and said (in normal, loud, and *very* friendly tones), "Hey, Coke. I come in peace. It's Nat."

Later on in life, Coke always felt a little twinge of guilt/embarrassment about that moment, and the next few hundred, say. Because, before he'd thought it through at all, he'd dropped the poker, opened up the door, and grabbed ahold of Nat in tears. Later on in life, he'd tell himself that he was drunk, which was at least a little true, and very near exhaustion, which was fact.

"Oh, boy," said Nat, a little awkward in his underwear, but not unsympathetic. "Everything's O.K. now, Coke," he said. "It's great to see you back."

He kept on patting Coke between the shoulder blades, until it crossed his mind that Coke might feel like he was being burped or something, so then he just hung onto him and said, "Yeah, it's O.K.," until he felt Coke's breathing get smoothed out a little.

When Coke felt slightly in control, he pulled away from Nat and took his handkerchief and blew his nose and started in, "Oh, Jesus, what a day . . ." And though he sounded near-hysterical, he got the story out. It was the only time he told it altogether truthfully.

What he'd found, when he arrived at Boynton Falls (almost) was that he was afraid to let himself be seen by *anyone*. At Nat's suggestion, he'd gotten off the road (and into woods or ditches) at the sound of any car approaching, and that had made him so completely paranoid that now he didn't dare to enter Boynton Falls and get aboard a bus. He also didn't dare to hitch a ride (every car that passed seemed to be driven by a homicidal maniac), and he surely didn't dare to face his parents. So all that he could think to do was start on back to Robinson's. Pretty soon he felt so tired that he couldn't walk another step, and so he had to curl up in some underbrush—a thing he also didn't dare to do *at all*—and pass a night of total terror, listening to passing steps of bears and wolves and cougars. When it got light, he started off again, now weak from hunger, too, and hoped at first to meet the Group approaching Boynton Falls. Then he realized Nat would know some shortcuts, wouldn't have to stick to roads—so he had to hike it solo once again.

The return trip took an even longer time. It seemed that there were lots more cars and trucks abroad (many of the latter group had rifles, right on racks), and also he was tired. Even when he finally made the house, he didn't feel too great. And less so, as the hours passed, and darkness came again, and they were still not back. He told Nat he'd imagined—he blew his nose again—a lot of awful things, including whips and cages. He'd found where old man Robinson concealed his booze supply, and so he'd had himself a pair of vodka tonics, really strong ones. He'd found some crackers, too, but he hadn't felt like eating much. (Might have had some trouble with the box, Nat thought.) But he was hungry now, he said.

And suddenly his eyes changed focus, really looked out there at Nat, away from all his inner hurts.

"Christ," said Coke, his voice quite near to normal. "Why're you dressed like that? And where's everyone else?"

When Nat explained, Coke dropped his head; his eyes went side to side. "Look," he said, "you won't . . . you know"—he waved his hand—"go into every-

123

thing with them? I mean, a lot of what I said . . . I'm really *bushed,* you know."

"Sure," said Nat. He opened up the door. "All they're going to be is glad to see you," he predicted.

That night they had to eat a lot of chocolate chip, to toast the prodigal's return and all. Coke's story got to be that he'd decided they were right. There wasn't any point in challenging his parents—nothing would be proved, or solved, by that. And besides, he said, he'd missed the Group. He looked at Marigold when he said that, wanting to be sure she got his meaning. She met his eyes and smiled.

When everyone decided it was time for bed, Coke found a way to say to her—he'd had to snatch the dish towel out of Ludi's hands—that maybe they could meet upstairs, after everyone had been in bed awhile. And she had nodded, quickly, not the least bit hesitant, it seemed. The sleeping plan that people had decided on, the day before, was that they'd just use both the bunk rooms on the kitchen level, one for males and one for females, just like Spring Lake Lodge. That way, they wouldn't get their stuff spread out, nor would they use the bedrooms that were clearly "family." The bunk rooms were the guest rooms of the house; it seemed as if the Robinsons had lots of friends who skied.

So, at something in the neighborhood of two A.M., Coke and Marigold slipped out of bunk—first him, and then, some minutes later, her—and tiptoed up the stairs. And when they met, beside the sofa in the living room, they didn't say "Hello" or "How are you?" They simply took ahold of one another, made a little sound like "Oh," and brought their heads together till they found each other's mouths. When Coke came up for air, his next move slowly forming in his mind, he was surprised—astounded, terrified, delighted—to find that Marigold just crossed her hands and seized her cotton nightie underneath the armpits, and pulled it up and over, off her head. And underneath, she didn't even have on rainbow underpants.

Marigold had never been too awed by sex; it was not an unfamiliar topic in her home. Her parents, "Roz" and "Toby" R_____ (also known, in other homes, as "Mom" and "Dad"), believed in what they called "demystification." They also "demythologized" the parent–child relationship.

"Parents aren't perfect," little Mark and Marigold were told—and shown in countless ways. Parents quarreled, suffered, cried, they learned; parents "let their anger out"; parents were unfair, got frequent headaches, picked on one another.

But parents also offered lots of information, much of it unknown to other children. Marigold (and also brother Mark) found out that there were lots of names for all the parts of them that certain silly other people thought should not be ever touched, or talked about. They learned that, far from being dirty, those parts were beautiful and fun. Neither Roz nor Toby ever hid those parts from either of their children, and even touched each other on them, sometimes. The showers in their house had clear glass doors on them, and any time there weren't guests, bathing suits were never worn inside their indoor pool. Like many little girls, Marigold enjoyed her father's daily shaving ritual—more, perhaps, because he did it naked, using a soft brush, and lots and lots of lather. He often put a dab of lather on her nose, or chin, and once (in quite a frisky mood) he lathered up his pubic hair, pretending he would shave it. But then her mother entered, also naked, and told him he should cut the exhibitionism. "Later on," she said to Marigold, picking Toby's penis up, as if it were an unimportant medal, "you'll see he hasn't got that much to brag about."

Her parents always had a lot of books around the house that told, and showed, what sex was all about, so long before she thought of doing anything, she knew the things there were to do. Both her parents told her many times they knew she would experiment, and that was fine with them. They also drilled her on precautions though, including those that went beyond mere birth control.

"Fucking's just like any other skill, you have to practice it," they told her. "But unlike racquetball, or golf, you can't just go right out and play with everyone you want to. You have to be discreet."

"Guys talk," said Toby, grandly. "You can take my word for that. And a lot of times they'll tell a girl they love her, when all they want's a little piece of tail."

Marigold first "did it" on the Saturday after her thirteenth birthday, half to get it over with and half out of curiosity. It went all right and she decided to keep on with it, but a lot of boys she knew reminded her of Toby some, and so she followed his advice and never slept around. She also never lost her head and "took a chance" with birth control, though in her fifteenth summer she'd hitchhiked to the Cape and gotten trapped inside a Winnebago by a guy. His plan was that he'd feed her beer and something else back there, but she had faked some tears and told him she was twelve. When he let her go, she hopped the bus back home. "Forevermore," she told O.D., and meant it.

Marigold had lots of practice in decision-making; Roz and Toby saw to that. From very early in her life, she often got to choose, instead of having to; to certain sorts of people, she seemed "spoiled." Her parents didn't make her do her homework every night, and understood when she said certain teach-

ers (or their subjects) were "a monstro-fucking bore."
She did high-honors-level work in classes that she
liked, and just scraped by in others. If there was
something in New York to see or do, she didn't have
to wait for weekends or her birthday. She always
starred in the plays at school, and she was interesting enough in one of them to catch the eye of Jack
duVivier, founder (and producer and director) of
something called the Harlequins, a local theater
group.

Jack duVivier was Roz and Toby's age, which
made him close to forty, but not entirely like them;
in lots of ways, it seemed that he was Then, instead
of Now. He didn't talk about himself, or see a shrink;
his clothes were loose, and muted—made of things
like cashmere wool and silk and cotton: single-knit,
if that's a word. He drove a vintage Jag, and never
joined a health club. He didn't ski, and neither did he
marry. He had the most exquisite manners in the
world, Roz thought; he always let her use the bathroom first.

Roz was in love with Jack duVivier. *In love.* Affairs were one thing; Toby was another. Love—which
she had clearly never known before—was something
else.

Roz and Toby had affairs; Marigold learned that
when she was nine or ten, and one of them came up
at dinner time. At first it didn't bother her that Roz
had "played around" with Mr. Gilman, or that Toby
"had a little on the side" with Mrs. Fish. Roz told
her that her parents were each other's "best-best-
friends," like she and Wendy (pre-"Odetta") were;
each of them had other friends, from time to time,
but both of them knew who was always best. Toby
told her people, like machines, were getting more
and more complex, and this complexity produced a
lot of different kinds of needs. He explained to her
he'd *always* like roast chicken best of all, but that,

from time to time, he had to have a piece of steak, "or Fish," he said, and laughed, and winked a big one, leaned and pinched her on the thigh.

Her parents seemed to talk about affairs a lot, their own and other people's, both, and in a little while it came to seem to Marigold that possibly affairs were not so harmless after all. She learned of women getting "knocked around a bit" by irate husbands, and men who'd "gotten took for every dime" by angry wives. Wendy's parents' marriage "came unglued," and Wendy's mother had to go and "get detoxed" at some place called The Birches.

By the time a few more years had passed, Marigold began to give opinions on affairs at dinner time. She told her parents she and Wendy (just about to be Odetta, now) had done a survey of their class at school. Fifteen sets of parents, out of forty, were divorced; another six were separated. "That sucks," she told her parents. "Over half the people who conceived the kids in this one class don't even want to live together now. What I want to know is: where do they get off, to have a kid at all, if they're so fucking immature they don't know what they want? And who's to blame the kid for feeling she might be the next to hear that Mommy and Daddy don't love *her* anymore, either?"

Roz and Toby listened carefully to Marigold, and also talked it over with each other. They realized they *had* been immature, and "were playing with dynamite," as Toby put it. So, at one roast chicken dinner, on one Tuesday night in March (Toby always cooked on Tuesday, when Roz stayed late at work), they told their children they were through with "all that fucking nonsense." Holding hands across the table, they vowed their faith in what they called "home cooking." Mark and Marigold rejoiced.

When Roz discovered, three weeks after that, she and Jack duVivier were "very much in love," she felt that Marigold would understand (if ever she found out). After all, her daughter was a woman now, and as a woman she would need love, too, and understand how there could be two people in the world who really truly—yes!—were made for one another. Jack had told her how he'd searched for her so long, so hungrily, and she had told him back how long she'd been there, waiting.

But neither one told Marigold they planned to find each other, once again, beside the indoor pool at her house, the early April day she missed the bus that took her class to Washington, D.C. She'd come on home, decided on a swim; she'd nothing much to do for two whole days, so maybe she would start to really get in shape, she thought. She undressed in her room and got a towel; a suit would not be needed. It was lucky she was barefoot. Roz and Jack were barefoot, too, all over, and busy on the double chaise beside the pool. So Marigold retreated noiselessly. She went back to her room, and dressed, and left the house. She spent the next two days at O.D.'s mother's place, waiting to be able to come back from Washington.

Two weeks later, Miss Marino, drama coach at school, told her that the Harlequins were looking for a juvenile to work in summer stock. It seemed that Mr. (Jack) duVivier had seen the play at school, and wondered if, by any chance, she might be interested.

Miss Marino made the introductions, and on the fourth of May, in the master bedroom of that lovely old Colonial on the corner of Maple and Prospect, Marigold tried out for a place in the Harlequins. If Jack duVivier had been the type to kiss and tell, he would have told the world she was "a little hell cat." Marigold made sure she left some marks on him.

On June twenty-eighth, she told her mother she was pregnant and wanted an abortion. She said she'd been "a little dope"; she certainly knew better.

But, she said, she thought her mother'd understand: she *had* been swept away. It was just that she was *so* in love, she said.

Roz was very understanding; she signed the forms the doctor'd given Marigold—the procedure would be done within the week. And just as Marigold was going out the door, Roz asked her if she knew the "boy" by any chance. Not that she was asking for the name, but, naturally, she wondered if she knew him, this "boy" her daughter loved so much.

Marigold had waited for that question. She smiled and said she thought Roz maybe did. "He's not a *boy,*" she said, "exactly. He's a man. I think I may have seen him at a party here, the first time. A Mr. Jack duVivier." And with that, she slowly closed the door behind her.

If Roz had not been "hopelessly in love," it might have been a different story. But, as it was, it meant that Marigold was entered in Group 6, at Coldbrook Country School.

"In lots of ways," she'd told O.D., before she took that bus, September first, "I'm glad I'm getting out of here."

O.D. agreed with that. She'd been sent to boarding school herself, in jolly old Virginia.

Chapter Six

Nat's roommate senior year at UVM had been a girl named Jen Maloney. Jen Maloney studied nursing. She thought that all B.A.'s were bores and bullshitters, except for Nat, most of the time.

"You're the best B.A. I've ever known," said Jen Maloney to her roommate, Nat, one day in May, "so please don't take this personal. But—have you learned one single thing the last four years that you would call important? From reading all those bullshit books, I mean." Jen Maloney was leaving for Cambodia in June.

"Why, yes," said Nat, "I've learned two things, I think." He held two fingers up, to show he came in peace, and had important things to say. He wiggled them: two things. He also smiled. "I learned that everything is pretty much like everything else. And I also learned that nothing is the same as anything."

Jen Maloney rolled her eyes around.

"Your witness, God," she said.

Nat and Jen Maloney had talked like that a lot, and so he was a little bit surprised when he thought of what he'd said that day in May, in Burlington, when he was sitting in the woods in mid-September. It was like all of a sudden remembering that there was a purple towel buried in the dirty laundry on your closet floor.

What brought it back, of course, was his discovery that while living in the woods with these five kids in such peculiar circumstances was certainly unique as an experience, it was also loaded with the same old set of stresses and conflicts and disagreements that always was a part of "ordinary" life.

For instance: Freedom vs. Control (or, if you will, spontaneity vs. planning, improvisation vs. discipline, excitement vs. boredom, my way vs. your way, or however else you want to put it).

Example 1:

"Well, I guess it's Friday morning," said Sully, the second morning they'd been back from Boynton Falls.

"Is it?" said Ludi.

"So what?" said Coke.

"You know what I think'd be fun?" said Marigold. "To try to just live by body moods, or your biological clock, or whatever they call it. I mean, eat when you're hungry, instead of at three specific times during the day. And sleep when you're tired, maybe only three or four hours at a time, like that."

"I knew a guy at college who tried to get completely into his body for a whole month," Nat said. "What happened was, he gained twenty pounds, picked up a case of VD, and almost flunked two courses. He was a psych major. So what he did was, he wrote it all up as an independent study next term, and got an A out of it anyway. By then he'd dieted the weight off and gotten cured of his dose, and the A averaged in with the low grades he'd gotten to leave him with his usual B minus. So it all worked out in the end. It was almost as if nothing had happened, he said."

Ludi laughed. "I bet you made that up," she said. "I bet none of that happened at all." She pushed at his shoulder. "Get out of here," she said.

"I guess that's what we all have to do," said Sara. Nat nodded, looked at his watch.

"What?" said Coke. "What for?"

"Because it's *Friday*," said Sully. "The Robinsons, remember? They could be coming for the *weekend*."

"Oh, Jesus," said Coke. The day before, they hadn't done an awful lot, other than to paint the Pumpkin olive green, with streaks, and make one trip to Spring Lake Lodge with some of their supplies. Coke was feeling sort of reckless, fatalistic; more than ever, he wished for a moustache. He thought he was in love with Marigold—"just blown away," he would have said, if he'd had someone he could talk about it with. And then he'd have grinned a little grin and gone "Phee-ew!" and shook his head respectfully. Sully wasn't right for talk like that, and Nat was just as bad, for altogether different reasons.

"What a pain in the ass," said Coke. Spring Lake Lodge was not set up for romance, so it seemed to him.

When all of them announced their readiness to go, Nat suggested one more final check of all the rooms, to see if there was any tiny thing they'd missed, some clue that they'd been in the place for days. They found a towel behind the bathroom door ("Yeah, Sully") and shampoo and conditioner beside the tub and a razor on the edge of it ("Marigold!"). Plus a compass on the mantelpiece ("That must be Sara's"), a sock beneath the sofa ("Nat—no, Coke!"), and in the freezer section of the gas refrigerator, maybe half a quart of chocolate chip ("Let's blame that on Nat, O.K.?").

"God, I can't remember how this kitchen was," said Ludi. "I think that there were glasses on the drain board, those old-fashioneds—but maybe it was tall ones. And how about that coffee pot? Was it sitting on the burner in the back, or what?"

No one could remember, quite. And no one really liked the thought of two trips up to Spring Lake Lodge, or maybe three, getting the supplies up there. Plus Nat would have to hide the Pumpkin somewhere.

There seemed to be a lot of sentences with words like "have-to," "ought-to," "double-check," and "be-real-careful" in them.

Example 2:

"Well," said Nat, on Friday night. "I guess we'd better get our act together."

He didn't know he'd used a different tone of voice in saying that, but he soon knew something'd happened. Suddenly, the Group took on a wariness it never had before: the sort of sullen and defensive style you often find in classrooms in a high school, when teachers speak of major tests to come, or dare to claim that students aren't working to "capacity."

"Huh?" said Marigold and Sara.

"How d'you mean?" said Sully.

Ludi looked at Nat and raised her eyebrows. Coke watched his own right foot move back and forth along the ground.

Nat laughed a nervous laugh and did a kind of wiggle with his elbows. "Don't look at me like that," he said.

"But *what?*" said Ludi, smiling now.

Nat laughed again, but this time he felt different, so it sounded different. Other people smiled, and shifted in their seats a little. Nat had got his white hat back again.

"But . . . well . . . it seems to me we've got to maybe do some things that aren't altogether fun . . . ," Nat started.

"O.K., O.K., just tell us what it *is*," said Coke. "It's obvious you've got a list. Let's get it over with."

"I haven't got a *list,*" said Nat, a little bit offended.

134

His father was the one for lists. He wrote them down in tiny little writing, in a tiny little leather book he carried in a pocket in his vest. "It's just sort of a bunch of things that are all more or less part of the same thing. . . ."

That incoherence got him sympathetic nods, so he felt better and talked on.

The "same thing" he'd referred to was how to keep from getting killed, and so he called it that, in just those words. Might just as well, he thought. It was funny, the way people's minds worked. The thought that anyone would try to kill them was, on the one hand, very real: a fact that they believed, the main fact in their lives, the reason they were where they were, with just this group of people. But, on the other hand, it was also so far-out, remote, impossible, they couldn't take it in, or dwell on it. At sixteen—even twenty-two—death was still a whole career away, some other people's business altogether. "This can't be happening to me," is what some inner portion of their selves kept saying. And here was Nat insisting that it was.

Coke hated listening to Nat. Whenever he was forced to think about . . . this "mess" (he always called it to himself), he'd also always think, "We've had it." Sooner or later, Coke had learned in life, the other people always won. You never got away with it, whatever it was. He and Nat and the others in Group 6 could plan and scheme and practice all they wanted to, but in the end they'd lose. The best thing, as far as he was concerned, was to just try not to think about it, and have the best time he could for as long as he could. Really.

What Nat was suggesting now was that they organize their lives in such a way that (a) they'd have an early-warning system of some sort, no matter how imperfect, and that (b) each of them would always know exactly where he was (or she) and how to get to

135

somewhere else where there'd be food and shelter. That was for openers. It'd also be good, he said, if everyone learned some rudiments of chopping, tracking, hiding, shooting bows and arrows, and first aid.

"Say, how about kung fu and calculus?" asked Marigold. "Or making lamps out of household waste? Not to mention modern dance and whitewater canoeing. Natty, you slay me," she said. "It sounds as if you want us to have seminars and sentries, and run around in the woods all day with contour maps and compasses."

"Well, I'd say it's either that or go completely native," Nat replied. "Try to pass for some lost Stone Age tribe that still ekes out a bare existence eating snails and grubs and one another's body lice. Of course, we'd have to mat our hair and bury all our clothes and not talk smart to strangers. . . ."

Sully and the girls all smiled, and even Coke made one quick semi-snorting sound that could have been a humorous reaction.

"It sounds," said Sara, "very much as if we've got a lot to do. And a lot to learn." She didn't sound displeased at all. Sully nodded, wrinkling his brow.

"I think we're going to need alarm clocks." Ludi smiled. "A schedule, perhaps. You really do mean posting lookouts and all that?"

"Yeah," said Nat. "I think we ought to. Certain places, certain times. It never will be foolproof, that's for sure. But we can make it harder to surprise us. As for a schedule"—he grinned—"I don't know. But I guess it'd make sense if we agreed on, *you* know, what we're going to do, and when."

"Wouldn't you know it?" said Coke. "It's bad enough that we have people trying to kill us, maybe. But at least it gets us out of all that chicken-shit routine you always have at school. So what do we turn around and do? Set up a fucking schedule that's just as bad as school, or worse. Jesus Christ."

"Well, what do you want to do?" said Marigold. "Sit around on your ass and wait for them to find us? Doing what, all day, may I ask? There isn't any dope"—she counted on her fingers—"or any soaps to watch or any booze to drink except what Robinsons are sure to miss. Or any phones, or any magazines, or stereos, or delis. The *least* thing we can do, until we've got a—whachacallit?—long-range plan, is be a little hard to find."

"All right, already." Coke waved a hand at her. "I get the point. But we'll see how you like it when it's four A.M. in the middle of a rainstorm and you're the one that's watching Cowshit Canyon, waiting for the other flop to fall, heh-heh."

He ducked the piece of kindling she flipped in his direction.

Example 3:

Group 6 went into training right away. Every day they rose at dawn and spent the morning doing map and compass work and traipsing through the woods, going out from Spring Lake Lodge in all directions. On these trips, they'd practice recognizing trees and tracks, and learning how to go a little quieter, or climb a tree with confidence, and copy certain bird-calls.

Afternoons they'd work on skills: shelters, fire-starting, axe-work, bow-and-arrow, carpentry (like building boxes they could cache their food in). At Spring Lake Lodge, they always had a lookout in a tree below the spruces. From that tree, there was a splendid northern view, looking down the side that anyone who wasn't partly mountain goat would come from, if they came. A sentry-turn would last two hours, and they'd sometimes try to test the person, one or more of them, by sneaking down the back side of their hill and coming up where he or she should see them. The sentry'd make a blue jay's call any time that something seemed suspicious; a second call was red-alert. The sentry would come down and join the rest of them at Spring Lake Lodge, and all of them would then evacuate. Packs for that were always packed and ready.

After spending four days at the Lodge, they decided to move down to Robinson's early Wednesday morning and, if all went well, stay on till early Friday afternoon again. That way, they could color in some large new sections on their maps, places nearer to the school and roads than Spring Lake Lodge was. And also take hot showers. They discovered that the Robinsons had not come up to spend the weekend after all; maybe they were strictly summer folks and skiers. Down there, the Group went out together in the woods all day, and so they didn't use a lookout. And then, when they got back, they merely kept a person on the porch, to look and listen down the driveway. In some peculiar way, they all felt safer in a house like that, and quite absurdly sure that anyone who looked for them would have to use the road. During supper, all of them were lookouts: they ate out on the porch.

So, Thursday evening they were eating brownies in the twilight when Marigold demanded their attention: three good knuckle-raps laid down upon the wooden railing she was sitting on. It seemed to Nat that everyone was talking softer than they used to and was sort of more alert for other sounds. Nat also knew that he'd been known to kid himself. He turned to Marigold.

"What I wanted to ask," she said, "was what other people were feeling about . . . well, about . . ." She looked at Ludi. "I don't know how to say this."

"Seeing as I don't know what you're talking about," Ludi said, "I don't either. Why don't you just say it?"

"O.K.," said Marigold—and, oops, there went a

giggle, half a one, a gig. She choked it off ferociously and said, "I think we ought to cool it with a lot of the boy–girl business we're doing. Like, I don't put my body in Spring Lake unless the guys are all a half a mile away, and Sully can't take a piss if he isn't fifty trees away from Ludi, and isn't-it-a-dreadful-thing if Sara goes into the boys' room when Coke is changing clothes. That all just doesn't make much sense to me, in the situation we're in here. It seems to me there may be times when we're just going to have to be a little more . . . I don't know, *relaxed* with one another. So maybe we ought to start now. Get used to it. I'd like to know what other people think."

Nat looked around the porch. Sully was looking at the deck and smiling; Coke was looking at the deck and frowning. Sara was looking at Ludi, and Ludi was looking at Marigold and scratching the side of her head, but also smiling. He was looking around at everybody, and so was Marigold. *They* smiled at one another.

"You're probably right," said Ludi. "I know that I'd feel funny at first, but I guess I'd get over it. I guess we all would."

"I don't know," said Sully, still smiling and looking at the floor, but also shaking his head.

"It might be just a little harder on the guys," said Coke. "Heh-heh. If you know what I mean."

"Gee, no," said Marigold, a finger on her cheek. "I don't believe I do. Maybe you could tell us, Coke. Or show us, better still."

Coke got up and grabbed her, made as if to throw her off the porch.

Nat said, "That whole thing scared me to death when I went away to college. Co-ed bathrooms and all. But it turned out it really isn't all that big a deal."

"God, I don't know," said Sully, still smiling and

still shaking his head, but looking all around the porch now.

"I'm as bad as you are," Sara said to him. "Maybe"—she checked the other faces—"we could just agree we don't . . . have any absolute no-no's, or whatever you want to say. But that people won't, well, push it. You know what I mean? Like make a point of trying to catch someone, or something. Not that anybody would."

"Sure," said Marigold. "The point is to be cool. A lot of it's in what you're used to, from when you're growing up and all. Mah people were so po' that none of us had clo's," she drawled, "and Pappy burned up all the doh's to keep us wohm." She switched back to her normal voice. "Like I said, I think the main thing is not feeling we absolutely-have-to this, or positively-can't-do that. That kind of thing's a bummer. But respecting someone else's feelings—hell, that's about the most important thing there is, it seems to me. Like now"—she got up—"I'm going to take my last hot shower until whenever we get back here. Completely by *moi-même,* if everybody *s'il vous plaît*s."

And that was pretty much that, to Nat's amazement and delight. It wasn't that things got a whole lot different, and everyone immediately went skinny-dipping with everybody else; the boys and Sara—so it seemed to Nat—were much too shy for that. What seemed to happen was that now it was O.K. to pass and look at naked people of the other sex, if not to stop and socialize. Or ogle. Mostly, that had to do with being in Spring Lake, or getting in and out of it. Marigold, and sometimes Coke, would go "Eeek!" in those situations, and make a big fuss about grabbing a towel or sinking underwater, but the rest of them (including Nat himself, he noticed) were almost yawningly casual. Quick, too, but casual. Nat found that he couldn't help noticing, of course, that the

140

girls in Group 6 had pretty excellent bodies, top to toe. Marigold had definitely put on the briefest bathing suit that summer, judging by her tan. She had real long legs and full, round breasts; her arms were sort of skinny, lacking definition, and she still had a little polish left on a few of her toenails. Sara had the big, broad swimmer's shoulders and those sturdy thighs, just a great athletic figure, hard and sleek and round. She could probably get fat, if she ever stopped exercising and started eating bon-bons—not a very likely set of circumstances. Sara did her stretches and her situps every day, and Ludi did them with her (both of them had ropy stomach muscles), and after a couple of days Marigold began to join them, making lots of grunts and jokes so everyone would know she wasn't serious. Ludi was in excellent condition, weighing maybe ninety-five. She did have small, just barely curving breasts, but still she seemed extremely feminine to Nat. She wore her body easiest of all of them: never bothered, never hurried, never showing off.

One day, Nat remembered he was looking at the "dregs," the "lemons" of the Coldbrook Country School enrollment. He almost laughed out loud.

Homer Cone had not come close to laughing for a good two weeks. Except in class, of course, where certain times you had to laugh to keep from crying. He really doubted if Euclid himself could simplify geometry to the point that some of Doctor's baby boneheads could contend with it on equal terms. But that was par for the course. Homer Cone was never one to overrate the clients of the Coldbrook Country School. Colleagues sometimes said that they were "teaching" English 4, or first-year Spanish, but Homer Cone preferred to say he was "conducting class," in business math or algebra—whatever.

"I cannot call this 'teaching,'" he would say,

munching on a jelly donut in the teachers' smoking lounge. "When someone 'teaches,' other people 'learn,' and that does not seem possible for this year's crop of moneyed melon-minds."

Older faculty would shake their heads and chuckle at these misanthropic musings. "There goes good old Homer," they would say. Younger teachers, fresh from Vassar and Purdue, would ask each other why a decent school would keep a moldy, big-domed, prehistoric fart like that around. "Back at Choate, when I was there," they'd whisper, sneaking sideways looks at Homer Cone, "they had this asshole by the name of Ackroyd. . . ."

Yet it wasn't just his classes that had Homer Cone annoyed; there also was the matter of Group 6. He'd said that he would "comb the woods" until he found them; he'd said they "had a date" with Homer Cone. But at the rate that he was combing, the date was very apt to start off with a "2." That's talking year, not month or day.

And that was only the beginning of his problems.

Most of all, there were these outside complications. Doctor had mentioned that he planned to get in touch with his so-called "leading authority in that particular field," the man who'd recommended Rittenhouse as someone who might . . . lead Group 6.

Well, Doctor *had* done that (he'd called up Homer Cone to tell him so), and (he further told H. Cone) he'd been pretty much unprepared for the "passion and, er, well, *vulgarity*" of that important gentleman's reaction.

The leading authority had advised Doctor (so Doctor said to Homer C.) that he had plans to "contact up" a certain relative of his, whom he would urge to travel, with dispatch, to Coldbrook (" . . . get his ass down there before I start to cut it into steaks and chops . . .") and sever all connections with young Rittenhouse as soon as he could find him (" . . . shoot that college prick right up his nose . . ."). The relative would be in touch with Doctor in an hour's time, to make specific plans for his arrival.

In fact, it was a *half* an hour later (Doctor made that clear to Homer Cone) when he got the call that he expected. The leading authority's relative's name turned out to be Emfatico. "Like 'emphatic,' with an *o*," said Doctor, in his gentle voice. "Arnold B. Emfatico. He'll be here in the morning . . . 'oh, what a beautiful day,' " sang Doctor.

To Homer Cone, that *was* unpleasant news, personified. It meant another hunter in the woods, and not a hunter, really, more a *killer*. A Mad Dog. A man with pointed, thin-soled shoes and submachine guns—an out-of-stater, even, more than likely. And even worse than all of that, a person who might beat him to his prey.

"Oh, Lord," thought Homer Cone. He really didn't have a prayer. And then he thought of something else. This man had been assigned to deal with Rittenhouse, but still, that didn't mean that he would calmly leave Group 6 to him and Mrs. Ripple. Definitely not. Homer Cone had seen Italian movies in his time, and there were certain things he knew, therefore, about Italian people. For instance, they were very big on children. In Italian movies, there were lots of children, always, and Italian adults yelled at them a lot and gestured with their hands in funny ways—but nothing more than that. So, if a person named Emfatico just *ever* came upon two people like himself and Mrs. Ripple, while they were doing . . . well, a portion of their *job* at Coldbrook Country School, why there was no predicting (but there was!) exactly what he'd do.

Homer Cone had all those thoughts in just a flash of time, but Doctor hadn't finished talking yet.

"On top of that," said Doctor, "there is a further complication. . . ."

As Homer Cone emitted sixteen soundless groans, Doctor then proceeded to explain that still another person would be joining them at Coldbrook. It seemed that this Emfatico, besides his duties as an agent for his kinsman, had also had another kind of job. He was, apparently, a bursar's clerk in Burlington, Vermont, at UVM, and thus a worker for the state. In this capacity, he'd had to deal with students there, and one of them—incredible coincidence—was Rittenhouse. To make a long story short, the two of them (one acting on his own behalf, the other on the state's) had made a most irregular . . . agreement. In fact, it was a wager, which made it so irregular there wasn't any way to enter it in Records and Accounts the Bursar kept. Yet, in spite of all of that, it still was crystal clear that Nat did owe the state a certain sum of money. The Bursar, Mr. Darling, wanted to make good and sure the state collected on this debt; historically, the state had never tolerated welching, he made clear, going back to Ethan Allen's time. He'd sent a bill to Nat at home, and got the letter back, "Address unknown." And so he'd run a routine check in nearby states and that way learned that Nat had bought a car, and it was registered at "Coldbrook Country School." Ah-hah. Mr. Darling ordered this Emfatico, who knew the man by sight, to go with him to Coldbrook, even as his uncle had (not mentioning accompaniment) the day before. The Bursar planned that certain papers would be served on Nat, and possibly arrangements would be made to confiscate his salary at Coldbrook Country School.

But, said Dr. Simms to this Emfatico (as he told Homer Cone), this Nat had "disappeared" the week before, and so there wasn't any point in any Mr. Darling coming to the scene with papers. But this Emfatico had said that Mr. Darling told him he was coming, and that Mr. Darling never changed his mind, the little sweetheart.

So, concluded Doctor, there would be not one but two new faces on the campus in the morning. Would Homer Cone, by any chance, be free to lunch with them? And him, of course, and Mrs. Ripple?

Homer Cone agreed to be on hand. He did not expect that he would like that lunch, or anybody at it, much; he was correct in all particulars. The meal included Brussels sprouts.

"I've explained to Mr. Darling . . . '*je vous aime beaucoup . . . ,*' " Doctor sang under his breath, "and Mr.—er—Emfatico that Rittenhouse was fired late last week. They could have saved themselves the trip," Doctor said emphatically, addressing Homer Cone, but turning at the end to Mr. Darling. The last thing Doctor wanted was a governmental presence on the scene.

"But yet," said Mrs. Ripple sweetly, "Mr. Cone believes he's probably still here. Not here at school, of course, but in the woods around, some place." Mr. Darling seemed like such a perfect little gentleman. He had on horn-rimmed glasses, and he smoked a pipe, and wore a pair of argyle socks with garters. Mr. Ripple, right up to the time he died, believed a gentleman wore garters with his socks, except while playing tennis.

"Apparently he's very fond of camping out, and did so, here, all summer," Mrs. Ripple added.

Homer Cone directed one swift kick at Mrs. Ripple's shins. Typically, except when rifles were involved, he missed. The kick connected with the calf of Arn-the-Barn Emfatico. Arn didn't give the smallest sign that this had happened, but he also made a mental note of where the kick had come from. So, round-face was a bigot, was he? Arn-the-Barn had had to deal with men like Cone before: men who took what he was prone to call "an attitude." People who figured that every person with an Italian–American

145

surname had to like the opera or Frank Sinatra, one, and have a mother who was fat and made him eat.

"Well," said Mr. Darling pleasantly, "that is an interesting thought. Perhaps, just for the fun of it, I'll start to motor down here weekends, have a look around. I'm quite a Ranger Rick, myself." He gave a modest chuckle. "And wouldn't I just love to get this thing cleared up—eh, Arnold?"

"Oh, you bet," said Arn-the-Barn to his superior. "In fact, I just was thinking, Mr. Darling. I've got some sick days due, and also that full week I didn't take this summer. I was saving that for deer huntin' "—Arn could say that like a native, now—"but this seems more important. In fact, if you could see your way to let me borrow from my next year's summer holiday, I could keep on hunting Nat until I found him, probably." His uncle had suggested something very much like that, although in somewhat different and more . . . urgent language.

"My word, that's very thoughtful of you, Arnold," Mr. Darling said. "Suppose, for now, we just say you're on furlough. We'll see how long it takes to get a line on Rittenhouse, and then adjust accordingly, O.K.?" He clapped his open hand on one of Arn's huge shoulders.

Arnold didn't understand what Mr. Darling said, exactly, but he thought it was, again, the same thing that his uncle said, except in Darling-talk. Regular English translation: "Find Rittenhouse, or else."

"Fine," said Arn-the-Barn, and smiled right back at Mr. Darling.

"I must be getting back to Burlington, today," said Mr. Darling affably. "But perhaps I'll see you—one or all—late Friday afternoon. I'll plan to slip on in and out with just a minimum of fanfare." Mr. Darling laughed out loud, and Mrs. Ripple joined him merrily. "I'll park my Rover right outside this building, if I may," he said to Doctor, "and then climb underneath my pack and disappear. If, by any chance, I, well, get lucky"—(Obviously, he meant: "If my superior skills pay off as I expect they will")—"I'll certainly report to you, sir."

Doctor nodded, with the shadow of a smile.

Mr. Darling shortly rose and wrung each hand, and bowed to Mrs. Ripple. Arnold had to drive him back to Burlington, so he, too, took his leave. "But I'll be seeing you," he seemed to say to Homer Cone. "Whenever."

"Why?" said Homer Cone to Mrs. Ripple, once the two of them were gone, and only three of them remained. "Why? Why? Why? Why? Why?"

"Why what?" said Mrs. Ripple.

"Why tell that stupid Darling I thought Rittenhouse was *here?*"

"I don't think he's a stupid Darling at all," said Mrs. Ripple. "He seemed like rather a dear. And besides that, it's the truth. Maybe he can find them, anyway, and if he does, it's no skin off your nose"— (bouncy-butter-buns)—"'cause all *he* wants is *money.*" Mrs. Ripple pouted.

"I know, I know," said Doctor. "The thing that *gravels* me is all this governmental interference in the private sector." Doctor laid one clean pink fist upon the table. "Even if a fellow looks like a Republican, you still don't know. Mark my words. Pretty soon, they'll have their forms and guidelines, rules and regulations. First thing you know, you can hardly recognize your own business anymore. It makes me just see red . . . 'red robin goes bob-bob-bobbin' along,'" sang Doctor, as he rose and toddled from the room.

In addition to the competition, Homer Cone had had to face another major problem: his own weakness as a hunter. Not the shooting part, of course; his shooting—it could take your breath away. And often did—that muskrat's, for example. But as far as having a sense of direction was concerned . . . well, Homer Cone couldn't point to the west while standing on Laguna Beach at sunset. And he certainly wasn't going to trust Mrs. Ripple very far; anyone knew that a woman couldn't even read a road map.

So what he thought was, just at first, they'd only search the *nearby* woods—woods that you could see a road from, or some section of the school. With Mr. Darling entering the hunt, this strategy made even greater sense, to Homer Cone. If, by any chance, the Group *was* near the school, they certainly didn't deserve to be found by this bird Darling right away—or that Eyetalian, either.

Here's the way that Homer Cone explained it to his colleague.

"My strategy," he said to Mrs. Ripple, "is simply to eliminate, eliminate, *eliminate*. Every time I know a place they're not, I'm that much closer to the place they are."

Homer Cone had once misplaced his gold electroplated pen (he said to Mrs. Ripple). What he'd done was take four sheets of graph paper, one for every room in his apartment; he drew a different room, to scale, on each of them. Then, with lots and lots of masking tape, he'd sectioned off each room in three foot squares, and started in to search. Every time he searched a square of room, and didn't find the pen, he'd make a big black *X*, right on the corresponding square of paper. Starting in the bathroom, he'd *X*ed out every square of every single room. Three weeks later, to the day, he'd found the pen.

"Guess where?" he said to Mrs. Ripple, through his nose.

She made a certain guess inside her head, but what she said was, "My, I can't imagine."

"It had slipped down in the lining of the jacket I

was wearing on the day I looked for it!" said Homer Cone triumphantly. "The system that I used was even better than I thought," he said. "That pen had been in not just one, but *every* square I searched!"

Mrs. Ripple smiled a smile of mere politeness. She wasn't much impressed by what she'd heard. "Eliminate" meant just one thing to her, and anyway, what worked for pens might fail for people, so it seemed to her. What was to prevent the members of Group 6 from coming back and staying in a place they'd . . . searched, already? She tried that question out on Mr. Cone.

"Most unlikely," said Homer Cone, shaking his considerable head. "They'd be crazy to stay so close to school, where anybody might bump into them. Rittenhouse may look like a freak, but that doesn't mean he's stupid, too."

"No," said Mrs. Ripple, "it does not. I think that Doctor said his father was at Harvard."

"I wouldn't be surprised," said Homer Cone. "I know that Elliott House is." Homer Cone knew a great deal about Harvard. During his own college days, back in a certain middle-eastern state, he'd ordered all his notebooks from the Harvard "Coop"; he thought that classmates would assume he was a transfer.

But, in any event, he and Mrs. Ripple combed a lot of woods within a short and easy walk from campus. Almost every day they combed. The huge young man, Emfatico, had come back to the area and stayed in Boynton Falls, at Valivu Motel. He drove a white Trans-Am to school and wore a dark brown canvas field coat with a collar made of corduroy—a rugged kind of garment, often seen in duck blinds down in Maryland. Duck hunters like a loose, full, easygoing jacket that doesn't bind a fella in the armpits. And so, indeed, did Arn-the-Barn Emfatico.

* * *

"I just realized something," Marigold said to the rest of Group 6 on the morning of the fourteenth day they'd been together. "I just realized that ever since I met you people, I've been in almost constant pain."

Everybody laughed, but no one contradicted her. She spoke a universal truth: everybody ached. But less each day.

"Listen," said Nat, "on you it looks good. D'you know that people pay real money for intensive physical training courses? It's a national obsession, fitness. So that makes us the hippest of the hip, and it's not even costing us a dime. Anyway, did I ever tell you my theory about good pain and bad pain?" Nat babbled on. "Good pain, see, like what you've got—while it may hurt, it also grows on you. Your muscles hurt, but not as if there's something wrong with them—you dig? Good pain's sort of greenish-blue, where bad pain's got a lot of red in it. . . ."

Coke remembered having "growing pains"—his mother'd called them that—when he was younger. But exercise had never been his thing. He'd never thought that he'd become a closet fitness-freak, yet that was almost what the situation was right now. What had happened was, he'd had to push himself so hard the first few days—that trip to Boynton Falls and back, on top of all the rest—it almost seemed a shame to waste it. And then there was this . . . well, *relationship* with Marigold. Wouldn't it be good for it if he were just a *shade* more of a specimen?

Yet he was still a trifle loath to give up any aspect of his image. His life-style, you might say. Coke had always specialized in lassitude; he was a boredom connoisseur, a laid-back, decorated veteran of countless Bore Wars. Campaigns like that were rather fun. You could find an element of boredom in almost everything that you and other people did, and you could talk about it endlessly. Boringly. Destructively. Bored people specialized in put-downs: every-

150

thing was so boring it deserved to be put down. Each other, themselves—mox-nix.

What Coke really wanted was the best of all possible worlds: to keep his image as the prince of put-downs, the baron of boredom, and at the same time be a stud.

Life was much, much simpler for Sully. Every day he had one plain and simple purpose: to do as many things as possible that Sara'd like. Any time he made her smile and say, "That's good," he was in heaven; every time she called his name, it was a thrill. Sully knew that Coke and Marigold were up to something, meeting one another in the middle of the night. Sully wanted to be up to something, too. He never really had been. Sara must be what he'd overheard a senior at his former school describe as "one boss girl." He could imagine himself telling another guy—not Coke or Nat—that he had met this real "boss girl" at Coldbrook Country School, and that they'd been "seeing one another" for a while.

Sully didn't know whether Sara could get interested in him or not. It seemed to be a fact she was impressed that he could sprint up mountainsides every bit as fast as she could. And shoot a bow and arrow even better. He seemed to have a knack for it. That was amazing: there'd never been a thing before that he'd been good at, from the first. But what he figured was that Sara'd known a lot of guys who specialized in being great at stuff that was a lot more *choice* than bow and arrow shooting. Like football, tennis, or lacrosse—things that people watched and rooted at. Though Sara wouldn't ever be a cheerleader, Sully figured. Hell, no—she'd be on a team of her own. One time, she'd mentioned being chosen swimming captain at her school, and Sully'd seen her take a few strokes in Spring Lake; you could tell she was for real.

Of course he'd quickly looked away that time, because he'd seen that she was naked and it wasn't cool to stare, but still he'd seen enough to make his throat go slightly dry and his heart start to pound, and for his shorts to . . . *you* know. Sully thought perhaps he was in love. He wished he dared ask Coke.

Sara was aware of Sully's interest in her. She'd begun to wish he'd *do* something, but she wasn't sure just what. *Exactly* what, that is; in general was easy. Maybe he'd just start by asking her outside, like Coke and Marigold. They could sit by the fire and talk and stuff, and it'd even be nice to kiss him, she thought. To hug *and* kiss him. She thought it'd feel great to just be able to hold on to someone—a guy— Sully—and feel herself held on to and kind of cozy, like that. Sara didn't want to do it with Sully or anybody else, though for the first time in her life, she started to get a little flash of "Why not?" in her mind, whenever she said to herself she didn't want to do it. And where before there'd always seemed to be a bunch of reasons, now there was—well—mainly (only?) one: birth control. She sure didn't want to get pregnant. But she'd seen Sully's body, and it didn't repel her at all; in fact, it gave her a neat kind of friendly little feeling. He'd be pretty good to touch, she knew that, and she liked it when he looked at her as if he had ideas and hankerings. Being hankered for was quite all right with Sara, at that juncture in her life.

Nat kept telling himself not to get overconfident with the way things were going. Two weeks wasn't any time at all; the whole gig was still in the "getting-to-know-you" period, the first flush—or was that *blush?*—of excitement. New people, new circumstances, a certain amount of urgency. Even a Coke could not be bored already, so it seemed to Nat.

He also felt they'd got a lot accomplished. Everyone was pretty good at how to get from *A* to *B* to *C* to

D to E—A being Spring Lake Lodge, B being the Robinsons', C and D being two supply caches, and E being the Coldbrook Country School. And their woodcraft and overall fitness were definitely improving. There was still a lot of land they had to learn the lay of, and a great deal of practicing they ought to do, but if they didn't lose their desire, and kept on acting like a group, it seemed that they would soon be . . . what you might call *competent*.

For what? Nat sometimes asked himself. He didn't know. It tickled his sense of the ridiculous to realize that the members of Group 6 were having almost exactly the sort of group experience predicted in the catalogue of Coldbrook Country School—though doubtless seldom realized in fact. But still, that didn't get them anywhere.

What they would need, before too long, was an answer to "For what?": a set of goals that went beyond survival. That's what Nat supposed, in any case. Maybe *he* didn't need those kinds of goals, but he was pretty sure that they did.

It was possible that he did, too. It didn't pay to be too certain—jinx yourself. One trouble with fun—finding, seeing, having fun—was that you didn't like to break the flow of it. There were times that he'd felt like Snoopy in those *Peanuts* cartoons, where all he's doing is dancing and dancing and dancing, while Lucy's raving all around him, shouting stuff like "Famine! Pestilence!" and so forth, and all that Snoopy does is dance a little harder. You got to stop sometime.

And then, this one day, they were all together on the slope above the Coldbrook Country School and looking down at it. They were trying to decide whether there was any sense in putting up an observation platform there, up in a tree, when Sully just happened to say, as a making-conversation little joke, "You know what'd make a good base for us?"

153

And Ludi said, "No, what?"

And Sully, pointing, said, "Down there. The school. If we had Spring Lake Lodge and Robinson's and *that*, I'll bet we could hold out for years and years." He laughed a little raucously.

"I'm not so sure," said Coke. "Schools are always full of germs. Diseases. Or maybe it's this allergy I've got. All I know is, every time I hang around a school, I start to puke. . . ."

"Or *it* does . . . ," Marigold threw in.

Sara interrupted. "Wait," she said. She turned to Nat. "I wonder if we could. Seriously."

And he, not serious at all, said, "What?"

"Take over the school," she said. "Just capture the place and tell everyone what they were trying to do to us. Make them listen. I don't know, threaten them with our bows, or get some guns, or something. I'm positive that everybody down there isn't in on this—they couldn't be. The other kids and all. And most of the teachers, probably."

"Oh, sure," said Coke. "I can just see everyone believing us." Coke's tone of voice was gentle, though. He didn't know if Sara was serious or not, but he did remember how freaked-out she'd been by learning all that stuff about their parents. *He* was a sensitive guy; he could understand her feelings.

"They *might* believe us," said Nat. "And if there was some evidence, they'd have to."

"Evidence? Like what?" said Coke.

"Well, like letters, say," said Nat. "Or some record of the money Doctor got from . . . well, *you* know, your parents."

"My God," said Marigold. Everybody turned and looked at her; it was her tone of voice. Until she spoke, the thing was strictly in the jokes-and-what-if's league; Sara'd sounded serious, but that was Sara. Marigold's "My God" was more as if she'd had a vision, looking way out there, above the school.

"Could . . . you . . . imagine?" she said now,
letting out the words one at a time. Her head came
forward, and she switched her gaze to them. "Just
think"—the words began to tumble—"oh, wow,
'cause if there *are* some letters down there that our
parents wrote and we could get our hands on them,
why then our parents"—she raised her eyes and eyebrows and began to smile; her voice slowed down
again—"would damn well *have to do* whatever
things we told them to. You name it. Send us to the
schools and colleges we wanted to be sent to—huh?"
She looked at Sara. "Get us the things we needed
when we wanted them. A little BMW, perhaps?" she
said to Coke.

"Blackmail," Sully had to say, but more in awe
than anything.

"Justice." Marigold spread her mouth in one big
super-sweetness smile. "We didn't start this shit.
But we could finish it, O.K."

Ludi looked at Nat. "You think she's right?" she
asked.

"Jeezum, I don't know," Nat said. Everyone was
looking at him now. "I suppose *so.* Provided you
could get the right sort of evidence, provided it exists
in the first place. And provided that your parents
would rather pay you off than have it all made public."

"Sure they would," said Marigold. "You kidding?
I'm not talking about anything they can't afford.
And anyway, before they decided to send us to Coldbrook, they were probably planning to do all that
anyway. For them, it'd be just going back to plan A."

"Except for the gun in their ribs, this time," said
Coke.

"Exactly so," said Marigold. "And you know what
else? I'd make damn sure that they knew I'd given a
lawyer or someone one of those 'to be opened in the

155

event of my death or disappearance' letters." She gave one strong, emphatic nod.

"Supposing we did that," Sara said. "Supposing we somehow—never mind how, for now—got into the school and found those letters, or whatever they are. Is there any reason, then, why we couldn't get rid of Doctor Simms and any other people who were—*you* know—in on it with him, and then just . . . keep on with the school? Like, let it keep on going, even go to it? The whole bunch of us?"

"If we wanted to, we could," said Marigold. "Why not? Can you imagine that? Having our own little school?" She grinned.

"Boy, would I like that, or *what?*" said Sully. "I think that's a *fantastic* idea, I really do. 'Principal Nat'—how does that sound?" He laughed.

Nat did, too. "Ridiculous," he said. "I don't even know anything about teaching at a school, never mind running one. . . ." He'd been keeping one eye down the slope, while all this talk was going on, and now he said, "Oh-oh . . ."

"What?" said Sara, turning toward the school. There were two people walking on the road below them, coming from the school. One of them had a long bundle balanced on his shoulder.

Nat took out his field glasses. "Everybody take a look," he said. "Those are two of the people who were waiting to . . . um, *shoot* me, week before last." He handed the glasses to Ludi. "The woman's name is Mrs. Ripple; I actually met her, once. I don't know the man's name."

Everybody got to focus on the pair before, quite unexpectedly, they left the road and stepped into the woods.

"Let's get out of here," said Nat. He pulled an ear. "Let's see. Sully. How about a little test? Think that you can get us to the cave from here, in . . . twenty

156

minutes, say?" One of their caches was in a shallow, ledge-rock cave.

Sully made a mouth. "No," he said, "but maybe thirty-five, if everybody's game to try. But just before we go—how about what Marigold and Sara said? You think that we can do it?"

Nat shrugged. He was very conscious of Ludi looking at him, waiting for an answer. And of the fact she hadn't said a thing about this big new plan.

"Let's talk some more," he said. "Anything is possible, I guess."

"Well," said Homer Cone to Mrs. Ripple, "this should be the last of it, I guess. Just one last X and then we'll know they're nowhere near the school."

"Yes," said Mrs. Ripple, stepping over, never *on*, a fallen tree. "Not a sign of them, so far." Homer Cone had seen an owl, day eight, and shot its head off while it slept. And she, while answering a sudden "call of nature" (as she said to Mr. Cone), had seen two students from the school, Shelly Wynn and Robert Fritchman. They were in a glade, below the place she took the call, and quite oblivious to anything. She hadn't mentioned them to Mr. Cone, because she didn't care to talk about the thing that they were doing in the woods. She'd never seen it done before (*never* by herself and Mr. Ripple), although she'd read that people did such things—and therefore knew a lot of names (she wouldn't think of saying) for it. Lucky thing for Shelly, she thought, that it was she, not Mr. Cone, who saw them doing that. It would certainly not be proper at all for a mathematics teacher, and a bachelor, to see a young woman in such a state of *deshabille*. Let alone position.

"Well, just as well," said Homer Cone. "It simply means we're getting closer." He made adjustment to his cap. "Here's my thinking on the thing. They aren't *near* the school, or we'd have found them. And

157

if they'd been holed up *a little ways away*—well, that Eyetalian would have seen them. Or maybe vice-versy, and they'd am-scray out of there. So, what my theory is, is we should go a distance, next. *Drive* to different places, *park,* and—"

"*That's* the way Levi Welch hunts deer," said Mrs. Ripple, interrupting. "He learned it from his father, as I understand."

"I don't mean *staying* in the car," said Homer Cone. "And I don't mean in the middle of the night. What I'm going to do tomorrow is drive way up to where those people from Long Island built that house, a year or two ago. The real nice place with all the sun decks. Looks like a Swiss chalet."

"But I have a class tomorrow afternoon," whined Mrs. Ripple.

"I'll just scout around," said Homer Cone. "And anyway, I wouldn't be a hog." He licked his lips.

Chapter Seven

GIVEN THE WAY that human nature operates, it pretty much figured that almost everyone in Group 6 was just crazy to talk about the Plan. That's "crazy" in the sense of "very-much-extremely-anxious," not "kah-ray-zy" in the sense of "off their gourds."

A few months later on, Nathaniel claimed he'd seen the writing on the wall: that that was when the Group began to come apart. But, naturally, he hadn't *read* it—not out loud, in any case.

"The major storms in life bring out the 'we' in people," he maintained, in rather plonking tones, to his companion of those months (and years to come). "But then, as soon as skies begin to clear, the 'I' pops out all over them, like spots, and off they go, each one to follow his or her own star. Which may, of course, be just a neon light, or a little shiny piece of you-know-what."

She took him by the nose, but didn't squeeze. "You better not believe that altogether," she replied, "unless you want to see a rain dance every morning during breakfast."

"Oh, we're a different kind of 'we' than that," he said. "We're just you and I, for always in the hallways. As the little Messrs. H said to tiny Madame O: without you, we couldn't even make water." And he

159

slid an arm around her shoulders, as if she didn't know that anyway.

"Do you think we ought to do it at night, maybe?" asked Sully, spaghetti dripping off his fork. He was sitting on the main porch at the Robinsons', with his legs crossed tailor-fashion and his plate on the deck in front of him. Much as he loved Ludi's spaghetti, he couldn't concentrate on getting it wound around his fork right, so eating had been a slow business for him.

"Ah, a commando raid," said Coke. "I can see us now: our faces painted so we look like cows and bushes. With a knife up every pant leg, and piano wire coiled around our torsos. Heh. Of course, I am a specialist in hand-to-hand combat, Sul." He turned to Marigold. "Wanna Indian wrestle?" He jumped his eyebrows up and down.

"Oh, shut up," she said. "This is serious. You're only making fun because you're scared; you can't fool Mumsy. Not that I blame you for that." She put a pointer-finger on her chest. "*I* just wonder if we might not be better off in the daylight, when we could try to look natural. Just sort of blend in with the other kids." She moved the hand behind her head. "Not that that would be so easy for some of us, need I add again?" Coke hissed.

"You know what'd be good?" said Sara. "If we could go in on a day they're playing some other school in soccer or something. I know that they have teams. Then there'd be bound to be a lot of strange kids around, from the other school, who came to watch the game."

"Strange kid," said Coke, and tossed his thumb toward Marigold.

"Yeah, that'd be the best," said Sully. "We could just look natural. You know something? I think the only person who'd recognize me in the whole school

160

is the kid I sat next to on the bus coming up. Robbie Something. I wonder if he ever wonders what's become of me."

"He probably thinks you got smart and ran away," said Coke. "But—you know something else? You're right. Seeing how they kept us with our group the way they did, no one got to really talk to any other kid, except on the bus, like you said. That's pretty smart, the way they did that. The guy I sat next to was a real zombie. Wayne. He wondered if they'd let him fly his kites up here. That's what he was into: flying kites."

"What do you suppose they all think happened to the *teacher* from the bus, though?" Sully asked. "The weird-looking blond guy."

"They probably figure he belonged to the bus company," said Coke. "Or that he had to take the TSAT and flunked it." Coke and Sully laughed.

"Wait," said Sara. "I hate to keep bringing up anything important, like the rest of our lives, but seriously . . . it seems to me our biggest problem, almost, is where to look for it. The evidence, I mean, or whatever you want to call it." She turned to Nat. "All the school that any of *us* saw was just two rooms and a bathroom, basically. The dining hall, and that place where we slept. Do you know where the offices are, and stuff like that?"

"I think I do." Nat nodded. "Yeah. I was in a room with a lot of filing cabinets and a couple of secretaries. That's one real possible place. Then, Doctor has his study, with another little office outside it. Of course, there's Doctor's house, as well. It might just be he'd keep the sort of stuff we want away from all the—*you* know—school stuff. That's the thing, like Sara said. They've got a regular *school* going down there. I mean, most of the teachers and all of the kids are absolutely out of it—the Group Six garbage, you know. In fact, I wouldn't be surprised if it was just

Doctor Simms and this Mrs. Ripple, and a guy named Lemaster, who's sort of the Dean of the school, and that other man we saw with Mrs. Ripple yesterday. Oh, yeah—plus that guy who was up at North Egg Mountain. I don't think he was a teacher, though; he sounded awful country."

"Do you think you could make a map of the campus?" Sara asked. She ate some more spaghetti. "This is *so* good, Lu," she said.

Nat nodded. "Um, yeah. I think so."

"You know what I think we ought to do?" said Sully. "I think we ought to start . . . I don't know, you might say *spying* on the campus, right away. Have people there from sunrise to sunset, and keep track of who goes where and when. Like, when Doctor Simms leaves his house in the morning, and who goes in there during the day. You know, to clean and everything. And the same with all the offices. Stuff like that. We probably ought to find out when they have their lunch down there—and all the other meals, I guess. And do those secretaries you talked about eat in the dining hall, or do they bring their own, or what? We ought to get that stuff all down on paper, so's we'd know what times'd be the best for us to look. Even if we pretend we're people from another school, like Sara said, we still have to search for the evidence."

"Sully!" said Marigold. "You're a regular Mickey Spillane. Ace detective."

"De*fec*tive," Coke simply had to say.

Sara said, "I think you've got a really good idea." She nodded, and sort of squinted through her eyes at Sully. Sully nodded back at her, wrinkling his mouth and brow, in the manner of a real idea man. "How about we start that right away? Tomorrow morning?" she asked Nat. "If you could make up maps tonight, we could split up into groups of two, and take three shifts. From up the tree where we were yesterday—that'd be a good place, wouldn't it? *I* wouldn't mind being on the dawn patrol. Would you, Sully?"

Sully almost shook his head off saying no, he wouldn't mind. And Nat agreed that he would make the maps at once.

They made a schedule. Sully and Sara would be in the tree by six A.M., which meant leaving the Robinsons' before four. Marigold and Coke would relieve them at ten-thirty—so they could sleep till eight. They smiled at one another. And even more so when they heard what Nat and Ludi planned to do. They decided they'd get up when Sul and Sara did and go on up to Spring Lake Lodge, and spend all morning working on a root cellar ("A *Ruth* cellar?" asked Marigold, incredulously). Then they would head down to the school, relieving Coke and Marigold at three-thirty.

It looked as if there'd be a big day all around.

Arn-the-Barn Emfatico enjoyed the Valivu Motel in Boynton Falls. The owners, Nick and Flora Vali, reminded him of his aunt and uncle on his mother's side—the side his uncle with the orders didn't come from. Nick and Flora were nice folks. He took care of the business end, and maintenance, and that, but she put in the special little touches. Like, all the beds had ruffles on the bottom that matched the covers on the easy chair. Stuff like that. Flora ran them up on her Kenmore, she told Arn; it wasn't a lot of trouble, she maintained. And in every room there was a painting that she'd done herself. She painted bird pictures on black velvet. In Arn's room there was a Yellow-Shafter Flickereds, just to give one example. How about that for a bird's name? Nights, Arn had gotten to sitting around in Nick and Flora's place— they had this apartment, real nice, right back of the office—and having a few Schaefers and maybe watching a little television. The ball game came in pretty good, so they watched that a lot. Nick had played a little in the Class-D Pony League. "Which stood for Pennsylvania, Ohio, and New York," he'd told Arnold, "and not that we was all a bunch of little horse's asses."

"Even if they maybe was," said Flora, laughing.

They all preferred the ball game to the TV movies they had on, movies that always seemed to show a woman looking like she was just about to pass out from fright, while a guy's feet and trouser legs come walking down the hall outside her room.

Arn also liked the drive from Boynton Falls to Coldbrook every morning. He'd eat his breakfast first: Falls Diner, he'd have it in a booth, toward the back, so's not to make the regulars self-conscious. They'd put him up a lunch there, too: two ham and cheese with mayo on the ham side, mustard on the cheese, two cans of Pepsi regular, and two Milky Ways. Then he'd pile in his Trans-Am, and slip some music in the tape deck, wheel on down in style. He liked Emmylou Harris (his "blue Kentucky girl" is the way he thought of her) driving on those country roads like that, with a .38 under his arm and not a worry in the world, except how to keep from using it and still survive himself.

Mary-Jean Emfatico had not brought up her boy to be a killer, and he wasn't. From time to time he'd—sure—helped out his uncle on the side, but never more than what he called a "maybe-you-should-oughta" sort of job. What that was was just to pass along a message, looking mean. Communicate, his uncle used to say. But never any killing, even any breaking bones, or merchandise. If someone swung on him, he'd cuff him once, to just remind him of his manners, but Arnold, like his mother, Mary-Jean, was not what you would call a violent man. He enjoyed a little action on a horse, or basketball, or certain games that you can play with decks of cards, but he also liked to be a worker for the state, in clean, intelligent surroundings, and a pension up the road. He had a girl friend, Ginnie, who worked downtown, New England Telephone, and it was pretty much set that they'd be getting married, year from June, when he'd be twenty-eight and she'd be twenty-five, and both of them would absolutely know their minds.

Aside from not wanting to kill Nat for reasons of personal style, Arnold also kind of liked the guy. Not that he knew Nat that well, but they had played some cards together, three, four times, and Nat had shown him you could be a student and from out of state and not an all-wool asshole. In fact, Nat seemed like a pretty regular nice guy, just a little strange with the haircut, not stupid, but not so smart you had to watch him all the time.

What Arnold figured, as he drove along toward Coldbrook once again, was that maybe Nat had got cold feet and jumped not just the job, but even state and country altogether. Extreme, but possibly the best, for everyone concerned. So far, Arnold hadn't had an indication otherwise. He'd got a map, way up to Suddington, and he was going hill by hill, around the school, and then a wider circle, and like that. He hadn't seen a sign of anybody yet, except for this one wet spot with some tracks along the edge of it. The ground was pretty gloppy so you couldn't be real sure of what sizes went in it, but one footprint seemed pretty small, no bigger than a kid would make. Arnold thought he'd search another week or so, and if he still was shooting blanks, he'd tell his uncle he'd found out that Nat had skipped. What the hell, the money wasn't all that much; his uncle'd have to bite a little pride and swallow, this one time. Arnold couldn't blame Nat all that much himself. Hell, he would never kill a kid like that; he and Ginnie planned to have a couple of their own.

He nosed the Trans-Am off the road beside a pasture. It was a gorgeous mid-September day, another one. He'd get a good sweat going on a day like this. Arnold liked to sweat: clean out all them pores. He checked his map and cut across the pasture; soon he found a deer trail, going up, following the line of least resistance. He took it, walking easily and quietly, a huge man in a canvas jacket, wearing tan Bermuda shorts and high-topped sneakers, black. He was having a nice vacation, even if "on furlough" meant no pay. He'd have to work on Mr. Darling, somehow, next.

Homer Cone conducted classes all that morning. At nine o'clock, he'd had "No More Mr. X; or, Getting to Know the Unknowns by Their First Names" (formerly Algebra); at ten, it was "Plane Without Pain: The Study of Some Great Figures" (a.k.a. Geometry). Finally, at eleven, there'd been "Math for the Mathes, or What Comes After Sixteen?", to which question, Mr. Cone always told his class in basic mathematics, the answer was "Seventeen," not "legal sex," as everyone at Coldbrook seemed to think.

With those chores out of the way, Mr. Cone went directly to his apartment, where he changed to old shoes and traded cashmere sports coat for a cardigan; then he picked his tweed cap off a hook and plucked a paper bag from out the fridge. The cap soon had his head in it, while the bag contained a box of Famous Ginger Snaps and a thermos of banana daiquiris. He'd put his rifle in the trunk of his car the night before, rolled up in a map of "Europe at the Outbreak of the Franco–Prussian War." He'd found the map in study hall the previous day; it didn't look like anybody used it, ever.

It was a beautiful afternoon, and Mr. Cone drove down the gravel road with a carefree heart. He saw the white car pulled just off the road, about two miles from school, and scowled at it—"Oh, look, a Trans-Eyetalian," he'd said to Mrs. Ripple once—but he really didn't think he'd see the owner. The driveway that he had in mind was still a mile or two ahead, and cut a long way through the woods.

It was after twelve, about a quarter past, when Mr. Cone pulled up and parked at Robinson's.

Sully made the four of them his famous whole-wheat raisin bread French toast (with cinnamon) for breakfast, which, as Nat said, was great with maple syrup on it, and thereby proved that *anything* was great with maple syrup. Actually, it wasn't all that bad, even eaten in the dark (outside) at thirty minutes after three, A.M. Everyone looked forward to the day that soon would break, even Marigold and Coke, who still were quite unconscious in their beds.

Sara and Sully left a little before four, taking a clipboard with Nat's map of the school and paper for the notes they'd make, plus the field glasses and Sully's adopted bow and arrows, which had become pretty much a part of his outfit. They were most enthusiastic about their mission. It was definitely something new and a step in the right direction, not being a defensive move, evasive action for survival; this was starting . . . well, real life again. More the way their lives were meant to be: getting out and taking charge. Sara didn't put it into just those words inside her head, but still she knew she felt a lot more *natural* doing things this way. More like herself. She hadn't been brought up to run and hide.

The greater part of Sully's happiness had to do with getting to spend so much of the day alone with Sara for the first time. One thing he knew he'd like was not having Coke around. Not that he didn't like

Coke; Coke was all right. But it'd be nice not to have that little smile and laugh of his, just waiting to make fun of something that you'd maybe say, or do. He knew he'd feel a lot more relaxed around Sara if Coke wasn't there.

Nat felt differently than Sully, but not completely differently. He looked forward to a day with Ludi; he thought she was amazing. She was the first person he'd ever met who didn't ever seem to be a jerk. It seemed to him that she naturally (could it possibly be naturally?) avoided saying and doing stupid, jerky things.

Nat had had a sort of a test, a game, he'd played with himself the last two years or so. It was definitely kind of childish (the way most of his games seemed to him to be), but it did have one good side to it: it had made him awful careful about birth control. What he did was, whenever he'd get tight with some new girl, he'd ask himself: "What would it feel like to wake up in the morning and find out that you and she were married?"

Well, whenever he'd put the question to himself, he'd always gotten the exact same answer—even with a smart, good-looking, sexy, funny girl like Jen Maloney. And the answer was: "Oh, *no!*" accompanied by this semi-nauseated feeling in the pit of his stomach. It wasn't anything against Jen, or any of the others—hell, chances were they felt the same about him, except twenty times more violently. It was just that he couldn't see himself and someone else getting along that well, that long. He was just too much of a jerk, and so was everyone else.

Now he hadn't actually asked himself that question about Ludi, because Ludi was just a kid, but what he realized was, there was a *type* of person (maybe you could say) who he could actually imagine loving to be around . . . forever. And Ludi *was* that type of person, the first one that he'd ever met.

Pretty amazing, Nat thought. Encouraging, too. Yes, he looked forward to spending most of a day just with Ludi, but it made him feel funny, too. It was not the sort of thing that he should get excited about (he told himself), for Christ's sake.

They left the Robinsons' a little after four, both of them in sweat pants and a flannel shirt.

"What're you going to wear?" she'd called to him. He'd said that it was chilly out, but later on they'd roast. When he stepped out of the boys' room, she was waiting in the hall, wearing just what he had on, except her shirt was tan and his was green. They'd laughed, and both of them had said, "His 'n' hers," together, so they'd linked their little fingers up and made a wish. Nat had learned to do that from his mother, and he'd never known anyone else who did it, before.

(Coke woke up when he heard the door slam behind them, or that's what he told Marigold, anyway, twenty seconds later.)

"You lead," Nat said to Ludi. "And zigzag, if you can, a little. I know it's hard when it's so dark, but circle any soft spots, if you see them." They used their flashlights for a while, just now and then, but pretty soon they didn't have to. Ludi walked on deer tracks some, but going on and off them, and always on the side where there were leaves, careful not to step on top of hoof marks. As they got higher, and the woods thinned out a little, they left the tracks and walked on side by side, a tree or two apart. Once, she stopped and turned around, with her hand on a smooth striped maple shoot. She frowned and shook her head.

"What?" said Nat.

"I'm not exactly sure," she said. "Whatever, it's been happening for days. Sara and all the others seem to be getting so much more relaxed. I guess it's because we haven't had a clue that anybody cares we're up here. Hunting us, I mean. Except for those two people down by the school yesterday. And they looked—I don't know—so harmless."

"So what are you saying?" Nat asked.

"I'm *sure* we're being hunted," Ludi said. "That's the only thing it could be. I keep getting this sort of paranoid feeling that doesn't seem to have to do with the Group of us at all, so I figure it's got to be coming from outside. It makes me feel"—she shook her head—"all *wary,* like an animal, almost. And it's always there"—she made a little snort of laughter—"even at five in the morning. Am I making any sense at all?"

Nat nodded. "Yeah, I think so. I used to watch my dog when he'd just lie there, smelling stuff or hearing sounds *I* couldn't get. Feelings even." He held up a palm. "Not that you're anything like my dog, of course. He had *much* longer ears."

Ludi almost didn't seem to hear. "I keep thinking everybody has them," she said, "had them once, when they were little. All those sixth senses that you hear about. What happens is they just get overwhelmed by all the so-called facts that people teach us, and all the things we have to *do,* that everyone says are so important." She took a deep breath. "Anyway. The feeling I have now, it comes and goes at different times, but mostly it keeps getting stronger." She laughed and was suddenly, entirely, in the world of here-and-now again. "You know how old people are meant to say 'I feel it in me bones'? Well, that's almost it. It really makes my skin crawl." She pushed up a tan, chamois-cloth sleeve. "I wish you could see what I'm talking about." Her arm was smooth, with soft brown hairs.

Nat said, "We really oughtn't to relax. You're right, we have been doing that. Me, too. We ought to talk about it some tonight. It'd be so ridiculous to forget why we're up here in the first place."

Ludi turned and started up the slope. "I know," she said. "The trouble is, we'd really like to. Forget the whole incredible scenario. Or all the grungy stuff, at least." She giggled, and went bouncing up the hillside, agile as a little doe, Nat thought.

They got to Spring Lake Lodge just after six. The sky was clear, and sunrise not too far away. When they saw the little clearing, with its dark, still mirror of a pond, and then the cabin, squatting safely there, untouched and solid, they looked at one another and they smiled. Hideout of the year, beyond a doubt, Nat thought; how nice that they could leave the kids at Granny's.

This root cellar project hadn't been an instant smash, when Nat first mentioned it. Most people weren't exactly, or even at all, sure what a root cellar was, so that was part of it. But even when he'd given them a breathless, graphic, illustrated lecture on the subject ("Food Storage Practices in Colonial America," yawn), there wasn't any rush of volunteers. Of course there was hard work involved, but that didn't seem to be the problem, the way Nat looked at it. The problem lay with all that was implied by the digging of a root cellar. Storing food? Terrific. Great idea. A few days' or a week's worth, here and there; ten pounds of rice and five of beans, a dozen jumbo jars of sauce. But storing food for the *winter?* Forget it. Who planned to be here in the winter? That was months away. Nat talked about how early winter came, sometimes, up north. But still, it seemed absurd. Even when they didn't have a Plan, they didn't think they'd be here *that* long.

Everybody else said sure, they'd help, but only Ludi asked when they'd begin.

They got a pick and shovel from the Lodge and started looking for a site.

"It'd be easiest to dig into a slope," said Nat. "But with all the ledge you find up here . . . I guess we'll

171

have to try and see." They marked three spots that looked like possibles, but then decided one of them was much too open, visible to passersby. The other two were fine until the pick hit solid rock, about ten inches down.

"Hmmm," said Nat.

And so they ended up on level ground, atop the knob but near the spruces. A tall poplar had blown over just that summer, and had fallen almost flat. Sometimes poplars rot and snap, but this one was uprooted. That meant its roots had dragged up quite a clod of earth with them, making what was like a little crater, seven feet across and maybe three feet deep. "Already," as Nat said.

They both took off their shirts and got to pick-and-shoveling. It wasn't easy going in the wet and clayey soil, well stocked with good-sized rocks. In about an hour's time, Nat hollered for a coffee break.

"Boy," said Ludi, wiping sweat, "I can't believe I didn't even think about a lookout. Talk about relaxed. And you doing all that grunting."

Nat shook his head. They were walking back toward the Lodge. "We must have got blissed-out, ma-a-an," he drawled. "I can't believe it either. Shows the value of a good talk. Let's get something to drink and go to the sentry tree, O.K.?"

They shook up tropi-fruit with cold spring water, one canteen's worth, and left their shirts and sweat pants in the lodge. Ludi's shorts were brilliant red and had a pocket in the back; Nat's were navy blue, and didn't. He had a plain gray t-shirt on; hers was yellow, double-thick, and it reversed to green. Both of them climbed up the sentry tree and sat on different limbs.

"You aren't saying much about the Plan," Nat said to her. They'd looked and listened down the slope and hadn't noticed anything unusual.

She dropped her eyes and made a little smile, and

172

shrugged. "What's to say?" she said. "It's certainly a thing to do. And it seems as if it has a chance to work. Don't you think?"

"Sure," he said. "I think it really will, provided . . ."

"Provided we can find the evidence—that always sounds like a story or something—and get away with it," she said.

"Yeah, I guess so," Nat replied.

Ludi said, "The whole thing's so incredible. It's gotten so I don't feel any . . . I don't know, regular emotions about it at all. Like, really furious, or sad, or sorry for myself. I think my father's sick; I guess he always was and just got worse and worse after my mother died. So I can't even hate him. And I certainly don't want them to put him in a jail and try to punish him. That wouldn't do anything for anyone. But I don't like him, either—I *really* don't like him. That stuff that Marigold was saying—I don't even want his money. Unless my mother left him some when she died. I'd take *her* money." She smiled a little crooked smile. "I'm not *completely* pure, am I? But as far as he's concerned, all I want is to never have to deal with him, or with his wife, or with what either of them thinks or feels or wants. There was a girl from Virginia where I used to go to camp, and she said she wanted to be 'shut of' things, or people, all the time. 'Ah jus' want to be shut of that woman,' she'd say—she hated this dance teacher they had. And that's exactly the way I feel now. Which is why I don't talk about the Plan too much. I wish I could just forget . . . oh, all that stuff. Be shut of the whole damn thing."

For a moment, Nat thought she might start to cry. But no, she looked at him and made another little smile. "And how about you?" she said. "I don't hear you saying a whole lot, either."

He smiled back at her and shook his head, and

173

waved a hand on down the slope. "I suppose that I'm a lot like you." Saying that made him feel very good. "That stuff is like a wire to another life. A time that I feel done with—I don't know, kind of like before you were old enough to go to school, those days. It was O.K. . . ." He shrugged. "Up here is different. Not that I'd want to hang out on top of this hill for the next hundred years." He wondered that he had to throw that in. "But I do plan to feel the way I do right now, a lot." Whatever that meant.

"Yeah," she said, and licked her lips.

Nat wanted to say something confident and optimistic to her. Give her a solution to her problems. Tell her how and why and when they'd work their way around the different obstacles they faced, and reach a stretch of level, peaceful ground. Trouble was, it wasn't all that clear to him. Nothing ever seemed to be, beyond the answer to the question: "How are you—right now?" And he was feeling very good—right now. He knew that much.

"You want to get back to work?" he said.

And she said, "Sure," and smiled.

They took turns picking and shoveling and keeping watch, until all the noisy work was done, or all that they had time for that day; later they would frame the cellar up and cover it. He'd asked her how her skin and bones were feeling, and she'd said that everything was fine.

"It's more or less as if they're out there, looking for us, same as always," she gestured with a hand, "but here I still feel safe. Maybe I'm just kidding myself, because I like it here a lot, or it's the first place that we came to, or something." They'd been carrying up rocks from the stream to make a floor for their cellar, and cutting a drainage ditch around it, and away. Both of them were pretty well mucked-up when it was time to stop.

"I'll get some brush and sort of hide it, if you like,"

174

said Ludi, "provided you take charge of making lunch."

"Deal," said Nat. "Let's see, what'll we have? Maybe I'll jelly a few eels. Or, no, I think I'd rather a pâté. I'll bet I can snuffle up a truffle somewhere." He went off, making pig noises.

But when he saw Spring Lake, he knew a bath was first on his agenda. He went and got a towel and soap. Ludi might be back before he'd finished, but that would be O.K.; everything was cool. He slipped off his clothes and waded in the water.

It was delicious. Pure and simple, you might say. Nat lay down in the water and wiggled, hands beside his body, feeling like a trout. Or maybe like an eel. He rolled onto his back and paddled to the shallow end. Sitting on a rock, he washed his feet and ankles, and then he stood and soaped himself all over, falling forward in the water when he'd done so, rinsing off. He loved to feel the water all around his body; it made him feel so naked. He stood again and soaped his face and hair, and then, his eyes still closed, he knelt and rinsed his hair off, two, three times, blowing like a monster from the deep. Then he stood up straight and turned toward his towel.

Ludi was just pulling down her underpants. Her boots and the rest of her clothes were beside her on the grass. She was looking straight at him, and she smiled a proud and happy little smile. What she looked was calm and certain, more than anything. There were smears of dirt on both her round bare arms, on both her muscled legs; there was a mud-streak all along her forehead, underneath her curls. She tossed her underpants aside and stepped into the water. Then she made a shallow dive and glided, arms outstretched, head down, across the pool, until her fingers touched his thighs. Oh, yes, she had a gorgeous back, Nat thought. When she touched him, she stood up and shook her head and wiped her face

175

with both her hands. Then she put her arms around his neck.

His face went down to hers. She smiled enormously, inclusively, and so did he. His arms surrounded her, below her arms; he lifted, and they kissed. He felt her slide one smooth, cool leg around him, then the other; she pulled up with her arms and climbed him easy as she would a maple tree. He slid his own grip down her back and lifted her still higher, holding on the cheeks of her behind.

Their heads moved back, eyes at a level now—his locked on hers, and hers on his. Both of them were back to smiling, just so very, very pleased with this, him, her, them, everything about the world, each other.

"Oh, my God, I love you," Nat exclaimed.

And she said, "Oh, dear God, I love you, too."

He set her down and washed her then, carefully, intently, thoroughly. That was how he got acquainted with her body, washing her all over, clean. He loved her perfect little body, and he kissed his work from time to time and made approving sounds. When he was done, she put a hand out for the soap, and then she washed him, too, though he was clean already.

"Slick," she said. "You're just so *slick,* you know that?" She hadn't seen or held a man like that before, and it was good.

They left the water, hand in hand, and dried each other, standing on the grass. Then they spread their towels and sat on them and, putting fingertips to one another's faces, they kissed again, looking at each other in an almost unbelieving way.

He took her in his arms, rolled back with her; she slid across him, graceful as an otter. On his back, he pressed her in the air, his arms straight up, his hands upon her hip bones; she split her legs apart, then shot them forward—she must have been a gym-

176

nast—and sat down on his stomach, straddling. He covered her small breasts with his strong hands.

"I wish we could make love," she said.

"I haven't any birth control," he answered, wrinkling his nose.

"Well, then, let's not," she said. "And that's O.K. I never have, but now I want to. I had to tell you that."

He brought her face to his again; she stretched out on his body. He rolled them over on the grass and propped his weight up on his elbows.

"I want to tell you that I've never felt this way," he said. "Not even close, remotely. I feel as if I'd just been born, but that I'll never be this wise, or good, again. It's a crazy feeling, but the best. You know what I want to scream? I want to scream, 'I *get* it!' This must be what it's like to be inside a miracle."

And Ludi shut her eyes and shook her head and didn't feel herself at all.

Marigold and Coke got out of bed at last, at eight— and realized they had to rush. They were meant to be above the school at half past ten, which gave them half an hour to have breakfast and get organized.

Coke said, "It doesn't matter if we're just a little late. Sara'll understand."

"You're such a fuck," said Marigold. "It isn't up to them to understand. If we say we'll be there by a certain time, let's be there. Suppose you scramble up some eggs, and I'll pack up a lunch for us."

Coke was pleased to do that. Now that he knew how, he liked to scramble eggs, and if he did that, she'd have to wash the pan, which wasn't all that easy. He wondered if Marigold was going to be a nag when she grew up. He hoped she understood that he did what she wanted most of the time because he chose to, and not because she told him. Being with her certainly made him feel great, as a general rule. He'd never known a woman like her before; all the other girls he'd known were babies compared to her. He was getting a glimmering that "experienced" meant more than having done something a few times. It was more a whole attitude a person had, what you might call a style. It wasn't something that he always felt about himself, with her, exactly.

They made it to the watching tree, by Coldbrook Country School, at 10:27, by Marigold's digital wrist watch, and Sully and Sara handed over the field glasses and the clipboard and helped them get the buildings straight and understand the method they'd been using to keep track of things.

Sara and Sully were happy to be getting out of that tree. Four and a half hours of staring and counting and making notes was a lot. They both felt a need for movement: running, cartwheels, jumping up and down.

Sully got an idea for a game that they could play going back to the Robinsons', a sort of hare-and-hound affair, or straight-line hide-and-seek. One of them would take off, in the general direction of the Robinsons' (no fair going way off line), and have four minutes to get hidden—watches synchronized; after four minutes, that person couldn't move at all. The other person would then have *five* minutes to find the first one. If, after five minutes, the hare was still holed up, unfound, he or she would give the blue jay's call, and the game would then regroup, start over. The name of the game—simplicity itself—was Chase, they said.

It turned out to be fun—and the perfect antidote for a morning in a tree. In the right terrain the hare might go just a little ways and wiggle into something dense—then watch the hound go whizzing by and chuckle. Or—Sully tried this right away—the hare could flat-out sprint the whole four minutes, and then collapse behind a tree, figuring no flea-bitten hound could ever match that pace.

About halfway along, they went through a section that the loggers had been in the year before. Hiding places galore. One time, Sully was actually standing on the partly rotted butt-end of a big old beech log, peering all around in search of Sara Cottontail, when his five minutes done ran out. And she had shrieked the blue jay's call from almost underneath his feet. She'd wriggled into space below that log—held slightly off the ground by two big branches—and he'd never had a clue that she was there.

The shriek had made him jump, all right, and Sara had rolled out where he could see her, laughing.

"You dirty snowshoe," Sully said. He dropped his bow and quiver of arrows and leaped right down on top of her. "You know what happens to people who go around scaring other people? They get a tickling, that's what. A tickling that they'll not soon forget."

Sara eeked and rolled onto her stomach, elbows tight against her sides. Sully rode her and tried to get his fingertips between her upper arms and ribs. It was hard to believe how strong she was.

"So," said Sully, doing his best to sound like Count Dracula, or some such fiend. He made a lousy Transylvanian. "I see that sterner measures may be called for here." And with his heart pumping wildly in his chest, he brought one open hand down, not *too* hard, on the seat of Sara's tight white cotton shorts.

"Eek, you beast," cried Sara, laughing still. She made one mammoth upward bucking-bronco heave, followed by a roll away from her tormentor. Sully dove and grabbed her, trying for her shoulders; one he got all right. His other hand came down on Sara's fine left breast.

"Oops," said Sully, more as an apology than anything. But then the only thing that seemed appropriate was just to kiss her, so he did, hitting just the corner of her mouth at first, but sliding quickly over so's to get things squarely into place. He smelled that sort of sweet and herby Sara-smell he'd noticed in the tree, when they had put their heads together, whispering.

Sully could hardly believe he was actually kissing her. Her lips felt wonderful under his, and—whoa—he'd forgotten to move his hand from off her breast. He was actually *feeling* her breast with his hand and *it* felt just fantastic, and then her lips were moving, and, wow, that was her *tongue*. . . .

They stayed like that for quite a time. Sara'd put one hand on the back of Sully's head, and actually slipped the other one under his t-shirt, right onto his sweaty back. Sully'd finally had to pick his head up, so he wouldn't drool too much into her mouth.

"Oh, gosh," he said, feeling there were some things to say and that he was probably just the guy to say them. "Boy, I'm sorry . . ." started out, though—that left-over apology from a little while before, and not the thing he meant to say at all.

Sara smiled and put a hand across his mouth. "Silly. No, you're not," she said. "And I sure am not, either."

And Sully wanted to just pound his chest and scream. If everyone could see him now!

"We've got to get going," said Sara, but before they moved, they kissed again—again, at length. This one felt like a promise to Sully: no accident this time, babe. He put *his* hand under Sara's t-shirt, in the back, this time; he thought his girl friend's skin felt wonderful. They walked together for a little ways, now holding hands, but that was hard to do on that terrain, so pretty soon they went back to playing Chase. It was good practice, and it got them moving fast.

After Homer Cone had parked his car beside the house Group 6 had named "the Robinsons'," he got out, walked straight up to the kitchen door, and knocked. After a suitable pause, he knocked again, a good deal harder, and called out, "Anybody home?"

Satisfied there wasn't, he got his cap and rifle from the car and made one circle all around the house. The blinds were drawn downstairs, except for in the kitchen, so he didn't learn too much—except that people from Long Island left their dishes on the drainboard by the sink, instead of putting them away in the cupboard, as his late mother would have done, or any of his aunts. Or, for that matter, Homer Cone himself, although he preferred not to dwell on his involvement with household tasks best left to females.

He made a second circuit of the house, this one at a greater distance, maybe fifty yards or so; it was then that he was struck by something odd. Not odd, perhaps, but out of order: there was a window open on the second floor.

It could have been an oversight; Homer Cone knew that. People who left dishes on the drainboard by the sink were certainly capable of forgetting to close a window. But . . . He walked back to the house and tried the kitchen door. It was unlocked.

Homer Cone went in. "Halloo!" he caroled cheerfully, his rifle at the ready. "Anybody ho-o-me?"

Unanswered, he moved quickly through the kitchen. He found three open sleeping bags in bunk room one; that made him start to smile. But when he found three more in bunk room two, he grinned a Cheshire grin. A *greedy* Cheshire grin that Mrs. Ripple would have found alarming, and unsuitable.

Mr. Cone went on upstairs, and out onto the big main porch beside the living room, the one that had a nice view down the driveway, and down a wooded slope from which the people from Long Island had thinned out a lot of trees and bushes, creating quite a nice cleaned-up effect, as well as lots of visibility.

He looked around, then went inside and fetched a

181

straight-backed chair. He set that near the sliding door, so that someone coming from an angle, and the uphill side, would never even know that he was there, until he'd seen them, too. His sight-line down the road was excellent—ditto through the cleaned-out woods in front of him. Rotten hunter that he was, he didn't even think about his car.

In fact, excited as he was, he didn't even think about his *lunch*. And that was most unusual, for such a big-domed little pig as Homer Cone.

Sara and Sully had kept on playing Chase. They knew that they were close to "home" and lunch, and both of them were good and hungry. They were also both feeling a little bit excited and a little bit nervous about the prospect of having the Robinsons' to themselves. Coke and Marigold did gosh-knows-what, exactly, at the Robinsons'; what would *they* do? Sara and Sully both wondered that, but neither of them knew that that was what the other one was wondering.

Sully was "hare" for what they thought might be the last lap of the game. The only reason they weren't sure was that neither of them knew exactly how far away they were from home in running minutes. They had a pretty good idea of how regular far it was, but time was another matter.

Sully took off. He decided he'd go hard again, really dig out, and try to make sure this was the last game. As a result, he saw the roof line of the house, at a distance, before even three minutes were up. He was coming from the northwest, angling down through the woods from the uphill side, on the side away from the road. He'd slowed to a nice quick, quiet walk, as he tried to decide on a hiding place.

One obvious possibility was not more than thirty yards from the house. It was a dark hunk of meta-morphic rock that stuck up out of the ground for all

the world like a titan's hassock: four-and-a-half feet
high, and half again as much across. Marigold had
labeled it "The Blackhead," although, in fact, it was
a lot more wartlike. Sully saw that he could hunker
down behind it and, when he heard Sara coming
through the woods, just move a little one way or the
other so she'd never see him. Unless, of course, she
came right to it—in which case he'd leap up and mug
her. Sully didn't want to prolong this last game. He
wanted to eat . . . and see what'd happen. He wished
he could remember if Nat and Ludi had said they
were going to come by the house on their way from
Spring Lake Lodge to relieve Coke and Marigold, or
what. But even if they did, there'd still be a good four
hours when they'd have the place to themselves.

Sully's palms were sweating as he dropped down
on all fours behind the rock and peered around it. He
checked his watch. Sara would have started.

She came on schedule, but farther down the slope
than he'd expected. She wasn't going full-speed, of
course, seeing she was looking for him, too.

Sully watched her moving. Even at a distance, she
looked great. She had a light tan t-shirt on that said
"Ski Trak Skis," in green, on it; her braid was bouncing, and she didn't have a bra on either, he knew
that. First-hand, you might say; Sully smiled. Her
shorts were from her school, these white gym shorts
that she was just about getting ready to outgrow, it
seemed to Sully. Put it this way: they would have
been uncomfortable on him, but girls were different.
Actually, they looked pretty good on her. They sure
were tight around the ass, but hers wasn't flabby
like a lot of girls' were. Sully couldn't imagine a
better-looking girl for him than Sara was. If they
ever got married, they'd have some really potent
kids, he'd bet. Not tall, maybe, but super-healthy,
and strong. And his kids, probably mostly boys,

wouldn't have to put up with the city, or any fags like McCorker. You could bet on that, too.

She hadn't seemed to guess he was behind The Blackhead; probably she thought he'd gone right in the house—and in the icebox, too. He watched her check her watch. She was just about straight downhill from the house, a little ways below the porch.

"Good afternoon," said Homer Cone to her. He'd heard her coming, from below and to his right. He'd stood up soundlessly and stepped straight forward, his rifle almost at his shoulders, his eyes just locked right onto her.

"Let's just don't move quite yet," said Homer Cone, as always, speaking through his nose.

Before, the house had hidden Homer Cone from someone kneeling by The Blackhead. But once he stood up straight and walked away from it, it didn't anymore. Sully knew exactly who he was, right off the bat; he'd seen him through binoculars, at Coldbrook Country School.

Arn-the-Barn had stopped to eat his lunch at quarter past the hour. The place he'd chosen was a patch of nice soft grass, a really thin, green, matted kind—a sunny island in between a bunch of bushes that he didn't know were blueberries, which was too bad. His girl friend, Ginnie, was nuts about blueberries, and it would have given her a kick to know that Arn had been sitting right where some had actually been, not in a box, a month or so before.

When things were going exactly right in Arnold's lunch, he'd open up his second can of Pepsi when he was about three-quarters of the way through his second sandwich. That meant that there'd still be plenty of Pepsi left to have with his Milky Ways. If he didn't have enough Pepsi left, the second Milky Way would seem to sort of stick in his back teeth, which'd make him feel as guilty as hell. His dentist,

Dr. Lombardo, had a poster in his office that *specifically* told you to lay off of candy bars and sodas. But soda didn't stick, at least.

This particular day, things were going A-O.K. It was one gorgeous day. The sandwiches had been perfect, really tasty; the Milky Ways were soft and fresh, but the chocolate coating hadn't gotten runny so's it stuck to the paper. And there were still a couple of swallows of Pepsi to swish around in his mouth after he'd finished the second Milky Way.

Arnold didn't even know that some people named Novotny, from Long Island, had built a house in the woods no more than three hundred yards southwest of where he sat.

But he did know what a .30-.30 sounded like when it went off, those same three hundred yards away.

Nat and Ludi went along beside an old stone wall, a wall so old that it had fallen, settled, sprawled. Ludi liked to think about whoever made those walls, and what they must have thought about when they were making them. Whoever made that wall had probably wished he had more kids, rather than less, she guessed.

The single shot was quite a ways away, in front of them. It didn't seem to get to her at first. She turned to Nat and said, almost distractedly, "The Robinsons'?"

He said, "Could be. Or right near there. It was a rifle, bigger than a .22, for sure. Jeezum. I think we'd better hustle." He started trotting, angling across the hillside. I hate to think and run, he thought, absurdly. Ludi was attentive now, running right behind him.

When they got close, he stopped.

"I guess what we ought to do is try to sneak in close and see if we can see what's going on. What *I* ought to do," he said. He looked at his watch. "It's just about time for Sara and Sully to be getting back. Jeezum."

Ludi shut her eyes and tried to feel what was going on. Of course things didn't work that way. Feeling—seeing—didn't have a thing to do with trying. Quite the opposite, in fact.

She whispered, "Could I just go with you?"

Before, he would have told her "no." Before, he'd made her wait below the house and take the car keys and his wallet.

Now he kissed her quickly on the lips and said, "Come on." She wasn't a kid anymore, and Nat had never been an M.C.P.

Chapter Eight

HOMER CONE was no fool. As such, he knew, for example, that where there's smoke, there's fire. He further knew that, in certain situations, when you've seen one, you *haven't* seen them all.

He also (finally) knew that he would much rather shoot all five members of Group 6, plus their (ho-ho) faculty advisor, than just one of them. There wasn't any question of his *not* shooting this one that he had right here in front of him, of course: this girl in the (ahem) tight shorts. He'd get around to that in just a moment.

In his own mind, Homer Cone was something of a humanitarian. When he returned a class's blue books, after an exam, he didn't build up the suspense—especially for marginal students—by handing them back in descending order, best to worst. Nor would he wander slowly round the room, seemingly at random, making vague remarks concerning summer school, or nature vs. nurture, the usefulness of wealthy, senile aunts, or the wage scale for illiterates in Portugal. No, he would march right in and say, "You flunked it, Livingston, you cretin. But you had lots of company: Swetman, Burdock, Remmeltree, and Norris. In twenty years of teaching, I've never had a dumber class. If you weren't all so ugly, I'd like to have you bronzed." The other members of the class would titter, sucking up to Cone. Little did they know that he was serious.

But, all that to one side, Homer Cone did know that he was going to shoot Sara (whose name, of course, he didn't know or care about). He wouldn't stretch things out, or change his mind. There wasn't any sense in taking prisoners, no matter what the situation. Sooner or later, you'd either have to kill them anyway or let them go, and in the present case they'd already let this group get away once, when they intended to kill them. "Not this time, my dear," thought Homer Cone, thinking through his nose. There was absolutely no logical or acceptable reason to keep this girl around, just to share her with Mrs. Ripple. Let Mrs. Ripple find her own girls. This one had a date with Homer Cone.

But first he had to have some facts from her, some information. It shouldn't take him long to get what he was looking for. His many years of teaching had transformed Olive Cone's bland little fat boy, Homer, into a subtle, shrewd inquisitor.

"So, where are all the others?" he nasaled down at Sara.

Sara'd had no trouble recognizing Homer Cone; she also knew that he was there to kill her, if he could, and that the means to do exactly that was resting in his hands. Before that moment, she'd never thought about being shot—in fact, she'd never seen any shooting, at targets, animals, or birds, in person. Films of shooting, yes; shootings on TV, sure, constantly. Without even counting some of the big, epic war movies, it's safe to say that Sara had probably seen over a thousand people shot in the course of her viewing life, some of them not even actors. And maybe another hundred people shot at and missed. Lucky for her, you might say.

For when she heard Homer Cone ask her where the others were, the part of Sara's mind that dealt with problems, plans, ideas, and reasoning shut down. She turned into an animal: the product of her culture.

Pivoting away from Cone and toward the shelter of the nearest tree, she just took off and ran, bent over, doing driving, zigzag steps, but not predictably. She didn't have to think about the proper way to do it.

Homer Cone was absolutely certain that "a bird in the hand is worth two in the bush"; that was one of those eternal verities. And, to make things even better, here was a little bird who challenged his authority. He had asked her a civil question, and she'd been rude enough to run, instead of answer him. Who did she think she was?

He raised his rifle to his shoulder, sighted through the scope.

Except for shooting rifles, Homer Cone had never been the least bit good at sports. The only positive thing that could be said about his career in Little League baseball, for instance, was that he was the only kid on his team who looked normal (meaning "same-as-usual") with one of those huge batting helmets on. But, for all of that, his baseball life had ended quickly, at the age of ten, when he was drilled in the ribs by a batting practice fastball thrown by David Rusterman, age twelve. He'd quit the sport that very day.

And for one small fraction of a second, standing on a porch, deep in the woods, not far from Coldbrook Country School, Homer Cone believed that he'd been HBPed again. His body felt a jolt and staggered to its left; his rifle lobbed a shot into the air that came down many hundred yards away. He started to look down, and to his right, to see if there could be, by any chance, a baseball on the deck beside his foot.

But what he saw, instead, was this: sticking out below his armpit, jammed between ribs five and six, was one round piece of dull aluminum, a hollow rod with feathers set in it, and a notch right at the end.

"Who killed Cock Robin?" Homer Cone thought that, and died. Sully's arrow'd touched his heart, as nothing in his life had ever done before.

When Sara heard the shot, but didn't feel it, even more adrenaline pumped through her system. It was like the gun lap of a swimming race, and she was leading once again. In just a few more strides, she'd be beyond the cleared-out space and into thicker woods. That would slow her down, but trees would also shield her from the next shot and the next. Her mind was coming back to her: use the contour of the slope, she told herself. Once she got that little ridge between herself and him, he'd never get her. Couldn't. What she would do was keep on going hard, until she knew she'd shaken him, and then describe a circle back to Spring Lake Lodge. Or, wait. Maybe she should head for School: warn Coke and Marigold. Nat and Ludi would be going there, as well, and she could catch the four of them and warn them all.

She stopped, now hidden from the house. All. All but Sully. Where was Sully? Back there somewhere. Hiding near the house. Maybe *in* the house? There hadn't been a second shot. Why not? Could the man have shot at Sully, not at her? And killed him, even?

Sara stood beside, behind, a big old sugar maple, breathing hard. She didn't have the slightest idea what she should do, and she felt as if she maybe couldn't move. Then suddenly, from not too far away, up-slope, she heard a call: not really loud, but terribly intense, you might say. Weird.

"Sara"—Sully's voice, she thought—"Sara"—Sully's voice for sure. "Sara. Please."

She ran toward it. He heard the noise and ran toward her. She saw that he was very pale; his freckles, on the other hand, were darker and stood out against his skin like oil spots on a clean white shirt. "Sul," she said, and ran right up to him.

He didn't seem to want to touch her. "I shot him with an arrow," Sully said. "I might have killed him. He's lying on the porch."

Sara tried to think what they should do. She made her mind behave. It was tempting to stick to the idea of heading on down to the school and meeting with the rest of them. But they had a lot of stuff at Robinson's they really needed, like their sleeping bags, and there *was* the question—sort of an important one—of was the man alone, or what? And was he dead . . . or what? "I guess we should go back," she said.

Sully looked as if he might pass out. She got him to sit down and put his head between his knees; pretty soon, he said that he felt better. Shook and functioning—but barely—Sara thought.

They angled up the hill and then around it, wanting to come down behind the house but to one side. So they could see that Homer Cone was lying on the porch, not moving, with an arrow in his side. No other person was in sight. They hurried down and saw the car that Homer Cone had come in, parked right where he had left it. They crept on up the outside steps that took them to the porch. The man was definitely not moving; his rifle lay a yard away from him, and seemed to breathe about the same amount that he did. They tiptoed toward the body.

The door from the living room slid open.

"Freeze," said Arn-the-Barn Emfatico, his pistol in his hand.

When Arn-the-Barn had heard that rifle shot, not far from where he was, he didn't either duck or holler. Instead, he tilted back his head and filled his mouth with Pepsi: two swallows' worth in one. Then he slid the empty can inside his little rucksack and stood up. He wanted to get out of brush and into open woods, where he'd be clearly seen by anyone. All he needed was to catch a "sound shot" from some crazy out-of-season hunter. He started in to whistle, loud as possible: "I've been workin' on the railroad . . ." That was a nice noncontroversial number, Arnold thought. He moved in the direction of the shot.

Pretty soon, of course, he saw the house and, coming from the east, he also saw Cone's car, which looked familiar, vaguely. He walked around the house; he called, "Hey! Everything O.K.?" and got no answer. He saw the steps that went up to the porch and used them. There was Homer Cone, his rifle by his side, his face averted. The head shape looked familiar, very.

"Hey," said Arn-the-Barn again. He walked straight to the body, bent, and saw the face. "Well, waddya know?" said Arn-the-Barn, by no means horrified. He'd never seen a victim of a violent death before, but he, like Sara, had been known to watch a little television. He knew exactly what to do; he felt at home and competent. He knelt and touched the body's neck, like Quincy might. He turned up one dead eyelid and put his ear down near the mouth, as either Ponch or Jon would do it. And then, of course, he stood and shook his head, like Colonel Sherman Potter. He went into the house to find a phone.

While he was looking for the phone, he also added two and two as best he could; he didn't always get an answer. This Mr. Big-Dome Bigot from the school had almost surely shot the rifle—he could check— and someone else had hit him with an arrow. Who? The possibility of Nat did cross his mind. The person hadn't stuck around, though; that was strange. You'd think they'd try to hide the body, wouldn't you?

Arnold found there wasn't any phone, and when he went upstairs again, to check the rifle on the

192

porch, he saw two kids out there. So how could he resist the chance to tell them "Freeze"?

They did. The man was much too close to make a run for it, and much too huge to jump on, even if he hadn't had that pistol in his hand. What they felt was overwhelmed, defeated.

"I suppose you're from the school," said Sara sullenly.

Arn shot up his eyebrows. "From the school? *That* place? Sheesh." He waved his empty hand. "Hell, no, I'm from . . . around. *You* know. What the hell happened here?"

Sara's hopes revived. She thought he might be a policeman, even dressed in shorts like that. Perhaps he was on some sort of undercover assignment and couldn't risk identifying himself.

"Well," she said, "this man was trying to kill me." She moved her chin toward Cone, but didn't look at him. Neither did Sully. "Is he dead?" Arn-the-Barn nodded solemnly. "My friend here saved my life," she said. "He shot him with his bow. The man was just about to kill me. I don't know why." That wouldn't even count as a lie, thought Sara. "I think he must be crazy. But I'd be dead if it wasn't for my friend. He saved my life. This man was going to shoot me down in cold blood." There, she thought.

Arnold turned to Sully. "Is that the way it went?"

"Yes, sir," Sully said. "I didn't actually try to kill him. I'm not that good a shot. But he had his gun up to shoot at Sara. I was down there." He pointed over the side of the deck. "I just grabbed an arrow and shot. I hardly even aimed it. Really." Sully was still in a daze. He felt as if his foot had gone to sleep, except all over. He could think, he could remember, but nothing had any meaning. He couldn't plan at all; he could just be wherever he was, answer questions, do as he was told.

Arnold was impressed. "Wow," he said. And then, "Hold on."

He went inside and got a blanket from the bedroom. He put that over Cone. "There," he said. He slipped the pistol back inside his jacket. Sara and Sully were just standing there looking at each other. She had thought about running—taking off—when Arn went in the house, but when she'd looked at Sully and seen how blank he looked, she knew that it was hopeless. She would never get him moving fast enough, and she wouldn't think of leaving him. What she'd have to do was hope the man *was* a policeman; maybe he would help them somehow. The thing was this, though: there weren't all that many ways that *anyone* could help them. Sara realized she was scared.

"So," said Arn to Sully, walking toward the railing to his right. "You were just down there. . . ." He was trying to get a completely clear picture of how it all had happened.

And then who should step out from behind a nearby tree but this guy Nat, with still *another* kid, another girl.

"Hey, Arn," Nat called to him. "What's happening up there?"

It was typical of Nat to think that Arn-the-Barn Emfatico, although an unexpected sight, would also be a friendly one. They'd always got along, and even if he owed the state and Arnold's uncle money, that didn't mean to Nat that they'd stop being friends.

"Hey, Nat," said Arnold, forgetting, for the moment, why he'd even come to Coldbrook. "How ya doing?" Nat, for sure, could clear things up, about this bigot teacher and the kids. Then, after that—oh, yeah, thought Arnold, to himself—they'd get to other matters.

* * *

You couldn't really call it a *summit* meeting. To begin with, Robinson's was only part way up a hill, and neither Nat nor Arn-the-Barn was like a head of state or president of anything. But still, in terms of sheer agreement and accomplishments, no summit meeting ever worked as well for everyone concerned.

It started with a shock for Nat and Ludi.

"Guess what?" said Arnold, before they'd even climbed the steps. "Your kid here iced that bastard Homer Cone. Bow and arra. You know the guy I mean, right? Big-headed son-of-a-bitch from the school down there? He went to take a shot at the girl, and the kid twanged him a good one. Right inna heart."

Nat and Ludi hurried up the stairs when they heard that, and went to Sully and Sara, passing the blanketed pile of Cone without a second glance. Sara cried then, feeling much relief, but Sully stayed quite stiff and pale and shook his head a lot, and said, "I can't believe it," many times.

It was Ludi who remembered Coke and Marigold and volunteered to go and get them, but Nat thought otherwise.

"Suppose," he said to Sully, "you and Sara go. Tell them just what happened and take them back to Spring Lake Lodge. Lu and I'll join you when we get through here. And maybe Arnold if he wants to. Probably we'll beat you back, in fact." Nat smacked his forehead. "Arn!" He turned to the big man. "Here I am, babbling; I didn't even introduce you." Arnold beamed; he knew manners when he saw them. "You met Sully and Sara already, right? And this is Ludi." He gestured toward Arnold. "This is Arn Emfatico. We were friends up in Burlington. Boy," he said, "that seems a hundred years ago."

"Hi," said Arnold, smiling all around. "Pleased to meet you. How ya doing?"

The kids all managed smiles of sorts and said

195

hello; Sully even took a few steps forward and shook hands, calling Arnold "sir" again.

Arnold turned to Nat. "And these are the ones they wanted you to . . . ?" He made a face and gave a shrug. ". . . *you* know?"

"Yeah," said Nat. "These and two others. It wasn't ever possible, Arn. I never should have said I would. The whole thing's completely crazy."

"I guess *so,*" said Arnold. "I see exactly what you mean. Before . . . like, I imagined . . . *I* don't know exactly what I thought they'd be like. But these . . . my God." He shook his head. And then, remembering, he made another face. "Hey, Nat. I just remembered. We got something serious to talk about."

"Just a second, Arn," said Nat. He turned to Sully and Sara again and asked them how they felt about going for Coke and Marigold. He felt sure that they'd be better off away from Cone's body and doing whatever had to be done with it. Especially Sully. And he wanted Ludi with him. Oh, boy, did he ever want Ludi with him! You want to talk about serious? *That* was serious.

Sully and Sara seemed to like the idea and left, Sully saying, "I'm glad to have met you, sir," to Arn.

"Now . . . what?" said Nat to Arnold.

"Hey, Nat," said Arn. "We got a problem, a bad one. What I'm doing here—my uncle sent me down, you got it? He sent me after you. And if that ain't enough, I'm also here on accounta my boss from the Bursar's office, Mr. Darling. He's looking for you, too; he wants that money that you owe us. But my uncle, he's the really bad part—he just wants no more Nathaniels."

Nat said, "No. You can't be serious. Because I didn't pay him what he said I owed him from that Florida excursion? That wasn't my fault, Arn. You know that wasn't my fault."

Arnold pulled his lower lip and shook his head.

"It's more than that. He feels his reputation's on the line. The Doctor from the school, he called him up and told him how you didn't do your stuff down here. My uncle got that job for you, and so, when you don't do it right, he thinks that's making him look bad. It's, like, he guarantees his help. Same with a Carvel's or a McDonald's—any franchise. They got this quality control, I think they call it. My uncle sends a guy to do a job for someone . . . the guy had better do the job. Right up to my uncle's standards, or he's out. Same with Carvel's. He don't take no excuses, Uncle."

"So you were meant to kill me, too?" Nat asked. "Is this another franchise deal?" He ran a hand along one cheek and shook his own head back at Arnold. "How can this be happening?" he said. "In twenty-two years, nobody even takes a punch at me. I've never been kicked or slapped, for God's sake; my parents never even *spanked* me. And now, all of a sudden, people want to have me killed." He looked at Ludi. "I hope this isn't catching, Lu."

She made a little pouty face at him and smiled.

"I was hoping I could tell my uncle you just skipped," said Arn. "I was hoping you were long since gone—you *and* the kids from here. But here you are. And all these crazies from the school—and Mr. Darling, weekends—running through the woods with guns and legal papers. I just wish you were a thousand miles away from here, the bunch of you. Believe me, Nat—if my uncle ever knew I'd seen you, talked to you, and didn't . . . *you* know. Well, then, I'd be on his list, and he wouldn't send no guy like me to cancel *me,* I can tell you that much."

Nat sighed and scratched his head, but when he did his eyes went down and saw, again, the blanket-covered heap that once conducted classes at the Coldbrook Country School.

"Hey, Arnold, wait a minute . . . ," Nat began. He

was sure he'd had the idea of his life. And so the Robinson Accords began.

Arnold checked it over every way that he could think of, but still the idea didn't leak a drop. Homer Cone had got what he deserved. Alive, he'd been a bigot and a killer and a prick; why not let him be a good guy, dead? Why not let him be Nathaniel Palmer Rittenhouse?

What Arn would do was follow his directions, do exactly what his uncle'd told him to: "Find this guy and finish him, and take what's left to Dunphy's." Dunphy's was a funeral home; the owner was a relative, by marriage, of Arnold's uncle's family, and Uncle tried to help him out and make sure business never got too slow. Dunphy would take care of all the paper work, as well; it would be certified that one Nat Rittenhouse had died an accidental death ("a fall") on such-and-such a date, at such-and-such a place. The family—Nat's family—would get an urn of ashes, via UPS, collect, and in a little while, a bill for Dunphy's services. Eventually the news of Nat's demise would filter back to UVM and Mr. Darling; Arn could see to that. But for a while, for Mr. Darling's sake, Arn would keep on walking through the woods around the school by day and staying at the Valivu Motel at night. Maybe Ginnie could come down for the weekend, he thought; motels kinda turned her on. As far as his uncle was concerned, he'd just be "off on holiday."

"But what'll you be doing?" Arnold asked his friend. "What I mean, the real you, not this eight ball, here." He flipped a thumb toward Cone.

Nat explained the Plan to him, and Arn-the-Barn agreed it maybe had a chance to work, provided they got lucky.

They stuffed the late, completely unlamented Mr. Cone into a garment bag they found inside the house, and all of that into the trunk of his sedan. What Nat would do was drive the body down, with Arnold, transfer it into Arnold's Trans-Am's trunk, and then drive back. Arn would go direct to Dunphy's, call his uncle the good news, and then get back to Valivu to spend the night. Ludi volunteered to try to deal with bloodstains on the deck: there were some bathroom cleaners in the house, she said, all of which were sure that they could pick up anything that mortal man could spill. Then she and Nat could organize the stuff that Group 6 had at Robinson's and start evacuation drill. Nat thought of hiding Homer Cone's sedan a ways away, but that would mean some extra time he didn't want to spare, and anyway, the chances were that Cone told someone else just where he planned to go, and so there would be searchers in the space around the Robinsons', regardless.

They accomplished all of that without a hitch. Although it didn't specifically say so on the label, one of the bathroom-cleaning products did a "fabulous job, my dear," according to Ludi, with bloodstains on a polyurethaned surface, and Nat and Ludi got all of everybody's gear moved up to Spring Lake Lodge in two fast trips. So, well before nightfall, they were all back at the Lodge again, trying to recover from the day's events and figure how and where to go from there.

At dinner there was a new seating arrangement. Marigold created it by sitting on the other side of Sara than she always did. That meant that she had taken Ludi's place, and wasn't sitting next to Coke. Sully then moved over next to Sara, in Marigold's old place, and Ludi, getting there last, sat over on the other side of Nat from usual, where Sully used to be. There were no comments on the changes.

"Nothing against the cooks," said Coke, "but isn't

there any other sauce for things besides tomato? I know I probably shouldn't talk, seeing as I never cook anything myself, but I swear to God, in another week I think I'll start to speak Italian and be full of seeds. . . ."

"Which might be quite a pair of pleasant changes," said Marigold to Sara in a mutter.

They were eating one of Nat's concoctions: dried lima beans and rice, with basil, cheese, and canned tomatoes.

"Well, let's see," said Nat. "There's always hollandaise, but for that you need special stuff to put under it, like eggs benedict, or asparagus, or broccoli. Or maybe Brussels sprouts. I don't think I'd like Brussels sprouts even with maple syrup on them, though. Of course, there's also white sauce, like you get with chipped beef . . ."

"Ugh—chipped beef," said Marigold. "Let's stick with the tomatoes, O.K.?"

"I like this," Ludi said, holding up a forkful. "It tastes like something you'd make," she said to Nat. Ludi was happy being back at Spring Lake Lodge; she hoped that maybe Nat would sleep outside with her.

"Are you implying all the food I cook tastes just the same?" said Nat.

"Not exactly," Ludi said. "But similar. Related. You know what I mean? It has to do with spices, mostly. Flavors, anyway. Like onions, or garlic, or herbs."

"I guess you're right," said Nat. "I never thought of it that way before. But I do tend to reach for the exact same seasonings all the time. If it isn't basil it's curry, and if it isn't curry it's garlic or onions, with black pepper." He looked around the circle. Except for Ludi, everyone was sitting looking at her bowl, or his, eating sort of stolidly. Not what you'd call fascinated with the dinner-table conversation. The "parents-are-a-bore" look.

Sara felt like they were losing ground, being back at Spring Lake Lodge, two hours farther from the school, thus that much farther from the Plan. Would they ever use the Robinsons' again? She doubted it.

Coke preferred it at the Robinsons', by far, and so did Marigold. It was more comfortable, let's face it, and you didn't have to be with . . . *people* all the time. They both got that idea, quite suddenly, that night. They'd gotten used to spending time with each other, but until that day, there'd always been a bunch of others with them, too. Those others were the bumpers in the pinball game of life: you could use them, in a way, to keep yourself in play, and scoring. A target for "asides," they were. A day with just the other one had gotten slightly irritating, like socks that wouldn't stay pulled up. They both thought it would be pleasant to spend time alone more often—and that was hard at Spring Lake Lodge.

Sully's mood kept swinging back and forth, a lot more quickly and enormously than he could say, or anyone could tell from looking at him. He sat there rather calmly, looking sort of stoned. At times he seemed a hero to himself; face it, he had saved his girl friend's life. It was right out of dreamland. And he could tell she was grateful, because she kept asking him how he was doing, and giving him little touches on the leg or arm; she never had before. If she didn't look at him adoringly a lot—well, that was just her way, and anyway, with all the other kids around . . .

And then he'd think he was a killer. A person who had been alive this morning—gotten up and brushed his teeth and ate and maybe laughed and took a shit was dead, and he had caused it. Maybe he was a murderer. Maybe the guy never would have shot at Sara

201

at all; maybe he was just trying to scare her, or make her mind. Before, Sully had thought that he wouldn't mind killing McCorker. He'd even run through different scenes in his mind, where he'd saved his mother from the guy, or even protected his own virtue, as the saying went. But McCorker always made the first move and it was definite, quite unmistakable, and Sully'd had to shoot him with this little pistol he'd imagined. Right between the eyes. McCorker'd look surprised and fall right down, but never bleed. He didn't look any worse than a parochial school kid on Ash Wednesday. And then the fantasy would end; there wasn't any "later on." Nobody to dispose of, no having somebody call him "Robin Hood."

Coke had done that when he'd first heard the story down near school. He'd first said "What?" like in amazement. And then he'd said, "Hey, neat," and looked at Sully in an all-new way. "Robin Hood, himself," he'd said. He'd gotten serious right after that, but Sully saw that he was acting, playing out the role of "sympathetic friend," making like he understood the situation all too well. Sure, Coke. He didn't understand a thing, as far as Sully was concerned. For Coke, it was more or less as if he'd been told about the latest episode on *Hill Street Blues* or a new Clint Eastwood movie: "Well, you see what happens is, there's this guy out on a porch who's gonna shoot this chick. An' just when he's getting ready to gun her down, this other kid, who's behind this rock . . ." That's what it was really like for Coke. He didn't understand at all, it seemed to Sully.

"What about today?" Sara'd had enough of talk about tomato sauce. She turned to Marigold. "D'you think you guys learned anything useful about the schedule down there?" She craned her neck and looked past Marigold to Nat. "And what about tomorrow? Shouldn't we think about setting up our watching post again?" If questioned, Sara would have said she *was* thinking of Sully. It was best for him to keep busy, get his mind off himself.

Marigold pulled folded papers from her pocket.

"We got a lot of numbers written down," she said. "It was pretty confusing, 'cause when we were there was when all the classes were going on, and changing, and then there was lunch. And a certain individual kept fucking around and screwing up the count."

"Up yours," said Coke. "It was already screwed up." He spoke to Nat. "The thing was, there're all these people milling around and going in and out, and back and forth, and forgetting stuff and going back for it. It got ridiculous. And I don't see where it makes any difference if twenty-five people or thirty-seven people went into Moorhead Hall at twelve-oh-five. You can just say 'a whole bunch of people,' and leave it at that."

Nat nodded, noncommittally. Arguments were so unnecessary, mostly. He wasn't going to get involved in this one.

Sara said, "We got a lot of numbers, too. But I guess the only ones that really matter are the ones that have to do with Doctor Simms's house, and Foote, where the offices are. Don't you think?" She was speaking to Nat again.

Nat said, "I imagine so. Like I said, Doctor has a study in both places, or an office, or whatever you want to call it. And the one in the house still seems like the most likely place to me."

"Is there a *Mrs.* Simms?" asked Ludi.

"Not so far as you can see," said Nat. "She may be locked away some place, of course. Down in a musty cellar maybe. But somehow I think Doctor is a widower. Or possibly divorced. He's too weird for anyone to live with for long, but he also doesn't seem like a bachelor. I don't know why I say that, exactly—"

"Well," said Sara, interrupting, "whatever he is,

203

no one goes into his house from eight-thirty in the morning till ten-thirty. Or, no one did today, I can tell you that much."

"*He* went in after lunch," said Marigold, looking at her papers, "and stayed for about five minutes, and then went back to Foote."

"Probably brushed his teeth," said Coke, "like a good little Doctor."

"There's a lot more traffic into Foote," said Sara, "but it doesn't really start till"—she ran a finger down a page of notes—"till eight-fifteen, when a fat woman—who drives up in a Vega, by the way—comes in."

"Oh, yeah," said Coke, "*that* one. She was first one in for lunch, too, and she didn't come out for over an hour. Remember?" he said to Marigold. "That's the one I said reminded me of the woman who taught 'Habits: How to Break the Baddies,' at the Institute."

Marigold looked up and nodded quickly, with a little smile. Coke had been pretty funny telling her about that woman, and how the flab below her upper arms swung back and forth when she was writing on the greenboard.

"After eight-thirty," Sara said, "there're people coming and going all the time, in and out of Foote. And it's all irregular, not just at certain set times, like when the classes change."

"No," said Sully loudly, and he gave a little jump, as if he'd scared himself. "They just come and go. I was thinking. Maybe kids get mail there. Or money even. Maybe there's like a school bank."

"Could be," said Sara. She touched him gently on the knee; then she patted the place she'd touched. "You know, I'll bet that's right," she said. "I seem to remember that some of them went in and out in just a couple of minutes' time. I'll bet that's exactly it." She smiled at Sully.

"What do you think'll happen"—Sully turned to Nat now—"when that guy doesn't come back?" He cleared his throat. "*You* know." He did some flutters with his hands. "D'you think they'll look for him up there, or what?"

Nat shook his head. "Gee, I don't know," he said. "I'm sure they'll look for him eventually. But when they start and where they'll start looking . . . I guess that'll depend on whether he told anyone where he was going, and—well—what his habits are, you might say. I mean, is he the sort of guy who'd stay out overnight? Stuff like that. I was thinking, as a matter of fact, that it might be a good idea to put the Robinsons' under surveillance for a while." He put his fist up to his mouth and spoke in it, as if it were a microphone. "Car eight-oh-two, let's run a check on five-three-nine Magnolia Drive. I want a stakeout round the clock." He laughed and shook his head. "But seriously. See if anyone comes, and what they do, and stuff like that. It *is* only a couple of hours from here, after all."

"Boy, I agree," said Ludi. "I was wondering about that actually. D'you think maybe we ought to consider setting up another—I don't know—major base, you might say? *Farther* away from everything? I mean, if we've lost the Robinsons', and if they're going to start searching from there . . . Before, it seemed as if Spring Lake Lodge was just about the end of the world, but now, well, it doesn't feel that way at all. I don't even like to think about them finding it, but . . . I don't know." She shrugged and looked at Nat, wanting to be sure he understood what she was saying.

"Hmm," said Nat. "Maybe we ought to talk about that. I know some other places that are pretty neat. There's one that's by this little waterfall. . . ."

"But how about *tomorrow?*" Sara said. "And watching the school some more? Don't you think we have to know what happens in the afternoons, for instance? I mean, if it is during a game that we go down there, like whoever it was said . . . ? And don't you think that maybe one of us could sneak in there and copy down the schedule? Of games and stuff. I'll bet there's one on that big bulletin board, and if I went in right at the beginning of dinner, I'll bet I could do it without getting caught. Without getting *seen*, I mean."

"Well," said Nat, "maybe we ought to split up again tomorrow. I think we ought to keep an eye on the Robinsons', like I said, and see what they may be up to—the people from the school. But if you and Sully want to go down to the school—or at least to our tree down there . . . I don't know. I'd feel a lot better if you didn't go into the place just yet, though. Would you humor me on that?" Sara nodded, and he looked over at Coke. "What do you guys feel like doing, do you think?"

"I don't feel like *counting* again, I'll tell you that much," said Coke. "Maybe we could go with you, or just hang around up here. . . ."

"I'll go with Sara and Sully," Marigold said. "It might be easier with three." She made a big thing out of licking the inside of her bowl.

"Well, then, maybe I could find another house to take the place of Robinson's," said Coke. "If you could more or less suggest some possibilities," he said to Nat, "maybe I could scout around and look at them." He wanted to give himself something dramatic and important to do. He wouldn't exactly hate finding some liquor or something, too.

Nat shrugged. He didn't much like the idea of Coke soloing around the summer houses in the area; most of them were pretty unremote and near a road. But he also found he loved the prospect of a Cokeless day, spent hanging out with Ludi. It had even crossed Nat's mind that if he got the chance to go

206

back into Robinson's, he'd remember to check out the . . . well, the birth control situation there. He wondered if he should be a little embarrassed by that thought. She was still sixteen; love didn't change that. Could she really know exactly what she wanted? Of course she'd think she knew—but doesn't everybody, all the time, except about college and careers?

"Well," he said, "there may be one or two. They're pretty near the road, though. I suppose it wouldn't hurt to look, if you're super-careful."

Coke nodded, coolly, cagily. Marigold looked interested. Sara was talking to Sully in a sort of private tone.

Nat got up. "I cooked," he said, "so I don't get to wash. I think I'll hit the sentry tree awhile. Just to be on the safe side. I'll make you a map in the morning," he said to Coke.

"Want company?" said Ludi. "I'll do a dish or two, first." Coke looked at Marigold.

"Why, shore . . . ," said Nat. He touched her head. "I'd *love* it."

He wandered off, hoping that he didn't look too happy. Being sentry wasn't all that big a turn-on, after all.

Chapter Nine

IF JEN MALONEY had had to choose one course, out of all the courses taken by her sometime roommate Nat, and label it "The Absolute Most Bullshit One of All," she might have chosen one called "The Collective Consciousness: Sounds and Styles of the Sixties." It was a little interdepartmental beauty, offered by some very junior members of the Music and Sociology faculties, and it included watching a lot of films, and listening to a lot of records, and reading (quite) a lot of jive about group marriages and other utopian experiments. The student nickname for the course was "Tunes and 'munes," and Nat would surely have got an A in it, if grades (or credit) had been offered.

But no matter anything that Jen might think, or say, Nat had gotten a lot out of that course. He'd learned, for example, that whenever people tried to live together, trouble always started in the kitchen or the bathroom, where the Cleans first quarreled with the Dirties over dishes, crumbs, and toilet bowls; and who ate whose last-thing-of-coffee-yogurt-I-was-saving and used up half-a-fucking-bottle-of-shampoo. He'd also learned that groups that had a good strong vow of chastity were apt to be long-lived, compared to those that smiled on pairing, mating, dating, or relating.

In the case of Group 6, there weren't any Clean

and Dirty Wars. It happened Nat and Sara, both, were energetic Cleans, and so was Ludi, when she thought of it. The other three were either neutral or unconscious, so principles did not become an issue; things were cleaned as needed, and no one felt a constant sense of loss-of-their-identity, or martyred.

Whether pairing (dating, mating, or relating) hurt Group 6 or not is quite another question. On the one hand, Nat thought not: he knew that he and Ludi didn't (*wouldn't ever*) talk against the others, or the Group, when they were what the French might call *à deux.* And he didn't think that other people did that, either. But yet, beyond a doubt, the "groupiness" of 6 just had to be affected by the separations and the stresses of the life-style it adopted.

The evening of the day that Homer Cone was killed was the first time that they didn't start the night, at least, with boys and girls in separate rooms. Nat and Ludi, sitting in the sentry tree, had talked about the matter thusly:

She: "You want to sleep outside tonight?"

He: "Yeah, sure, let's do that. Excellent."

And so, when it was getting dark, they walked back to the fire, hand in hand. The conversation there shut down as they approached, but Nat continued holding Ludi's hand. He checked expressions when they got in range; Marigold's was pure "I told you so" when, after greeting them, she smiled around the circle. Nat thought that she and Coke had semi-made it up; she'd been lying semi-propped on his lean stomach. Sully and Sara were sitting very close together, touching hip bones, actually. Sully still looked pretty strange and miserable, but Nat figured that might be partly because he couldn't get up the nerve to fling a casual arm around sweet Sara's shoulders. Coke and Marigold's being so-o-o cool and so-o-o relaxed wasn't helping the poor guy one bit, either, so it seemed to Nat.

"Well," he said, "we've decided it'd be fun to sleep outside tonight." He hadn't meant to say that "fun" part; what he'd meant to say was "we've decided to sleep outside tonight," but the rest of it just squeezed in there. Probably because, in some retarded corner of his mind, "fun" was always "wholesome," too.

Marigold, however, wasn't having any "wholesome," thank you very much; she rolled her eyes around and said, "I wouldn't be surprised."

"I'd like to do that, too," said Sully bravely. And, looking at the person to his right, more softly, "You want to, Sara?"

She smoothed her hair back. "Sure," she said, and touched him on the shoulder, keeping her hand there for a moment.

"We got dibbies on the far side of the Lake," said Ludi. "You can see the stars out there."

"Oh, sure," said Marigold.

Nat and Ludi went and got their sleeping bags, and pads, and a poncho to put under the whole affair. While Ludi was brushing her teeth and going to the bathroom, Nat managed to zip their sleeping bags together, and when he got back from similar errands, she was curled inside their bed already. He got his boots and jeans off, then turned and asked her what her night dress was.

"The minimum." She smiled.

"The bare minimum?" he asked.

She nodded.

"Ah," he said, and grinned and got his clothes off. "What a day," he said, when he was in beside her and had her smooth, light body in his arms.

"If I didn't feel so sorry for Sully, I think I'd just light up with happiness," said Ludi. "Even as it is, it feels like I'm smiling all over me."

Nat stroked her gently, said "I'll check," and kissed her here and there for at least an hour's time.

* * *

Sully and Sara were the next to go to bed. It took a lot of "might as well's" and drying of their palms on thighs to get them started, but finally they were settled in a spot back in the spruces that wasn't on the way to anywhere that anyone would have to go to—as well as out of sight, and earshot, of the fireplace.

"Can we put our sleeping bags together?" Sully wondered, meaning, mostly, "would you like to?" He'd never slept under the same set of covers with a girl.

Sara answered, "Sure, I'll bet we could." And they did. She knew that Sully wanted her (whatever "wanted" meant), and maybe even needed her, that night; she was quite a bit less clear about her own feelings, which was unusual for her, she thought. She knew she wanted to help Sully, and that wasn't just gratitude, either; even if it had been somebody else's life he'd saved, instead of hers, she'd have wanted to help him. But whether she just plain wanted him (in all those senses) . . . well, she wasn't sure, still. The different ways of wanting complicated matters.

They both slid into bed with underpants and t-shirts on, and seeing that they'd kissed that afternoon, they kissed again, and that felt good. Sara found she was enjoying the warmth of Sully's body, and the way he felt and smelled. Their kiss came to an end, but they kept on hugging one another. And then Sara felt Sully's body start to shake, and she knew that he was crying.

He'd buried his face in her shoulder—in her hair between her shoulder and her head, and he was holding onto her very hard, and pressing his face into her hair to muffle the sounds that he was making.

She held him very hard, herself, and stroked his head and murmured to him. "Yes," she said, "I know," and that surprised her, saying that, so she said "It's all right," which sounded more traditional.

Sully was just saying "Oh, God," over and over, and moving his head in little shakes, almost as if he were trying to burrow into her and disappear.

"Sully, it's O.K., dear; it's O.K. now," Sara said. She shifted slightly, got her hand on one of his, and slid the two hands, hers and his, right underneath her t-shirt. She put his hand down on her breast, and her hand over it, and told him, "There. Now everything's all right. None of it was your fault, baby." She'd never called anyone "dear" or "baby" before, and the words felt strange and awkward in her mouth. Everybody said words like that: her parents and Robert Redford and Meryl Streep and everyone. She knew they were the right words, but they still sounded funny, coming from her. But having him touch her felt good and right—again—and she was pleased to feel his gasps and sobs subside, in time, and *very* pleased to feel so good, in such a sexy way, herself.

"I'm acting like such a baby," Sully said. He had to blow his nose.

"Don't be silly," Sara said. "You're acting like a person."

"I don't know what I'd do, if it wasn't for you," said Sully softly. He was now really touching her breast and sort of blown away by that reality, and pretty much confused by feeling so great and so terrible at almost the same time.

Sara had her own confusions. She knew that Sully's crying didn't bother her—if anything, the opposite. And neither did his touching her, and the effect it clearly had on him; it seemed to her she loved them both. What she wasn't sure of was the way he seemed to depend on her so much—although (she reminded herself) at the crucial moment it was he who'd acted, she who ran.

Rather than try to figure anything out just then, it was easier to pull her t-shirt up a little, and run her hand around his side, onto his belly. He was surely breathing different—better—now.

"Well," said Coke, "I guess we've got the kiddies all tucked in."

"Now don't be cynical," said Marigold, "I think it's kind of cute."

Coke shook his head resignedly. "These wartime romances," he said, and smiled his foxy smile. He smoothed Marigold's bangs; her head still rested on his stomach.

"Well, what do you think ours is?" Marigold asked.

"I thought you'd never ask," said Coke. "But seeing as you have, let me ask you one now. Suppose—just for the fun of it—that we *could* stay at the school here. Like Sara was saying that time. Would you want to?"

"Would you?" she asked, tilting her head around so she could see his face.

"I asked you first," he said.

"Well, suppose I said 'Yes,' then," she said. "What would you say?"

"No 'supposes,' " Coke said. "That's not fair. You have to say, one way or the other."

"O.K., yes," said Marigold. "I think I would. It might not be too bad. In some ways, I feel better now than I've ever felt in my life. So, now, how about you?"

"If you stayed, I'd want to," he said. "Even if you weren't my girl friend, maybe you'd be my friend. It's sort of weird when you think about not having a home to go to anymore. Not having a family."

Marigold reached up and touched Coke's cheek. "You know it," she said. Suddenly her eyes were full of tears. "I've thought about that, being alone. You always knew it was going to happen sometime: that your parents'd die before you did, and maybe your brother'd be living in Seattle and never see you or write. But you don't expect anything sudden, like this. It's the same as an airplane crash or something, but it isn't your parents who're killed, it's you. Most of the time, I can handle it, but then, all of a sudden, I feel so incredibly *lonely,* you know?" She shook her head and pinched the corners of her eyes.

"No shit," said Coke. "So I'd like to ask you something. Would you be my family?" he said, and looked away from her, as if it weren't dark out there and he had had to look at something.

"O.K.," said Marigold. "I will. Sure; I really will. And you can be mine." She sat up and offered him her hand to shake. Then she took a breath and grinned, fighting off the mood. "And that'd give us a chance to play Instant Incest—first ones on the block." She looked around and did a double-take. "Hey. Here's a switch. Everyone in this group's in bed with each other except us."

"Copycats," said Coke. And then he said, "If you'd rather just sleep in your bunk tonight . . ."

"Are you kidding?" said Marigold. "Someone might think I was losing my"—she put one hand on the back of her neck and did a little sitting bump—"stuff. Or that *you* had lost your mind." She laughed and stood up. "This has to be one of the most difficult weeks in the history of innocent young girlhood." She held out a hand. "Come on, bubba," she said, "I've got to be in shape to *count* tomorrow."

Coke sighed and made a face, but the sigh was more relief than anything.

In the morning, everyone got up together, more or less. Marigold had found the little tin flute that Ludi had, and played "The Worms Crawl In" on it, to make sure people were awake. Nat and Ludi had had to wiggle into shirts and pants while still in bed, but nobody was watching anyway.

When they all sat down to Marigold's French toast, each couple seemed to make a point of its own bondedness, although before they'd even had a glass of juice, the girls had gone together to the Lodge "to dress—no men allowed." Each of them had wanted to be sure that the other two were "feeling good," and until they each knew that, none of them could feel—or act—real happy. Marigold had said, "You know, I've never liked that 'sisters' bullshit that you hear sometimes. Just 'cause someone's female doesn't mean she isn't an asshole, as far as I'm concerned. But you two . . . I really wish you were my sisters, and I just wanted to tell you that."

Well, that made all three of them nod and hug and feel their eyes burn, and everyone insisted she felt fine and dandy.

By seven, under cloudy skies, they'd gone their separate ways. Sully, Sara, and Marigold headed for the school, where they would watch all through the afternoon, and not get back till after dark. Nat and Ludi aimed for the Robinsons', and Coke went with them, almost all the way. The houses on the map that Nat had drawn for him were farther than the Robinsons', and on the side away from school. He'd promised Nat that he would take no chances, and he knew he'd keep that promise. He was no hero. But whatever he was, he sure felt different than he used to feel. The strange fact of the matter was that Coke was starting to feel healthy.

Mr. Cone was not at breakfast. Mrs. Ripple knew that 'cause she looked, although she didn't have to. Homer Cone ate breakfast at a table just behind her own; he always took hot cereal with cream, and toast, and coffee. Though lacking rural roots herself, Mrs. Ripple had some knowledge of the language of the farm: agricultural idioms had an earthiness that pleased her. So, even if she didn't know what "sloppin' hawgs" might mean, exactly, she thought that she would recognize the sound of such a happening, not unlike the breakfasting of Homer Cone on oatmeal. And that morning there was no such sound, a rare event. Mr. Cone was seldom one to miss a feeding.

Mrs. Ripple thought she should investigate. She'd been a little miffed, the day before, when Mr. Cone had failed to seek her out and tell her what he'd found, or hadn't found, when he'd gone hunting on his own. And now he hadn't come to breakfast. Could he be avoiding her? Could he, by the blindest luck, have finished the whole job himself? That bulbous-browed B.M., thought Mrs. Ripple.

She knocked on Homer Cone's apartment door. No answer. She knocked again, a good deal more emphatically. He could be in the bathroom, she supposed. She went away and then returned ten minutes later, knocked some more. He surely would be finished in the bathroom, Mrs. Ripple thought. She tried the door. It was unlocked; she entered.

"Mr. Co-o-one," she called. She craned her neck. He wasn't in his little kitchen, either. Should she go into the bedroom? Mrs. Ripple wondered. Would that be proper of her? Having been a married woman, Mrs. Ripple dared.

There were no heavy drapes, no mirrors on the ceiling or the walls, no movie screen, no water bed. Rather a disappointing bachelor's bedroom, Mrs. Ripple thought. Not even heaps of loathsome magazines, and scatterings of cutout underwear. The bed looked undisturbed, uninteresting—unslept in. Mrs. Ripple touched the counterpane; it wasn't even warm, nor did it vibrate. She hurried off to Doctor's office in Foote Hall. That gentleman had just arrived and now was drinking coffee, brewed (incredibly) by a Mrs. Olson.

"Oh, Mrs. Ripple," Doctor said. "Yes, do come in. Perhaps a cup of coffee? Mrs. Olson made it; it's the best."

"No, thank you," Mrs. Ripple answered, "I've had my tea." Coffee was an after-dinner beverage, in her opinion. "I hate to bother you so early in the day," she said, "but Mr. Cone, I fear, has not returned."

"Returned?" said Doctor, eyebrows arced and raised. "Returned from where? Since when?"

"Yesterday," said Mrs. Ripple, lowering her voice, "he went up, just at lunch time, to that new house in the woods. The one that people from Long Island built, with all the porches? People named Novotny, I believe?"

"Ah, yes," said Doctor, matching left-hand fingertips to right. Once again, they came out even, to his great delight.

"And insofar as I can tell, he never did get back," said Mrs. Ripple.

"I take it Mr. Cone was . . . on a mission," Doctor said discreetly.

"Yes," said Mrs. Ripple. "And that's what makes me think he may be lost. He wouldn't be familiar with the woods up there, you know, and besides . . ." She stopped. One shouldn't speak ill of a colleague, ever.

"And besides, as Levi always says, he couldn't find his sock in his galoshes," Doctor chuckled.

Mrs. Ripple smiled her very thinnest smile. She'd overheard what Levi "always" said one time. Levi should have his mouth washed out with good strong laundry soap, that sharp-nosed donkey's dork. "It's true that Mr. Cone does not possess what my late husband called a 'bump of direction,' " said Mrs. Ripple. "He *has* been known to lose his way."

" ' . . . down upon the Swanee River,' " Doctor

sang, " 'far, far, away . . .' That's true, for sure," he said. "Well. Now. Let's see. How's your schedule look this morning, Mrs. Ripple?"

"I have no *formal* classes till eleven," she replied, "though students often seek me out for special help and counseling at *any* time. Yesterday, for instance, I couldn't go with Mr. Cone because my schedule was *much* too tight. In fact, I didn't get to bed till after midnight, as it was. I still insist on weekly themes from all my classes, unlike some others I could name." Mrs. Ripple sighed. "It must be wonderful to teach math, and just go *C* and *X*, right down the page. Isn't it ironic that the teachers who have lots of time to read just don't, while those of us—"

"Yes, fine," said Doctor, slapping both his hands on chair arms, meaning that the interview was ending. Ripple always did run on about how overworked she was. "Suppose you just go round to Maintenance and tell young Levi that *I* say he should run you up with him to Br'er Novotny's. Tell him to take a bullhorn, too." He chuckled. "Homer'll be mighty glad to hear a friendly voice, I'll wager. Bet he's feeling grouchy as a silvertip without his breakfast." Doctor liked to salt his speech with Rocky Mountain lingo. He'd never been west of Philadelphia, nor higher than the highest point on the Massachusetts Turnpike. He looked down at his fingernails and counted to twenty, to himself, lips moving; by the time that he'd looked up, she'd gone.

Mrs. Ripple found Levi drinking coffee in the Shop beside the big garage. The men in Maintenance had chipped in for a Mr. Coffee, and they all had their own mugs with their names on them that hung on nails when not in use—or hardly ever, as it seemed to Mrs. Ripple. She'd like to work *their* hours, she could tell you that much. Actually, the cups didn't have the men's own names on them, but the names of people they particularly admired. Levi's, for example, had Jesse Helms's name on it, whose views he shared on crucial legislative issues, such as gun control and some other stuff, too, that he couldn't usually think of right then. Other cups belonged to "Genjus" Kahn, Bo Derek, Joe DiMaggio, the U.S. Hockey Team, and Zonker Harris, whoever he was.

Levi shook his head and acted real concerned to hear that Homer Cone had not come home all night, and that maybe he had spent it in the woods and lost. Actually, he thought: too bad it didn't snow. He got the Rover and a bullhorn, though, and in less than twenty minutes time, the two of them were parked beside the Robinson-Novotny house, right next to Mr. Cone's sedan.

"Well," said Mrs. Ripple, "at least we know he got here, anyway."

"Unless somebody stole his car," corrected Levi Welch. "Or had another one just like it."

Mrs. Ripple looked at Levi sharply, wondering if he was being fresh or merely stupid. Presumably, he might be both at once.

"Perhaps," she said, "we now should use the . . . hailer. Ask that Mr. Cone discharge his rifle, if he hears your voice."

Levi raised the bullhorn. "Hey, Cone, if you c'n hear me, shoot your gol-danged gun off!" He shouted that four times: up, down, and across the slope in both directions. Then, after a moment's discussion, they began to walk almost due east, away from the school and away from Spring Lake Lodge. Levi Welch and Mrs. Ripple both knew Homer Cone, and the walking . . . it was *much* the easiest, in that direction.

Nat and Ludi had to smile as they watched Levi Welch and Mrs. Ripple disappearing with their bullhorn. Pretty soon, they heard "Hey, Cone . . ." again, four times, and shortly after that another set.

219

They wondered just how long they planned to keep that up.

"Do you think we ought to follow them?" said Ludi.

Nat shrugged, with both hands deep in jacket pockets. It wasn't all that great a day for walking in the woods. One pocket clinked: something hitting up against the little bottle he had got from Doctor; that seemed an age ago. He fished around to find the clinker, and his hand came out with car keys: Homer Cone's.

"Hey, Lu," he said. "You want to take a ride?" He held them up before her face. She saw, then, for the first time, the way he must have looked before he flipped that quarter with the state and Arn-the-Barn: the part of him that got him into this. She decided that she loved it, too.

"Come on," he said. "How about it? We can leave it somewhere else where they can find it when we're done, and maybe get them searching farther from the Lodge."

She grinned and nodded, started skipping down the slope. "Can you imagine the looks on their faces when they get back? And think they missed him, maybe?"

He opened up the door for her and bowed. "Your carriage, princess," he announced.

They coasted backward to the road, and then drove carefully to Boynton Falls. Every time a car approached, Nat would cover up his mouth and duck his head, as if he had a cough; Ludi would sink down below the dashboard. But once they reached the major highway there, they felt anonymous, and headed on to Suddington quite merrily.

"What fun," said Ludi. "I feel as if we're playing hooky."

"Our first date," said Nat. "Ya gonna take me to a show?

"Well, actually," he cancelled that suggestion, "we shouldn't stay away that long. We wouldn't want the others getting jealous, would we . . . hmmm? But seriously. How about some shopping and a picnic . . . ?"

"Yay," she said, and pounded fists down on her knees. "And presents. For the other kids, O.K.? And treats?"

"Definitely treats," he said.

They got some necessaries first: more flashlight batteries, shampoo and conditioner, two different kinds of pinch bars of the type that might be great for breaking open desks and filing cabinets. Then they found a thrift shop and got presents for the stay-at-homes: a houndstooth vest for Coke, a purple chiffon shirt for Marigold, a checkered-wool visor-cap for Sully, some almost-surely-handmade leather sandals for Sara. "Though it's almost the end of sandal season," Ludi said.

When they were back on the street, she said, "I want to get something for you, too, but I don't have any money."

He said, "Listen, I'm the original man-who-has-everything. Forget it."

She said, "No. Come on. Please. Just five dollars or five minutes, whichever comes first. Ple-e-eez."

Of course he gave in. They agreed to meet at the Burger King in ten minutes. He went to a freaky little gift shop and bought an Indian necklace made out of little tubes of colored clay and other bits of polished stone. She found the biggest drug store in the town and chose a pack of condoms and a red bandana. "The-man-who-has-everything," indeed, she said to herself. She had no idea that there were that many kinds and styles and colors (yet!) of condoms, so she had to spend a little while at the display rack trying to figure out what kind he'd like the best. And, at the cash register, she had a bad moment when it looked as if the clerk—dapper, with a huge moustache—was going to ask her for I.D., or perhaps some sort of permit, like a marriage license. But she ran all the way to Burger King and was only a couple of minutes late.

They decided to stick with the picnic idea, in spite of the chill in the air and the lack of sunshine. "At least the ice cream won't melt too fast," they told each other happily. Even not-so-good things are just what the doctor ordered some days.

Suddington may be a town, the county seat, but still it has the same old village green, complete with bandstand. On one side is the county courthouse and the jail; on the other side is the school, which has been added on to, twice, but all of it is brick, the same as the original. Nat and Ludi sat near the center of the green, on a plaid wool blanket that had been in the back seat of Mr. Cone's sedan, where it was called a lap robe.

"Have you ever noticed that a lot of jails look like a lot of schools?" said Nat. "Or maybe the other way around?"

"I guess that's right," said Ludi. "And wasn't that place where the Winter Olympics were held—Lake Placid—isn't that a jail now, where everybody lived up there?"

"Yeah, I think I remember that," said Nat. He helped himself to french fries. "We used to call our high school a jail."

"God, so did *we*," said Ludi. "And in a way it was. In lots of ways, actually. They always said they were teaching us how to take our place in society and be good citizens. That's what jails are meant to do, too, right? But they'd never let us decide anything for ourselves—nothing important, anyway. We were 'too young' to do that, or we didn't 'know enough.' They always had The Answer, and it was really the only one we were allowed to give." She ate another bite out of her Whopper. "At our school, The Answer to 'What goes with hamburgers?' was 'ketchup.' 'Mustard' was wrong, so you couldn't have it. I'm not kidding."

"Right," said Nat, "and The Answer to 'What kind of a world is it out there?' "

" 'Dog eat dog,' " said Ludi promptly.

"And, 'When should a person go to college?' "

" 'Directly after high school, or you'll never go'— everyone knows that," said Ludi. "That's as stupid as asking, 'If you know how to do the homework, and it isn't graded, must you hand it in anyway?' "

"Of course you must," said Nat. "Otherwise you'll flunk. 'The homework is *required.*' So. What's a person called who doesn't date?"

" 'A queer,' " said Ludi.

"Right," said Nat. " 'Is more better?' "

"Always," she said. "Except in the case of zits, cavities, and pants-tightness."

"Excellent," said Nat. "Now, 'How many kids in a happy family?' "

"At least two," she replied. "The 'only' child is always spoiled, or lonely, or both. And even though you didn't ask, men who make beds, or clean a house, or cook—except for outside, in the park or in their own backyards—are either fags or henpecked. Unless they're Black or Hispanic, in which case they can do those for a living. That proves that 'some of them are all right,' by the way. The others all are welfare cheats."

"Very good," said Nat. "But why aren't there more women high school principals—or business executives, administrators, or government officials?"

"Because it's traditional," she said, "and, anyway, women can't command respect. They're just not tough enough to compete in the marketplace or to talk turkey to the Russkies. And besides, they menstruate and have babies all the time."

"So any ones that do get good jobs . . . ?" he prompted.

"Suck up to men, to put it tastefully," she replied. "That's if they're good-looking. Otherwise they're dykes."

"Yes, gee whiz," said Nat. "You really know The Answers. You must have been great in school."

"Well," she said, "I was a model prisoner in lots of ways. I didn't talk back or smoke in the girls' room. But I just didn't do a lot of things I was told to. And that made people furious, because They Knew I Knew Better."

"That's like giving The Wrong Answer on purpose, isn't it?" said Nat.

"I guess so," she said. "it's funny, you know? When I got into Coldbrook, I decided that I *would* conform up here. I'd do whatever 'They' wanted me to, mend my low-down ways. Be a Good Girl. And then I discover 'They' had got tired of waiting. It was too late for that." She ran her fingers through her mophead curls and stretched. "Now I wonder if I'll ever want to be good again. That *kind* of good. Which reminds me—how would you like your present now? Your pres*ents*, as a matter of fact."

"Great," he said. "If you'd like yours."

She nodded, trying to look greedy, but not making a very good job of it; her face was just too sweet, her eyes too huge.

Nat handed her the little paper bag that had her necklace in it. She squealed for joy and looked at him, her head cocked to one side. And then she leaned forward and kissed him, with tears in those huge brown eyes.

"It is *so* beautiful," she said, and put the necklace on. "Now open yours. It's beautiful a different way." She handed him the drugstore's paper bag.

Nat smiled and took the condoms out. Ludi smiled and dropped her eyes. He rocked onto his knees and

224

hugged her, and when she raised her head, he kissed her, too.

"What a wonderful, wonderful present," he said. "Much the best I've ever gotten—not to mention the sweetest and most generous." He grinned. "My absolute best color, too." He licked his lips. "You know something? I can hardly believe that I could love you any more than I do this minute, but I bet I can. And when the time comes"—he held up the package—"I promise you." He sank back on the blanket.

She cocked her head again, this time with a wrin kled brow. " 'When the time comes?' You make it sound like that's a ways away."

He nodded with a smile he hoped looked sweet and gentle, like he felt it, really. "Well, not too far, I hope," he said. "But I've been thinking, Lu. We've known each other—what?—two weeks and some. And under what you might call unusual conditions. Like, never knowing what tomorrow has in store for us, if anything. I'd just hate it if you jumped into something that you'd regret later on. That'd make you sad, or pissed, or disappointed. I know sex isn't that big a deal with a lot of people, but I want it to be, with us."

She shook her head. "But it is," she said. "That's the whole point. It's a fantastically big deal, just the way it should be. Loving you is much the biggest deal in the history of my whole life. It always will be, Nat; I absolutely know that. Every so often *some-body's* lucky enough to meet their own true love at sixteen, you know." She gave a little laugh. "And I think at this point I'm meant to say 'Look at Romeo and Juliet.' "

Nat stuck with the nod and the smile. The ridiculous part of all this was that he actually believed everything she said. "I know," he said. "But you've got to admit that the circumstances are so bizarre that they're enough to mess up anyone's . . . perspective. How can you tell whether you'd even *like* the everyday me, when I'm just hanging out and coming home from work, always going bowling, and there isn't anybody hunting us and trying to shoot us up the nose and all that jazz. I mean, it stinks, but it's exciting, right? And it isn't even remotely real—and so we all act differently than normal."

"That depends on how you look at it," she said. "*I* could argue that it's *super*-real. That is makes everything clearer, instead of more distorted—or whatever it is you're saying. I could say that if you really want to know someone, watch them under pressure, if you can. Maybe that's when the real you shows up."

"Yeah," he said, "maybe. But don't you see I have to feel responsible a little? Turn it around. Suppose you were the teacher here, and I was the kid in your group, and you fell in love with me, and I seemed to be in love with you. . . ."

Ludi was carefully packing away the trash from their meal, folding it all into the original Burger King bag. "It sounds as if you're telling me you know The Answer, in this case, and that it's 'No—no making love.' And that the reason that's The Answer is that one of us knows what he's doing and the other one doesn't, so that the one that does has to decide for both of them." She didn't look up from this careful, deliberate work she was doing.

"Christ," he said, "I know it sounds that way. But it isn't. Can't you see that I love you so much it makes me scared to death I'll mess it up some way?"

She looked at him then. He was sitting tailor-fashion on the blanket, with his hands interlaced in his lap and his body leaning forward. By any standard he looked miserable.

"I don't know how upset I really am," she said. "I think a lot. That may prove you're right and that I am just a kid, and I don't know what I'm doing. Or it may be because I didn't expect this from you—which

226

may also prove that I really am too young or too stupid or inexperienced or something to fall in love with anyone." Her eyes were glistening again.

"Oh, Lu," he said, "don't talk that way. It isn't anything like that. Look. You know what you feel, right? And I know what I feel. For each other, I'm talking about. That's what we have to hold on to and believe in. Really. Nothing else matters but that. When the time's right for making love, we'll know it."

"But you mean *you'll* know it, don't you?" she said. "Because I thought I knew it already." It all seemed pretty clear to her. "But I don't think I know it anymore," she went on. "And I kind of have a rotten feeling that maybe I never will again."

"Whoa," he said. "Hold on. Ludi, please." She heard a wild and desperate stridence in his voice. "Don't *say* that. We've got to be able to make mistakes and not get killed for them. Don't you think I love you? Look. If I didn't love you like this, it all would have been easy. That's what's so stupid. I've *made* love before, but I've never *been* in love before, don't you see? Jeezum." He battered the sides of his head with his fists. "I'm such a jerk I don't know *what* to do."

Ludi shook her head. What had seemed so clear a moment before had gotten clouded over again. "O.K.," she said. "I take it back. The last thing that I said. I didn't mean that; I'm just hurt. I *know* I love you, Nat. And I guess that means I'm scared, too, and in a hurry, and I want to be your woman . . . absurd as that may seem."

He dared to look at her. She was shaking her head and smiling a sad little smile. "You see, I think *I* know The Answer, too," she told him, "so I suppose I ought to be willing to wait for you to find it for yourself. I mean, if it's the right answer. . . ."

They finished getting all their stuff together. Nat

tied the red bandana on, and as they left the green at Suddington, they hesitantly held hands.

They drove back through some intermittent silences; "communications blackouts," in the space age. Nat was thinking that perhaps he'd blown it: that now there'd never be another time for him. Certain things had a way of hanging over a relationship. He could just see it: when he wanted to say "yes," she'd have to say "no." Give him a taste of his own medicine. That's the way it worked, wasn't it? He looked at Ludi sitting next to him. She wouldn't do that, not Ludi. She was that exceptional. If he'd blown it with her, he deserved the worst, the very worst. What a moron.

Nat thought of leaving Cone's car up by the place where they'd grounded all the earlier Group 6's. He thought he could find the spot, from what Lemaster had told him, and that'd give Doctor something to wonder about, all right. But the trouble with that idea was that the place was *too* remote, too seldom visited. He'd rather that they find Cone's car and have to try to figure out what it was doing *there*—wherever. They left it by a summer home, right on the road to Boynton Falls and far from Robinson's. Somebody would see it there, for sure, the next day at the latest.

They had a long walk back.

"You know," said Ludi, near the start of it. "You always think that when you fall in love—why, everything'll be O.K. Nothing more to worry about, and so on. But it isn't like that at all, is it?"

"Don't ask me," he said. "I've never been in love before, remember? I'd guess there's always stuff to worry about, though. It wouldn't be like life if there wasn't. But if I love you, and you tell me that you love me, there's this kind of O.K.-ness in the background of everything that sort of changes the way I worry. I can see all the shit and stuff, but I'm not

228

buried in it, you know? I'm not destroyed by what a jerk I am."

"Well, I can tell you that I love you, for whatever it's worth," she said. "I really, really do, Nat."

"Still?" he asked. They'd stopped.

"Always," she replied. "Just absolutely always."

He wrapped his arms around her, closed his eyes, and squeezed. "Always and all ways and everywhere, I promise you. Be patient with me, Lu. You're the most amazing woman in the world."

The silence that they walked in after that was soft and comforting, and everything seemed possible again.

At three o'clock that afternoon, Coke tried to remember if he'd ever spent that many hours completely by himself before, without any cigarettes, liquor, or drugs (including TV), and without calling anybody up on the telephone. He didn't think he had, ever. Not counting time he was asleep, of course.

It would have been easy enough to get his hands on some . . . distractions. One of the houses he checked out had had a bunch of bottles in plain sight—including both Drambuie and Tia Maria, which were big favorites of his. All he'd have to do was break a pane of glass in one of the windows, unlatch it, and climb in. But he hadn't done that. What he told himself was that having a drink just wasn't all that important to him. True, there was also the matter of maybe cutting himself when he broke the window, and the possibility that there'd be an alarm of some sort, or a prowl car. But, besides that, it'd be pretty mean to mess up someone's house that way. Birds and different things might get in—squirrels, for instance—and rain, when it rained, which could be any time, from the looks of it. Coke could see the house wouldn't be of any use to the Group, either; as Nat had said, it was much too near the road.

The second house Coke looked at was really pretty swanky: gardens and a pool out back, with a sort of little house on the back lawn, a little house with no real walls and some woven metal furniture. Coke sat there to eat the lunch he'd brought. Marigold had told him that her house had an indoor pool. He guessed that all the kids in the Group came from pretty rich families, but none of them seemed spoiled, Coke thought. That made him laugh inside, when he thought about it. *Spoiled,* sure. It'd be hard to call anyone spoiled whose parents wanted to kill them. Not "I could have killed him." The real thing. How unspoiled can you get?

Coke decided, as he had before, that he liked the kids in the Group about as much—face it, more— than any bunch of kids he'd ever met. It'd really be good to be able to stay with them, at the school, if that was ever possible. They would have some fun. And, it occurred to Coke, he might very well do some studying, too. He felt an odd little thrill go through him at that thought. He'd always kind of known he was smart; everyone had always told him that. But now—*now*—it made sense to use his smartness, to study and do well. It'd be just for himself, no doing what someone else wanted him to do, no pleasing his parents. Of course it wouldn't hurt anything to have Marigold and the others be impressed. She'd be smart herself, Marigold, and Sara would be, too. Sara looked like a worker, the type that puts in a lot of hours; he used to hate that particular type of kid. Sully was harder to tell about, as far as how smart he'd be, but he was a good kid. Sully-the-Kid; he'd killed a man. Bet that felt weird, thought Coke.

Ludi seemed real smart, too. A lot of quiet kids were smart. She'd surprised him with how strong and . . . well, *mature* she was; she was probably real good in school. It was . . . interesting, her and Nat getting together. Coke wasn't sure he exactly went for that. It seemed as if Nat was maybe taking advantage. It didn't seem possible that he'd be . . . well, sincerely interested in a sixteen-year-old girl. *Screwing* a sixteen-year-old, maybe, but not anything more than that. Actually, it was surprising he hadn't made a play for Marigold, who seemed lots older. Coke realized how lucky he'd been to get it going with Marigold real early like that. She was such a bombshell—but also his friend, his family, now. Wouldn't it be a riot if they got married some day? Coke wouldn't rule it out; they had a lot in common. No, Nat was all right, but Coke decided he'd feel a lot better when Ludi got to hanging out with guys her own age. If, by any miracle, that school idea worked out . . . well, Nat would probably just go on about his business somewhere else. He wasn't a teacher, really—never had been, never planned to be. No, he'd go off and do something else, which'd be too bad, in a way, just on account of the Group. But it was basically all right with Coke. Ludi'd get over him before very long. Coke knew; he could probably help her. And she'd be better off in the long run.

Coke had heard Levi Welch calling to Cone through the bullhorn. For a while, the calls were definitely following him, but way before noon they'd gotten more distant and then stopped altogether. Coke concluded, correctly, that the searchers had retraced their steps and maybe gone back to school. And at a little after three, having visited all four houses on his list, Coke did some of the same—the retracing part. He'd have lots to tell about the places he'd checked out, and why he felt that none of them would do for the Group. Much as he regretted it, of course.

"You can imagine our surprise"—Mrs. Ripple spoke to Luke Lemaster—"when we discovered it was gone."

The time was nine P.M.; the place was Doctor's study, in his house. Present and accounted for were Doctor, Mrs. Ripple, Levi Welch, and Luke Lemaster. Doctor had been asked to imagine their surprise over ten hours before, when Levi Welch and Mrs. R. had just got back from the Novotnys' with the news: Homer Cone had disappeared, and now his *car* had, too. Mysterious occurrences, indeed. Levi Welch had been there, been surprised himself, so there wasn't any point in saying that to him. But Luke Lemaster was a nice fresh set of ears, and Mrs. Ripple was enjoying herself, filling them right up with news and commentary.

"I almost pinched myself," Mrs. Ripple said, imagining herself being pinched, not by herself, but by the seven finalists in the Belleville (N.J.) Iron-Pumpers Body Building contest, all glistening with olive oil and wearing satin jock straps. " 'How can this be possible?' I asked myself." Their pinches were more presumptuous than painful; such a group of healthy, handsome boys, joking with their traineress.

Levi Welch pinched the neck of his beer bottle, which he'd set between his thighs. "How about a beer?" Doctor had said to him when he'd come in. He'd been the first to get there, right on the stroke of nine, with his face washed and his hair slicked down. And he'd thought that was pretty good of Doctor, and he'd said he didn't mind if he did, and Doctor had opened up this bottle of Millers and handed it right over. But then, when the other ones come in, Doctor asked them what they *wanted,* and one of them had one thing and the other had something else, and Doctor made himself what looked like a big rye highball, while Levi was left sucking on that Millers without even a glass to pour it into. There were times when Levi Welch just about wished he'd stuck with the army, after all.

"What I says to her, at first," he said to Luke Lemaster now, "was that he must of finally got himself straightened out and come back to his car and headed right on home. But turns out he sure as hell didn't do that. Not yet, anyways." Levi put a finger down the neck of that danged Millers.

Mrs. Ripple frowned at Levi Welch's interruption of her story-telling. *Obviously,* Mr. Cone had not come back to school. If he had come back to school, he would have been in this room with them, telling what he'd seen and done. If she was going to have to compete with Levi Welch for Mr. Lemaster's attention, she just wasn't going to bother. Let them do without her theories on the disappearance, based on quite a bit of firsthand knowledge of the individual involved. She rejoined her regularly scheduled daydream, measuring some rock-hard oily muscles. Let Luke Lemaster try to make sense out of that toothless manure spreader's stories.

Luke Lemaster pulled his ear and looked into the distance. "So, where does this leave us?" he said to Doctor in his slow, deep voice. "What's become of Homer, in your view?" His years of teaching had given Lemaster the ability to ask every question in a tone that made the person questioned think Lemaster knew the answer to it. He also often said, "I'd like to have your thinking on that," in a way that was meant to make people feel enormously flattered that so wise a man should care what they thought, then or ever.

Doctor was much too slick to fall into Lemaster's little traps, though. "Whatever happened to Baby Jane?" Doctor said, and held up both his palms. Then, much more seriously, "I'll tell you this much, though: wherever he is, there's a reason for it."

"Maybe we could get the Guardsmen come and help us look for him," said Levi Welch. "I know this one fellow, over to Boynton Falls; he's in the Guard. He's got to go most every weekend, seems like. I could speak to him, right after this, and maybe he could talk to his captain about them coming over here and helping us. Tomorrow's Saturday, you know."

"So it is," said Luke Lemaster thoughtfully. "So it is, indeed."

Doctor smiled a little rosebud of a smile. "Well," he said, "assuming Mr. Cone is lost—rather than *mislaid,* as I still think of him"—Mrs. Ripple looked up sharply—"it seems to me that we should search for him ourselves. What does the Good Book tell us about the shepherd and the poor little lambs who have gone astray? Mr. Cone is one of ours, and we should find him. What better all-school activity could anyone imagine than the entire student body out searching for one of its devoted and beloved teachers? I'll bet the kids would jump at the chance to go on a treasure hunt like that. With maybe a nice barbecue thrown into the deal. Breast of chicken, say, your strip sirloins, homemade pie with ice cream . . ."

"Choice of beverage?" asked Levi Welch.

"Why not?" said Doctor grandly. "And a prize for the lucky one who's found him . . . 'never let him go,' " sang Doctor.

"And where, may I ask," asked Mrs. Ripple, forced to break her latest vow of silence, "would you possibly think to look?"

"Everywhere," said Doctor simply. "We'll comb the woods for him. Just as he did 'Cone' them for Group Six." That drink was Doctor's third since dinner.

"And what, may I ask, about Group Six?" said Mrs. Ripple. She knew she spoke tartly, difficult as that was for a lady like herself.

"Ah, yes. Group Six," said Doctor, laying a finger on the side of his nose and speaking slowly, softly—wisely. "They're never out of my mind, of course.

Just like those hostages in Eye-ran were for President What's-his-face. Here's my thinking, now, folks. It's been three weeks. We haven't had a peep from them, not even a postcard. Nor have their families, poor people."

The other three shook their heads sympathetically, and Mrs. Ripple echoed him: "Poor people."

"Emfatico and Darling haven't seen a sign of 'em," Doctor went on, "and neither have good Cone and Mrs. Ripple. Add all those facts together and you get—what? That Cone was right: that they're still here, somewhere. If they were safely in Saskatchewan, or Baja California, we'd have heard by now—at least a 'nyah-nyah-nyah' from one of them. I know kids and I know *that;* it's human nature, people. And if one of them had headed home, we'd sure have had a jingle from the Better Business B. And if they *weren't* in the woods, we'd've been bound to find some sign of 'em by now: a Twinkie wrapper, a banana peel, an empty thing of Clearasil. You see? They're being careful as coyotes at a turkey shoot. And finally, folks, I ask you this—going by the law of averages, isn't it about time that Homer Cone was right? No, good friends and neighbors"—Doctor beamed around the room—"as far as Group Six is concerned, it's only a matter of time . . . 'on my hands,' " sang Doctor, and he took a merry swig of his highball. All around the room, people were nodding; Mrs. Ripple might have actually dropped off. But for all his joviality, Doctor knew it just wouldn't seem like a new school year until they got that grounding in. "Now here's what I propose . . . ," he started up again.

The atmosphere at Spring Lake Lodge that evening was far more mellow and laid-back than, say, the day before. It wasn't being too dramatic (so it seemed to Nat) to say that everyone had lost a little

235

childhood in the day just past. Whether they liked it or not, they'd all moved up one level in life, become a bit more like their parents, maybe. Certainly as copers. Knowing how to cope was great (thought Nat) at times, in certain ways; the trouble was that copers sometimes coped too much, when they should let-alone and cool it. Or just admit they didn't have the answer.

In any event, the members of Group 6 had drifted into moods that weren't so extreme on either end— closer to a happy medium. The presents were a great success—each immediately tried on and named a perfect fit. The shirt they'd got for Marigold was absolutely see-through, which made for a certain amount of good-natured, and even flattering, comment, most of it by Coke, and Sara said her sandals *were* handmade, she knew it, and very much the best she'd ever owned. Sully said he liked the fact that they were see-through, too.

There was also some discussion of the possible effects that "everything" had had upon the Plan. Nat wondered if they might not all go down, quite early in the morning, to see if they could guess what form the search for Cone was going to take. He was curious to see if they had found the car, and whether they would ask for any (skillful) local help, like Rescue Squads or Fire Wardens: people who had known those woods since childhood. Sully, Sara, and Marigold had seen Levi and Mrs. Ripple return and go to Doctor's office, but after that the day seemed normal, insofar as they could tell. Mrs. Ripple spent it in the classroom building, Levi in the Shop; Doctor wasn't seen at all. He had—although of course they didn't know it—a Jackson Pollock jigsaw puzzle on a table in his office in Foote Hall.

When they were washing up the dishes on which they'd eaten an outstanding, gourmet, fresh-food meal (Corporal Nat's North Jersey Broiled Chicken),

Sully asked Nat if they could talk, and the two of them wandered up to the top of the little knob above the spruces. Their departure was observed approvingly by all the others, and even a little proudly by Sara and Ludi.

"I'm sure you can guess what I want to talk about," Sully said. He looked steadily at Nat as he said this, and he spoke in a flat and neutral tone of voice.

"Yeah, I imagine," Nat said. "How're you doing?"

"Better," Sully said, and nodded once. His eyes left Nat, but came right back to him. "Much better. But I can't quite seem to get over that I actually killed a guy. You know? That if I look in the mirror, I'm not just seeing a person who *could* do that, or *might* do that, but who's really done it. Gives me a weird feeling, I can tell you that much."

"I'll bet," said Nat. "Just having been there at all'd give you a weird feeling. I mean, suppose you hadn't shot. You'd still feel a hell of a lot different than two days ago."

"My God," said Sully, "I guess so. I never thought of that. If he'd killed Sara, and I'd just stood there and let him . . ."

It was Nat's turn to nod. "That's the thing. No matter what you did, or didn't do, just being there . . ." He made a wry smile. "I'm sure if it were me, I'd rather live with what you did than the other. And those were your only choices, Sul. Let's face it. You couldn't have shot the gun out of his hands, right? Even if you'd wanted to and had all the time in the world to aim and everything." He thought of something else. "Look. It isn't any of my business, but . . . you really like Sara, don't you?"

"A lot," said Sully, still looking right at Nat and talking very matter-of-factly. "I don't mind telling you that."

"O.K., then, answer me this. Suppose the roles

were switched around, and you were the one about to get shot, and she was the one with the bow and arrow. What would you want her to do?"

"For whose sake, hers or mine?" asked Sully.

"Either one. Both. Any way you want it."

Sully looked down at the ground and took his time. "If I'm going to be honest, there's no question about it. I'd want her to shoot him. I really would." He took a deep breath and crossed his arms, rubbing his hands on his shirt sleeves. "I can't tell you how good it makes me feel to say that. She really isn't going to blame me, is she?"

"No," said Nat. "Not hardly. I don't think so."

"I guess that's been bugging me as much as the other," Sully said. He dropped his eyes again. "I think she's *so* great. But what I do is, I keep wondering if she really likes me, or if maybe she's just trying to make me feel good. If she thinks I saved her life, well, I guess she's got to be grateful. But that isn't what I want. I wouldn't want her hanging out with me just because she thinks she ought to, or because she thinks she owes me something. You know what I mean? I'm afraid that maybe she's doing that, whether she knows it or not."

"Listen, Sully, um . . ." Nat hitched his weight forward a little, and clasped his hands between his knees. "You'll never figure that one out. You'll never know. So you might as well forget it. Things just turn out, you know what I mean? Look. You say you like her a lot. O.K., just act like it then. And as long as she's acting as if she likes you, too—well, believe it. Don't waste your time with that other stuff; it's hopeless. Does-she, doesn't-she; will-she, won't-she—waste of time. Enjoy what you have; believe what she says. She knows what she's doing. Hell, if you like her—love her—you've got to believe *that.*" Suddenly he heard his own voice, his own words of wisdom. What an incredible fucking *jerk* he was.

Sully looked at Nat again. He shook his head—in wonder, not denial. "Of course," he said. "I see exactly what you're saying. And that's completely right. It's hard, but it's completely right. That's the way I want to be, Nat. That's the sort of person I want to be." He dropped his head and said, much softer, "Like you, you know?"

Nat reached out and rumpled Sully's hair. "Yeah? Well, I'm going to try to be like *you,* Sul."

Sully shook his head some more. He didn't understand, but smiled at Nat and touched him, feeling awkward, on the shoulder.

When they got down to the Lodge, only Coke was still beside the fire.

"They said they had to get their beauty sleep," he told his fellow feminists; his thumb jerked toward The Ladies Room.

Chapter Ten

THE TREE that Group 6 used for looking down on the Coldbrook Country School was what Nat called a good old-fashioned Robin Hood tree. When he was a kid, he'd seen this Robin Hood movie with some huge old oaks in it, enormous things, each of them with space for . . . hell, a *score* of merrie persons dressed in Lincoln green. What they'd do was get up in these trees and wait a little while, and then drop down on top of the Sheriff of Nottingham's goons, all of whom wore chain mail and couldn't fight worth a lick. Other days, they'd wait until some fat-pursed merchants palfreyed by, and then they'd drop on *them* and take their little clinking bags of gold away for later distribution to the local widows and orphans. Another thing the merrie persons also did a lot was whack the merchants and men-at-arms across the fanny with the flats of their swords and then bend over, with their hands on their knees, and laugh and laugh and laugh.

But that was a movie; this was real life. And so, instead of there being a lot of strapping varlets in the tree, each on his own fat, spreading limb, there was a band of five suburban–urban high school kids and their slightly older "teacher," crowded together like monkeys and squabbling over the rights to a single pair of binoculars.

For there *was* something worth watching on this

morning bright: the Coldbrook Country School was getting ready for a Treasure Hunt.

Doctor had announced it in the dining hall at breakfast. Saturday classes were all canceled; instead, there would be Fun, and also Games: a frolic in the woods, a Treasure Hunt, a contest. With Homer Cone, that priceless pedagogic gem, the prize!

The place erupted with excitement: Cone *was* lost; he hadn't been arrested (as the rumors went) at all! Cries of "Yay!", "I told you so" were mixed with "What's the second prize?" and "Do we have to keep him if we find him?"

In fact, beamed Doctor, Cone was not the prize at all (though certainly the Treasure!). Whatever dorm found Cone would win itself a brand new Betamax TV recorder! But even those that didn't would also get Prizes, Doctor promised, and everyone would Feast that night, for sure!

Once again, the dining hall went wild, but quieted again to hear the rules. After breakfast, from the steps of Daughtridge Hall, Luke Lemaster, Dean, would run some Raffles. What he'd raffle off would be the Searching Rights to different Sections of the land around the school. The night before, he'd made a Map, on one big piece of Sheetrock, and that was right beside him on the steps. There were six Sections (just as there were six dorms), each of them boundaried by this road, that brook, et cetera. Whichever dorm won the first Raffle would win exclusive Searching Rights within the Section that it chose. And so on. Everybody clear on that? Oh, yay! Each dorm would have to try to figure out what sort of place a guy like Homer Cone would be most apt to find himself completely lost in. And make its choice accordingly.

So what Group 6 observed, between the leaves of its great oak tree, was something that looked like part medieval country fair and part sheer bedlam—or, in other words, pretty much the way that local folk defined the Coldbrook Country School. They saw the Raffle getting ready to begin.

It had finally rained the night before, starting after midnight. But in the early morning's light, the wind had turned around and broken up the clouds and carried in a day so cool and clear and bright that even Mrs. Ripple must have felt like dancing on the diamond-studded lawn. She didn't, but a lot of others did. It wasn't formal dancing—no, indeed—but rather more a floating, weaving, chasing, arcing, soaring, banking, bumping kind of play. The gusts of wind were strong enough to push a person slightly off her balance, and with that kind of start . . . why, well, why *not* put out your arms and fly with it? Play some leapfrog, maybe, with those people over there, or, following the leader, roll your body to the side and make some perfect cartwheels clear across the lawn. The campus dogs jumped all around them, barking, bouncing up and down as if their feet were strapped to springs.

The kids who went to Coldbrook Country School were colorful to start with, and on occasions such as this they let their outfits match their natures, yes, indeed. Ludi, Marigold, and Sara looked on with something very close to envy in their hearts; three weeks of shorts and jeans were apt to cause a little dress-up hunger. The Coldbrook girls had gotten into colors for the hunt: purple shirts and orange ones; long, full, flowing skirts in pastel pinks and mauves and greens, with hiking boots beneath them; sashes, shawls, and capes of all descriptions, fluttering. A lot of boys wore masks with cowboy hats: the Cone Rangers would be riding, *kemo sappy,* side by side with certain Cone Heads, just a few of those, in fact. "It's perfectly possible to be a Dead Head and a Cone Head at the same time," a boy named Rushton told his roommate, Gabriel, a little stridently, defensively; maybe he was ruining his reputation for a cheap laugh. Gabriel, a Star Trek freak and heavy-metal man, could not care less.

Doctor, in the spirit of the thing, had got himself up as the Master of the Hunt: hard hat, red coat, riding pants, and all. Slim, black, shiny boots. From time to time, he'd bellow "Yoicks!" or "View Halloo!" The students, much more tolerant of weirdness, paid him no more mind than usual, but younger faculty were forced to wonder. In many of their secret hearts, of course, there lived the hope that Cone would never be recovered. Then, too, they doubted that he was in the woods at all—unless, perhaps, some angry students, fed up with his insults, had beaten him to death with geometric solids and then buried the remains. Such things did happen; Cone was insensitive, for sure, but not invulnerable. No, what they really thought was: Cone had just flipped out and taken off. That happened, too: older teacher sees the writing on the wall—he's not communicating anymore and starts to hate the job, the kids, the school, and vice-versa. Exit him—good riddance. And the Director is saved an unpleasant duty. Of course (as Matt Wampler, History, put it to Missy Coleman, Dance) it might well be that Doctor'd fired Cone and then, wanting to avoid reaction/gossip, just decided he'd be "lost." Was it not significant (asked Matt) that no "authorities" had been involved so far? Perhaps (said Missy), but it really didn't hardly matter, did it? A Treasure Hunt was just a "*fab* idea."

Finally, Luke Lemaster called them all to order and got six dormitory delegates to mount the steps beside him and his map. He made them pump their fists in time with his: "One, two, three—shoot!"

A lot of fingers stabbed the unpolluted morning air. Luke quickly totaled up and counted off. A girl named Marci Bronson was the winner. In a loud voice, she made her choice: "On behalf of Drumby

House, the intellectual and athletic center of the school, home of the perceptive, the privileged, and the pulchritudinous, core of creativity and charisma"—(general booing and hissing in the background)—"I choose Section Four!" She pointed west, toward an enormous stand of soft wood in the distance. "Drumby House is certain," she screamed, "that Cone will be found in the pines!" And floating on a great soft pillow of sound (groans, boos, laughter, and applause), she left the steps to rejoin her gifted cohabitants. Section Four was a long, long way away, and a rotten place to even *maintain* your tan, but Drumby'd felt the joke was worth it, what the hell.

The rest of the raffle was completed without incident and pretty soon the exodus began. All the dorms were taking sandwich lunches from the dining hall, but Doctor, capering about, was promising a dinner to remember. "Roast ox!" he cried. "Slumgullion! Haggis!" "How about some poon-tang for dessert?" Richard Wanamaker shouted. And Doctor, hearing "marzipan," or possibly Chinese, replied, "Why, shore, m'lad; why, shore."

They left in all directions, blowing horns and whistles, flashing mirrors in each other's eyes, and waving so-called signal flags. Darwin House had even whipped up some lyrics and sang, to the tune of "Home on the Range":

"We're looking for Homer, that fat little roamer,
    where the deer and the beaver do play.
He's always absurd,
    he's a schnook and a nerd,
    and his eyes, they are cloudy all day.
Homer, Homer you're so strange . . ."

There was no question what was going on down there; the people in Group 6 were all pretty bright, but you didn't need to be bright to figure that one out. An all-school search for Cone was taking place; even Mrs. Olson and her cohorts were unplugging their coffee pots and getting out of there; and because of the barbecue that night, the kitchen staff was off for the day and free to head for Suddington and have a wine or two.

Group 6 looked at one another. Would there ever be a better time, a better moment, for their mission? Surely not. They waited for ten minutes after the last straggler from the last dorm seemed to have disappeared, and then—look out below! They headed straight for Doctor's house and study.

The doors to both were open, country-style. They closed them both behind them. In character, they rubbed their hands together, sensitizing fingertips, perhaps. Ah-ha: so this was Doctor's study.

It was a good-sized room—once upon a time a formal living room, the biggest in the house. Stretching over halfway down it, from just inside the door, was one enormous cherry table, big enough for almost any kind of meeting you could think of, or (from time to time) for Doctor's Hot Wheels track. Grouped around it were twelve heavy captain's chairs with ugly steerhide seats; large windows on the left looked out upon an apple tree that bloomed in May, a path, and also lawn that led to Foote, where Doctor's other office was, and sometimes Mrs. Olson.

At the far end of the room was Doctor's royal desk, a large mahogany affair with a high-backed leather swivel chair, in black. It faced a canvas-covered sofa, tan, flanked by matching canvas-covered easy chairs. The sofa had a glass-topped coffee table between it and the desk, and both the upholstered chairs had little tables that looked like nail kegs beside them. Wherever you looked, there were plenty of cork coasters and big ceramic ashtrays with pictures of game birds on them. Directly to the right of.

Doctor's desk chair and along the wall behind it was the dry sink that served as his bar, with the Titans of the Turf glasses on the first shelf over it. In the matching space to the left of Doctor, there were two three-tiered wooden filing cabinets, and beyond them, going down the lefthand wall from Doctor's desk chair, was the lavatory door that Doctor liked to put his Nerf basketball hoop up on. Past the lavatory was the large walk-in closet where he'd hide the ball and hoop when people came, and where he kept his cars and track and lots of other things including outdoor clothes. There was a pole across one side of the closet, with jackets and rain gear hanging on it, and backed deep against the wall there was a small pine chest of drawers, with scarfs and gloves and woolen hats and sweaters in it.

The members of Group 6 headed straight for the desk, their pinch bars in their hands, their faces grim. But, to their disappointment, the drawers were unlocked. They contained the following items, period.

—one small, square puzzle in which you moved the numbers 1 to 15 around and tried to get them to come out in order. Whoever'd been playing with it was either having a whole lot of trouble or had just rejumbled the numbers so someone else could try.

—a three-pound box of Fanny Farmer assorted chocolates, about five-sixths eaten and with crescent-shaped indentations in the bottoms of all the remaining pieces.

—a Nixon–Agnew button.

—a deck of playing cards from a child's magic set.

—various manufacturers' coupons.

—a cartoon book titled "So Much More Mary Worth."

—twelve unused legal-sized yellow pads and a box
of really sharp wooden pencils.
—a framed photograph of two middle-aged women
standing outside the Luray Caverns in Virginia.

The filing cabinets were next. They actually contained a number of folders, some of which had to do
with Doctor's job as Director of the Coldbrook Country School.

There were, for instance, carbons of letters he'd
dispatched to various foundations, trusts, and corporations (". . . I'm sure we can agree that private
schools are no less vital to our nation's interests than
whales are to our oceans . . ."), along with their re-
plies (". . . directors cannot quite convince themselves that Coldville's mission, worthy as it is, is
quite in tune with that of Runcible and Co.'s. As you
must know, we manufacture only bayonets these
days . . .").

There were also letters sent by applicants for
teaching jobs, which ran the gamut of formality from
standard Xeroxed résumés to handwritten notes on
cheap lined paper ("Hey, I'm a free-and-easy guy,
who's mostly into leathercraft, just now . . .") and
Doctor's standardized reply to all of them, which was
. . . exactly no reply at all. It was still a buyer's market, Doctor knew, and stamps were twenty cents and
climbing.

Above and beyond those, there were folders full of
catalogues for Eddie Bauer and L.L. Bean and Moor
and Mountain, mixed in with those from Denison
and Hobart and Tulane. It also appeared that Doctor
took the PSAT's every year and kept the question
books, if not his answer sheets, on file. On the outside of each booklet he'd scribbled his reactions to
the test, like "tricky little bastard," "math a pisser,"
and "what the hell's a 'paradigm,' anyway?"

But, in spite of all the interesting reading in those

files, there wasn't a thing that had to do with the members of Group 6, individually or collectively. Where else could they look?

Nat and Coke went into the lavatory, opened up the tank behind the toilet, and the medicine cabinet. Marigold swung wide the doors below the dry sink, and peered inside among the bottles buried there, while Sully took out all the drawers in Doctor's desk, to see if there were papers taped or tacked across their undersides. Sara and Ludi tried the closet, going through the pockets of the jackets first, and then the little dresser in the back.

The letters from their families, and all the other things that they were looking for, were right where they belonged: under the sweaters in the bottom bureau drawer. That's where Doctor had always hidden stuff all his life—and no one'd ever caught him. But there was always a first time for everything, as Mr. Cone could have told him, if he could have told him anything at all.

"I've got them," Sara said, and held the folder up. On the outside, it said: "Wide-Row Planting— 6th Edition," but Sara had peeked inside and seen Coke's father's letterhead and one or two key sentences. And, deeper down, an application to the school, typed on her old portable.

"God, let me *see,*" said Marigold, and rushed across the room to her.

They should have left at once, of course. They should have just made sure they had the letters (five of them, plus Doctor's deeply moving answers) and then got out of there. But no, they had to read them right away—or, all of them but Ludi did. Sara passed them out and everyone sat down around the table and began to read. Ludi didn't. She just sat and watched the others, her father's letter placed face-down in front of her.

And so she was the first to see the door swing open, admitting Doctor Simms and Mrs. Ripple, Levi Welch and Luke Lemaster.

Just as the word "freeze" fit as naturally in the mouth of Arn-the-Barn Emfatico as Wednesday night's spaghetti dinner, so did the expression "My, my, what have we here?" feel exactly right in Doctor's. What *he* had "here" he quickly pointed at them: a Smith and Wesson .38 automatic, an executive model called "The Hilton Head."

Not to be outdone, Mrs. Ripple, Levi Welch, and Luke Lemaster also showed that they were armed. Lemaster's gun was very much like Doctor's, lacking just a bit of scroll work on the monogram; Levi Welch wore a revolver, which he quick-drew from a low-slung leather holster, while Mrs. Ripple had, of course, a lady's gun, "Enchantress," by Marlin.

It might, perhaps, be thought—considering that large display of ordnance—that Doctor had expected that he'd find the Group exactly where he did: that somehow he had lured and trapped them there. Nothing could be farther from the truth. The facts were that the night before, in a burst of boozy good fellowship, Doctor had invited his associates to join him in a "Hunt Breakfast" on the following morning: "Bloody Marys, biscuits, coddled eggs and bacon, bran flakes for the so-inclined. We'll get the main show on the road and then slip back to my house, do it up in style!" Running into Group 6 was just dumb luck. They all had hand guns with them because that's the kind of people they were.

But Doctor was smart enough to try to make it appear otherwise. "My friends," said he, "our guests of honor are on time." He cocked his wrist to check it out with Seiko. "Ahead of time, in fact." He turned toward his colleagues, little ham. "Last night I told you where they were and why they had to be there;

249

today"—he snapped his fingers, magically—"I hab their corpuses." He made a sweeping, courtly gesture with his gun toward the other empty chairs set round the table. "Let us join our company, dear colleagues." He frowned to see the folder and the letters on the table.

"My word, how rude of them," he said in mock dismay. "It looks as if they've started in without . . . 'a song,' " sang Doctor, and he chuckled.

Everyone sat down. At first the members of Group 6 looked closely at the guns the other people carried. They were the sorts of guns they'd seen before, a lot of times, in movies, on TV, but somehow they looked different. Marigold, who'd been in half a dozen plays, could tell that these guns weren't acting. Stage guns had a kind of lightness to them: prop men twirled them by their trigger guards around a finger and made jokes; *these* guns only pointed and looked heavy. Marigold's parents had a "Ban Handguns" bumper sticker on the Audi, and here was their daughter maybe about to get shot and killed by one. That was ironic, Marigold guessed; her getting shot by this bunch of fucks while her parents gave money for gun control. A minus times a plus equals a minus: one less daughter. She was about to be killed by some people who didn't even look as if they'd be good at it. What she felt was pissed, and also scared to death. This wasn't the way it was meant to turn out, the way O.D. and she had talked about their future lives and happiness.

Luke Lemaster cleared his throat. As far as he was concerned, there was no such thing as a comfortable silence when you were sitting around with a group of teenagers. When kids were silent, they were being surly, sulky, stubborn.

"Well," he said, smiling at the members of Group 6, "you certainly have led us quite the merry chase. Where on earth have you *been* all this time?" Ask

250

them questions, get them "rapping," that's the ticket.

People looked at Nat.

"Oh, here and there," he said. "Um, up in the hills. You know. Different places." He didn't know why, but he was absolutely determined not to tell them about Spring Lake Lodge. Fuck *them.* But he also felt that he should keep talking. Part of it was the old where-there's-life-there's-hope business, and as long as there was talking, it meant that everyone was living still. But another part of it was, like, a responsibility—almost as if it were a social duty of his to hold up their end of the conversation, not have any awkward silences. "I saw you up at North Egg Mountain," he said to Levi Welch and Mrs. Ripple. "You and the other gentleman."

"Hey," said Levi Welch. "Maybe *you* can tell us. What the hell's ever happened to Cone? That feller that you saw us with? When we wasn't lookin' for you, we been lookin' all to hell and gone for *him.* That's where all the students are right *now,"* Levi babbled on.

Mrs. Ripple had found she didn't enjoy looking at the members of Group 6, beyond the first quick glance she'd taken. She'd told a friend once that, quite frankly, she didn't think she could enjoy a nice roast chicken dinner if she'd gotten to know the chicken first. "Stupid as they are, one forms attachments," she had said. So, because she was looking at Luke Lemaster (quite a hunk, a Duke Wayne sort of stud, she'd always felt; she bet he had a big old one), her sharp eyes didn't register the way that Levi's question hit the Group: the little shifts of weight and looking down—the way that Sully's freckles seemed to darken.

Sara stared at Mrs. Ripple and felt better. She'd been saying to herself "This isn't happening," and looking at Mrs. Ripple in her neat white blouse with a gold circle pin on the collar and her lavender monogrammed shetland sweater . . . well, she *knew* this was a dream, or somehow not the thing it seemed to be. She couldn't begin to imagine what was going to happen next, or how it would turn out, but there was no possibility that this nice-looking older woman would ever let her get killed. She wondered if Mrs. Ripple would like to know that her mother was a member of the Junior League.

Nat answered Levi with a shrug and shake of head. "I'm sure I couldn't tell you where he is, exactly, now." It wasn't hard to say a truthful thing like that. "The last *we* saw of him, he was heading away from those people's house up at the end of that long private road. You probably know the place, the one with all the sundecks? He was going *down* the road from there, actually, but he might have taken off into the woods for all we know." He paused. "But that was a couple of days ago, or three. How do you know he didn't keep on going down that road and . . . well, just split? Maybe he got sick of teaching school, and decided that he—"

Doctor rapped his pistol on the table, interrupting. "Mr. Cone would not do that," he threw at Nat. "Mr. Cone was under contract. Not a written one—we've never had to use them here. But we had our agreement. Unlike *some other people I could name,*" said Doctor, "Mr. Cone would always do what he'd agreed to do."

Ludi wasn't really listening to what was being said. She felt peculiar: very nearly numb, as if she couldn't move, but also she was full of . . . not quite *sound,* a sort of warm vibration. She kept her eyes on Nat, which made her happy. He was there, and he was her beloved, come what may. They'd always be together. Maybe this was the life she was meant to have: a short one, with such sweetness at the end. She didn't feel as if she was just about to die, but she

252

didn't feel that things were going to go on from there, either. She would have liked to say something to Nat, but she didn't think her mouth would move.

"Look," said Coke loudly. "I've got something important to say."

Sully's head jerked up. He'd been sitting looking down at his folded hands in his lap. His hands were greasy with sweat, and his mind had been saying "Oh, no" over and over again. Being startled by Coke's loud voice made him want to jump up and start punching someone, maybe Coke. But no, it'd make better sense to just launch himself across the table, right at Doctor, yelling, "Run for it, Sara," or something like that. He almost did, too. But then he picked up on what Coke was saying.

". . . this uncle of mine, Jeffrey Milliken"—Coke was speaking at Doctor, and at Luke Lemaster—"my Uncle Jeff. He's my mother's brother, and he's really, really rich. He's got a townhouse just off Sutton Place, and a summer home on Shelter Island, and another big old place down in Palm Beach. And he's always liked me a lot. If you'll let me call him up on the phone, I promise you he'll give you *double* what my parents paid you . . . wait, no, make that *five* times as much, if you'll just let us all go. He really will; I know he will," said Coke. "And we'll put anything down on paper you want, that'll say you're innocent of doing anything bad to us, or planning to, or whatever you want us to say." He looked over at Levi Welch then. The guy was obviously a hired man, a townie, but he had the biggest gun, and a pinched and greedy look about him. "You'll get to keep all the money that our parents gave you, and have all this extra, too. Do you realize what your share of that would be?" he said to Levi Welch.

Levi turned part way around, toward Doctor. That didn't sound like too bad of an idea to *him*. Maybe it

253

was about time he got a share of whatever it was, which'd probably be more than his straight hundred and fifty a week, cash, plus room and board, he'd bet. Why, Judas Priest, if he got his hands on a couple of thousand dollars, he could put something down on an old skidder, and get to drawin' logs some place, an' . . .

But Doctor was just sitting there, with about a half of a little smile on his face, shaking his head back and forth.

"I'm very sorry, Coleman," Doctor said. Marigold blinked and looked at Coke. *Coleman?* Him? "But we don't run our business that-a-way. Which is why we stay in business, my young friend. Like Mr. Cone, I honor my agreements. Even if you had an Uncle Jeff who values you that much—and from everything I've heard, that isn't very likely—it's now a little late for any other players in our game. *Les jeux sont fait*— that's what they say in Monte Carlo, Coleman. *Rien ne va plus,*" said Doctor, *petit prince* of Coldbrook Country School.

"Well, speaking of that kind of thing," said Luke Lemaster, heartily, "maybe we should . . ." His head jerked quickly toward the door; his eyes rolled upward to the hills just past the school.

"Tut, tut, no—nonsense," Doctor said. "There's no big rush, good Dean. We came back to enjoy ourselves and have a nice Hunt Breakfast. Now we have a cause for celebration. You know, I wouldn't be at all surprised if Homer Cone shows up today, as well." In great good humor, Doctor cocked his head and cupped a pink and shell-like ear. "I *thought* I heard a . . . yes! This *does* call for a drink. Bloody Marys all around, I guess?"

Levi Welch thought of asking for another Millers, at that hour, but what the hell (he also thought). If they were going to have some sissy drink, then so could he. So *would* he, by Glory. The other two

254

just licked their lips and nodded. Knowing Doctor Simms, when he was in a mood like this . . .

Doctor pocketed his gun and rubbed his palms together. Then he toddled over to the dry sink, got out a pitcher and ice, and a large can of tomato juice, then lined up Worcestershire, Tabasco, lemon juice, and vodka. He was singing under his breath: " '. . . is the girl I love, now ain't that too damn bad . . .' "

Nat was trying to make his mind work right and get a plan together. Levi Welch was probably his own age, more or less; lean and wiry, he'd be, physically, the strongest of their captors and the hardest to disarm, but he also might be the weak link, the one that might be worked on, somehow. The way he'd talked to Cone and Mrs. Ripple up on North Egg Mountain (and they to him) had made it pretty clear that he was just a stooge, the one they teachered around and snotted on—and he obviously wasn't getting properly cut in on the profits. The problem was that he couldn't invite Levi to his house for the weekend, or to play a little racquetball, or to drive on down to Florida over Easter break—in other words, make friends, like you would with another guy at school or somewhere. This had to be done fast and publicly. Oh, hell, he thought, maybe he'd better just try to jump Doctor or Mrs. Ripple and "grapple for their guns," like it always said in the newspaper. The trouble was it usually also said that "the gun apparently went off in the struggle, killing . . ." Who? Nat decided that the moment wasn't now, in any case. Let them mellow out a little, relax; no telling what a drink or two might do. He was pretty sure that they'd want to make them all walk out of there, just to cut down on the lugging and dragging part. If they had any sense at all, they wouldn't kill them until they had them all the way up at the grounding place. That'd make the most sense. There were tinkling and gurgling sounds to Nat's rear, from the direction of the dry sink.

And then a gasp from Mrs. Ripple.

"Oh, dear. Darling," she said.

She was looking out the window. And there, sure enough, was Mr. Darling, dressed in country tweeds. Having crossed the lawn from Foote, he was just about to enter Doctor's house and join them.

Doctor scuttled back across the room, his pistol in his hand again. He sat at the far end of the table and slid the Hilton Head beneath it.

"Don't anyone get foolish." Doctor said this softly, but quite clearly, too. "The smallest peep, and we will start to . . . send you little disapproving messages from underneath the table. Think about how much you'd like . . . some bullets in your lap." Doctor smiled, as if he'd said Angora cats or puppy dogs.

"Doctor Simms?" Mr. Darling's voice from down the hall.

"Yes, right in here. Keep coming, Mr. Darling," Doctor caroled out. Then, in a stage whisper, "Remember, mum's the word, or you'll . . . 'never walk alone,' " sang Doctor softly, pointedly.

The door swung open. "Doctor Simms . . . ," said Mr. Darling. "Oh, ex*cuse* me, sir. I didn't realize you were in a meeting. . . ."

Doctor showed him one flat, guileless palm. "That's quite all right, sir, quite all right. Just— er—my Student Council. With their faculty advisors, yes. Important, to be sure, but interruptible. How may I help you?"

Luke Lemaster, Levi Welch, and Mrs. Ripple all glanced up at Mr. Darling, the first and last of them with smiles, one hearty, one demure. Levi Welch didn't know if a faculty advisor did a lot of smiling, so he just tried to look smart. Sully was wondering if he should make his move right then, while they were looking at Mr. Darling. But by then they'd stopped

256

doing that. Oh, Lord, he didn't want to get shot where Doctor had said; he crossed his legs the other way.

"In fact," said Mr. Darling, "I have tidings—ti*ding,* really—won't take but a minute. I could have telephoned, but I was just close by . . . and it's a lovely day to drive. I spent last night in Boynton Falls—at that new inn, The Bread and Bundle?—and got the call this morning. But anyway, my news: Rittenhouse is dead."

Levi Welch sat up and made a strangled sort of sound, the sound of an emotion being choked, perhaps. Mr. Darling looked at him and shook his head in phony sympathy. This bumpkin was a friend of Rittenhouse? He shouldn't be surprised, he guessed. He wondered what on earth he taught. Poetry . . . or pottery; some artsy-craftsy nonsense, Mr. Darling thought.

"Sad, but true, I guess," continued Mr. Darling. "I thought you'd want to know. An accident, my office said; they didn't have the details." He straightened up a bit and touched a tweed lapel. "As Bursar, I am *never* out of touch; I leave a number when I'm going out of town. That's the way you have to play it in 'Accounts, Receivable.' " He shook his head and smiled a thin-lipped smile. "I'll miss the hunt, the tonic of your woods, this air—I must admit it. We'll put a lien on the estate for what he owes us, maybe sue the parents, too"—he sighed—"but that's a different kind of fun."

"I know," said Doctor solemnly. "I know. I had to fire him, myself, but still . . . *De mortuis,* and so on, so forth." He slapped a hand down on the table in a sudden change of mood. "I've got an idea! Let's drink a toast to the poor young man! Say, *Bill*"—his eyes were daggered straight at Nat—"suppose you pour for us—good fellow! I've got a little something ready in the pitcher right behind you, if you could add a bit

257

more ice and give it just a stir. . . . You'll join us, Mr. Darling, in a Bloody Mary, won't you?" Nat got up to do as he'd been told.

"Er, no," said Mr. Darling. "Can't stay another moment; have to run. Sorry to have interrupted, really." Peculiar school, he thought, extremely. Having drinks in front of students at eleven in the morning? He had a hand upon the door knob.

"Oh, just one last thing," he said. "My man Emfatico, remember? *If* you see him anywhere, *would* you be so good as to . . . inform him of this sad . . . development? Well, thanks so *very* much." He gave the room a wave, a smile. A *most* peculiar school. He'd have to ask Admissions if they'd ever had an applicant from there. "Sorry for the interruption, all. Good-bye!" And he was (finally) out the study door. A moment later, they could hear the front door closing, too.

Nat had their glasses on a tray: Bold Ruler, Native Dancer (she scowled, but took it anyway), Gallant Fox, and Buckpasser.

The four pistols were back atop the table once again, but loosely held, relaxed. "*Well,*" said Doctor, and he shook his head in the manner of a man who's just been hearing gibberish, "so much for Mister Know-it-all."

He cleared his throat and raised his glass. "I have a toast, but it's a slightly different one than what ̈ said when *he* was here. Here's to *us,* my friends, and to Group Six (better *late* than never, kids!), and to a job well done. And to teaching, maintenance, administration, free enterprise, and the real beginning of a new school year. And to you, Rottenhouse, and to you, Homer Cone: so long and hurry back, respectively."

With which he raised his glass and took a healthy swig, in concert with Lemaster, Welch, and Ripple.

But maybe not a *healthy* swig, at that. Luke Lemaster didn't look so good, and Levi Welch (whose last thought was: "I should have had the Millers"), he looked even worse. With Mrs. Ripple it was hard to say; she always looked a good deal less than great, to Doctor.

"My God"—Doctor looked at Rittenhouse, comprehension dawning in his darkening eyes—"there's . . . there's . . . 'a shadow hanging over me,' " he sang, and fell, face-forward, on the table.

Mrs. Ripple stayed upright the longest. Women are the stronger sex, there isn't any question. Paralysis was taking over her; she couldn't squeeze the trigger. But still she had a sentence left, and if it wasn't ladylike, you couldn't blame her, really.

"Mr. Rittenhouse," she said, her lips a-quiver, fighting for control, "you are a plecklerucker micklestitch," and, looking disappointed, she expired.

Chapter Eleven

IT WAS several days before anyone at the Coldbrook Country School was sure that Doctor, Luke Lemaster, Levi Welch, and Mrs. Ripple weren't anywhere around. That they, in point of fact, had disappeared, exactly like the man that they'd been looking for. Schools aren't—or shouldn't be—perpetual motion machines, but once you get one started, it'll run all right, even when it's missing parts or has some out-of-order.

There were, of course, some instances that very day of people noticing that one or more of them was not in place.

Example 1:

"Have you seen Doctor Simms? I gotta ask him something." This Lucy Bishop said to Francie Foster at the barbecue.

"No," said Francie. "Anyway. I can't imagine *any*thing that he would know that you don't." With a giggle.

"Where he got that yummy jacket he was wearing," Lucy said.

Example 2:

"This steak is pretty good," said "Ripper" Roth to "Bingo" Broadstreet.

"You know why?" said Bingo, through a mouthful

of the stuff. "They let old Carlos cook it, 'stead of Luke the Puke. Even my old man can grill a steak better 'n Luke."

"That's right," responded Ripper. "Where is old Luker, anyway, I wonder?"

"Who the fuck cares?" said Bingo Broadstreet.

-Example 3:

"Mrs. Ripple! Mrs. Ripple!" Gerry Remmeltree knocked urgently on her English teacher's door. There wasn't any answer, and the door was locked.

"You seen Ma Ripple anywhere?" she asked a passerby.

"She didn't get back from the Hunt yet, I don't think," the girl replied.

Gerry smiled and bent and used a nail file to stuff wet toilet paper into the lock of her English teacher's door. She wasn't going to have her themes called "puerile and banal" by anyone.

Example 4:

There is no fourth example. Maintenance was closed down for the weekend, so there wasn't anybody to notice that Levi Welch was not around.

On Monday morning, though, Mrs. Olson had to face the fact, by noon, that Doctor hadn't had his coffee yet. She knew it couldn't be the coffee, and so she took a walk across the lawn to see if he was in his house; he wasn't. Next she went and checked with Mrs. Chilton, Dean Lemaster's secretary. Not only did Mrs. Chilton not know where Doctor was; it seemed her own boss was also, oddly, missing.

And so, at lunch, both ladies sought out Sandra Reynolds-Nix who, as the school psychologist and head of Guidance, was pretty well recognized as the most agreeable powerful person on the faculty—or perhaps the most powerful *agreeable* person, it didn't matter a hell of a lot. Either way, she was a slender, attractive woman with close-cut brown hair and lilac-tinted glasses, in her early thirties and married to Prosper Nix, the novelist, who had nothing to do with Coldbrook other than eating and living there for free.

As was her wont, Sandra Reynolds-Nix stayed cool. Being a trained and practicing psychologist, she knew a genuine nut when she saw one, and Doctor (she was sure) was salted, shelled, and boxed—the works. Luke Lemaster came from off a different tree, but he could also qualify; anyone who'd been around a school as long as he had could lose it all at once, though in Lemaster's case (it seemed to Sandra) there hadn't been that much to lose. The kicker in the case—that Sandra knew about but Mrs. Olson and her friend did not—was that Mrs. Ripple, also, couldn't be accounted for.

"Orgy," Prosper Nix, the novelist, opined at supper. "Can't you see it, hear it, smell it?" He smiled, while reaching for the pot roast and his ever-handy notebook, both at once. "The three of them at that motel in Suddington: the one with the vibrating water beds and three-D special movies round the clock? If I were you, I'd give 'em a few days before I panicked."

"I'm not going to *panic,*" Sandra said. "What's to panic over? But I do agree with you as far as time's concerned: I think I'll wait awhile before I buzz the Missing Person's even. There shouldn't be any problem here at all, until Friday at the earliest. That's when the salary checks are meant to get signed."

"Jesus Christ," her husband said, in obvious distress. "I didn't even think of that. Look, you better get on the horn to the school's attorney and find out who can sign them in case the Doctor isn't back. This is serious, Sandy. Really. You can't mess around with people's *incomes,* you know." As a man without

262

an income other than his wife's, Prosper Nix could speak with both authority and feeling.

Just to get him off her back, Sandra Reynolds-Nix found out that Mr. Kulman, lawyer for the school, was authorized to sign the checks himself, and would be pleased to do so, if necessity demanded. She instructed Mrs. Olson to make them up, as usual, on Thursday, and then if Doctor wasn't back by Friday, to take them into Suddington for Mr. Kulman's signature first thing in the morning.

The day before that happened, though, there was some real excitement on the campus. On Thursday, just as lunch was ending, six strange people wandered in the dining hall and asked for Doctor Simms. Five of them were kids and one a blond young man who looked a touch like Peter Martins of the New York City Ballet, Sandra thought. They had that unwashed look about them that you see on hikers near the Appalachian Trail, and, in fact, they'd left some heavy packs outside the dining hall.

Sandra Reynolds-Nix identified herself to them. By then, these strange new kids—two boys, three girls—were greeting certain students who were members of the school as if they knew them. The blond young man seemed very much at home, as well, and answered her in quite a friendly way.

"Hi," he said. "I'm Nat Rittenhouse and this is Group Six. I'm afraid we got tired of waiting for Doctor to call us in."

The story was quickly told. The five kids and this teacher of theirs had indeed come up on the bus from New York almost four weeks before. All the other new kids from the bus remembered having seen them. But Doctor had, apparently, given them a different set of instructions than he had the other groups. He'd told them to stay in the woods—some spruce grove, maybe fifteen miles away—until he sent for them. Which he never had done yet. So, finally, the Group had gotten tired waiting, and they'd came in on their own. They wanted to start school *sometime,* they said.

To make things even stranger, it appeared that Doctor had never entered these kids' names—*or* this teacher's—on any of the school's official lists, or rolls, or files, even though a folder containing their applications and carbons of Doctor's letters of acceptance were later found in a drawer of his desk in his study.

At first she had to improvise like mad. She got the kids all placed in rooms by making use of space reserved for VIP-type visitors and medical emergencies. Nat she put in Homer Cone's apartment, warning him it might be just a temporary thing, depending. She also asked if he would substitute for Cone in Basic Math and also, if he didn't mind, in two of Mrs. Ripple's classes. That was *really* good of him, she said. The following week, she called up the parents of each of the five new students and, imitating a confused and apologetic secretary (it *was* handy to be a woman sometimes!) asked them if, by any chance, they'd gotten back the canceled checks they'd used to pay tuition. All of them avowed they had, and even offered to send copies. And three of them informed her they had drawn the checks to Doctor Simms in person, which *had* seemed slightly strange, until they realized he owned the school himself.

When Sandra Reynolds-Nix hung up, she called the local sheriff's office, and the state police.

As soon as Mrs. Ripple's forehead hit the table, the members of Group 6 started to look at each other again. Up until that moment, no one dared.

But only Ludi seemed to comprehend what she had seen.

"They got our poison, didn't they?" she said to Nat.

He nodded solemnly. "I couldn't think what else to do," he said.

Coke said, "They're dead?" And he started to reach out for Doctor's hand before he caught himself and got up fast and walked on down the room, as if he'd just then thought that being dead was catching, maybe.

After that, there was a lot of motion in the study. Everybody got up from the table (except, of course, for Doctor, Luke Lemaster, Levi Welch, and Mrs. Ripple). Nat started behaving like a person in a detective story, Ludi thought. He took all the glasses, and the pitcher, into the lavatory and washed them thoroughly, washing his hands a few times in the process. Then he dried the glasses and the pitcher, and wiped the bottles with the dish cloth. Ludi watched this closely, nodding.

Sully watched him, too, but he also kept sneaking glances at the dead people. Killing them was something Nat had had to do, he thought; no question about it. Sara touched his arm, which made him jump.

"We're safe, aren't we?" she said. He'd never seen her look so white. She looked sick. "Can't we get out of here?" she said, and looked around, sort of in a panic, as if she were in a cage or something.

Marigold had gone and sat down on the sofa, and leaned over and put her head on her knees. Coke stood beside her and put his hand on her head.

Nat finished wiping the bottles, and he put them back on the shelf, holding them with the dish towel.

"I had to do it, didn't I?" he said to Ludi.

She nodded.

"Can't we get out of here?" Sara said again. She looked around at everyone, and she spoke much louder this time. "Can't we just get out of here?" This time she spoke to Nat.

Sully and Coke looked at Nat and nodded.

Marigold sat up and shook her hair in place. She took a deep breath. "I think the thing we have to do is ground them. Drop them into those bottomless holes in the ground you were telling us about. Just the way they were going to do to us. I was thinking. I thought it all through. They were going to poison us, and they got poisoned. They were going to drop us in those holes . . . well, that's what should happen to them. That way"—she shrugged—"they'd disappear, you know? Just like the one that was going to shoot Sara." She looked at Nat and Ludi. "What do you guys think?"

They looked at each other. Ludi put her lower lip between her teeth, but they both nodded. Clean up as you go along. The campus was deserted; they could do it.

"Then we ought to go back to the Lodge," said Marigold. "That's what I was thinking. We need a couple of days. Go somewhere and call our parents—tell them we have the letters, so here's what *they* have to do. *Then* we show up at the school. Here's our story." She flicked at her bangs. "We're tired of waiting for Doctor to send for us. What's going on? When does school start? Et cetera, et cetera, et cetera. We're just a bunch of innocent kids." She smiled a crooked smile at Nat. "And an innocent teacher, of course. I've thought it all through," she said again, "and we have to get rid of the bodies."

Everyone stared at Marigold. They wouldn't have been more surprised if they'd seen Jerry Lewis cast as Arthur Wellesley, first Duke of Wellington, telling how he planned to stick it to Napoleon at Waterloo.

But Sara was moving her head back and forth in small shakes. "I can't touch them," she said to Mari-

266

gold. "I really can't. I don't even want to look at them. I just can't do it." She started to cry, and she walked over behind Doctor's desk with her back to the room and put her face in her hands. Coke followed her. He wasn't too crazy about the idea of touching them himself. How the hell would they *feel?* Might anything come out of them? Better he should make himself useful consoling Sara. Sully followed Coke. Sara was his responsibility, not Coke's. If she was going to cry . . . well, he would tend to her, because he could understand her best. She was his girl friend, wasn't she?

Nat said to Marigold, "I can get the car, the Pumpkin. I'll do it. You all head back to the Lodge, and I'll meet you there."

Ludi made a mouth. "Are you kidding? I'm going to help you. It'll take two, you know that." She turned to Marigold. "Really. I can do it. You go with them. That'd be the best."

Marigold nodded, and the three of them walked over to the other three. They didn't have to do a whole lot of convincing.

"I'm really sorry," Sara kept saying. She had to keep her head turned away as they left the room.

"Are you sure you don't want me and Coke to help you?" Sully had to ask. But his eyes swung back to Sara.

"Sure I'm sure," said Nat.

Coke nodded judiciously. He could see the present plan was best, all things considered.

Nat and Ludi walked through the woods to where the Pumpkin was, not saying an awful lot, but not at all isolated from one another either. They both were thinking, some, about the job they had to do. Nat didn't think he was bothered by the thought of doing it at all; he just didn't want to get caught. He also didn't want it to do bad things to Ludi—give her nightmares or something. He wondered how come it had been so easy for him to put the poison in the Bloody Marys, when he'd always thought, and said, he was a pacifist.

Ludi was hoping Nat was all right. He'd taken on so much, and none of it really for himself. If it were just him, he wouldn't be within a thousand miles of this place, probably; he never would have had to kill those people. She sort of knew how it seemed to him, how it must be to *be* him, but not completely, yet. As was so often the case, she didn't think much about herself at all.

It didn't take long to do the job: getting the car, loading the bodies into it, driving the short distance they had to go. At the end, they made four trips on foot, carrying the bodies the last two hundred yards between them, resting once along the way. They left no tracks that anyone would notice.

When they had hidden the van again and were hiking back to the Lodge, Ludi said, "They were just like my father. Just as bad, and just as crazy."

"Yeah," said Nat. "If bad is crazy; I don't know. They all thought they were doing the best thing, I guess."

"I suppose you're right," Ludi said. "That makes it a little better. A lot of times, people think they know what's best for kids." She smiled and gave him a shove. "Older people, mostly."

"What gets me," Nat said—he was lost in his own thought—"what gets me is, after a while, kids start to agree with them, and act the same way they do. I've seen it happen to me sometimes." She gave him another shove, a harder one. "Oh, I get it," he said.

"Of course, in your case," Ludi said, "the condition might respond to therapy."

Nat rolled his eyes around.

They walked a little farther in an easy silence.

"Nat," said Ludi.

"What?" he said.

"Are we going to go to this school?"

"How do you mean?" he said, but of course he'd been worrying about the exact same thing.

"You know," she said. "It seems to be getting all arranged. That all us kids are going to make our parents send us. And I *assume* that you'd be staying, too, and be a teacher. . . ." She left that open, wanting at least to hear him say that of course he was, if she was.

"Providing that they ask me, I guess I will," he said.

"Well," she said, "I don't know if I *want* to stay. Do you? I don't know what it'd be like. Except for one thing. They wouldn't let us live together." She looked away.

"I guess not," he said, and barked a little laugh. "Coldbrook may be a far-out little school, but I doubt that it's *that* far out. We could probably see a lot of each other, though. I mean, the Lodge isn't going anywhere."

She smiled. "That's a nice thing to think about. But still . . . I've still got this other thing about taking money from my father. Remember?"

"Yeah," he said. "But look at it this way. He's already given Doctor Simms a whole ton of money, and God knows where it's gotten to. It's like he's already paid your tuition two or three times over. And besides, you've got to finish school sometime. . . ."

"And if I don't finish now, I probably never will?" She was smiling, but not as if she found it all that funny.

He smiled, too, and shook his head. "Aw, Lu. I don't mean that. You know I don't. I just think you ought to wait and see. Make sure it's a bad deal before you decide to bag it. Hell, it might be just the perfect place for us. . . ." He wasn't all that sure that he'd like being a teacher, at this school or any-

269

where, but if it was a good thing for her, he figured he could stand it for a year, no problem.

"Well," she said, "let's act like I'm going for the time being, and then we'll see, O.K.?"

He smiled and reached for her and kissed her. It was something he hadn't thought of doing in a few hours, but as soon as he let go of all the things he'd had to think about, and just kissed, it felt wonderful in a way that he'd forgotten about, because it couldn't be remembered, only felt, and only given in to.

When they stopped kissing, *he* wanted to say, "Let's bag the school, O.K.?" But she said, "As long as I'm with you," before he could open his mouth, and the moment passed, and when he started to think it out logically again, it seemed best to stay.

On Monday, they all drove to Suddington. Marigold was the first to call her parents—actually her father's office—and the others watched her from outside the phone booth, hearing bits and pieces of the conversation, too. She did it so well, so confidently, so cheerfully (reading snatches of her mother's letter, just as if it didn't say such awful things) that Coke asked her, *sort* of in a joking way, if she would call *his* father, too.

She answered, "Sure, why not?" and took his letter, made the call, and told them, "Piece of cake," when she was done. So Sully asked her also, and she did, and Sara asked her also, and she did, again.

"How about it, Lu?" she said to Ludi, after that one. "Want to use me while I'm hot?"

"I guess so," she said. She took Marigold by the arm and led her away from the others first. "But tell him . . . tell him that I won't be wanting any more from him than he's already paid Doctor Simms. And that this'll be the last time he hears from me, indirectly or otherwise."

270

"Wow," said Marigold. "You mean that?"

"Yes," said Ludi, "cross my heart."

"Boy," said Marigold. "Roz and Toby . . . well, I wouldn't do that. They're still my parents, after all." She smiled. "It's funny. Now that I'm in charge, I feel a little different toward them."

Ludi looked at her. "I guess that's good," she said, "I don't know." She turned and walked away.

Doctor's will—they found it in the files behind his desk—provided that "in the tragic and unthinkable event of my death," the school would cease to be a proprietary institution and become nonprofit (as a good school should be). A group of local businessmen and bankers, plus a minister or two, had, in fact, agreed to become its board of managers, if and when. And a new set of Articles of Incorporation had been drawn up and was ready to be filed.

But before any of that could happen, Doctor had to be dead, and when there is no (pudgy) body, or proof that one exists, "dead" takes years and years before it is a *legal* fact. The state police had come and stayed awhile, and nosed around and questioned everyone in sight. Group 6 and Nat stuck to their one simple story: they'd been at Spring Lake Lodge, this camp that Nat (and, later, they) had made. The officers could come and see it, if they liked; Nat reckoned it was fifteen miles "up there." On hearing that, most state policeman flexed their toes inside their shiny riding boots and said they'd take his word. But Sergeant Sturgis didn't. Sergeant Sturgis had ambition. Nat led him and Trooper Wallick up to Spring Lake Lodge the long way, and Sergeant Sturgis had the trooper check out underneath the outhouse and some other stuff like that. They only found what you'd expect. Because he'd hated all his teachers when he'd gone to school, Sergeant Sturgis was convinced that there'd been murder done, most

271

likely by some students other than Group 6, the ones who'd got to know the teachers good. He had motives coming out his you-know-what, but still, unless he found some bodies . . .

Captain Johnson, officer in charge, was a professional executive, and so he thought in larger managerial dimensions: grand theft, instead of pedagogicide, and plane trips to Brazil and "dummy" corporations, hidden assets—never mind what the accountants said, that all the cash appeared to be in place. The case, he said, would bear the label "Missing Persons," and he, himself, would keep on working on it. He wasn't ruling out Brazil at all, he said, nor even the Bahamas or Jamaica. He might just hop a plane down there, perhaps in February—by which time "they" might have gotten careless, overconfident, he said.

So, for the time being, the school was still a kingdom, but without a king; something had to be done about that.

At a faculty meeting hastily convened during the first week of this second mysterious disappearance Sandra Reynolds-Nix explained about the salaries, first off: no problem, whatsoever. Mr. Kulman was prepared to exercise his power of attorney for as long a period of time as proved necessary. The faculty applauded in relief, and then, relaxed and grateful, it importuned Sandra Reynolds-Nix to serve as regent, as Directress, *pro tem.* She obliged them in a flash (though saying she was sure that it wouldn't be for long) and, in her turn, appointed Carlos Pennywell as very temporary Dean (his steaks *had* been delicious), pending Luke Lemaster's surfacing ("at any moment," she was sure). The next day, she called her first community meeting.

"I'm delighted to tell you," she smiled out at the students, faculty, and staff, "that we've now gone over a week without losing a single faculty member"—(laughter)—"although I *did* hold my breath when somebody told me they'd seen Freddy Noble stepping out of Larkin House at half past twelve the other night." (Gales of laughter, and applause. "Frenzied" Freddy Noble was the younger faculty's most shamelessly self-advertised philanderer.)

"But seriously," Sandra Reynolds-Nix went on, "I do want to tell you I've been dazzled—simply dazzled—by the kind of ego strength I've seen in this community the past two weeks. Deaths diminish us, as the poet said, but disappearances are just plain scary. We don't know how to handle them; they're hard to incorporate. There's always that nagging little fear—and not so little, sometimes—that there's a list out there, somewhere. And that maybe our name's on it, too." (Nervous laughter.) "There is no news of Doctor Simms, or any of the others, I regret to say. No one has the smallest clue where any of them went, or why. None of them appears to have taken any baggage with them and—let me set your minds to rest on this, once and for all—the assets of the school are one hundred percent intact." (Enthusiastic applause.) "Not that any of you thought for a moment that Doctor Simms was an embezzler." (Laughter.) "Now, Mr. *Cone,* of course . . ." (Laughter and applause.)

"Of course I'm just kidding." She rolled her eyes and got the laugh a second time. "But getting serious again," Sandra Reynolds-Nix continued, "I want to clue you in on what we're thinking—Carlos and I—about the possibility of replacements on the staff." She dropped her eyes. "If the worse comes to the worst," she deadpanned. "We need advice on this; it really does affect us all. . . ."

She went on to talk about the options as she saw them: immediately hiring temporary replacements from a pool that "might not be too promising, let's face it"; standing pat with the present personnel and

273

increasing class sizes, maybe even dropping a course or two; or holding off on hiring new people ("which we won't have to do—God willing—anyway") until they could be sure of attracting "the Coldbrook type."

A goodly number of people wanted to address that point, students and staff alike. The head of Maintenance, Mr. Busby (since the disappearances, only secretaries, kitchen help, and maintenance people were still called by their last names), said that it wasn't up to him to say what the missing *teachers* were worth, but that if anyone had a hill of beans to spare, he could use that in place of Levi Welch, and then some. (Gales and gales of laughter and tumultuous applause that didn't stop until Mr. Busby rose again and waved his cap. "*That's* Mr. Busby," everybody said.)

Sandra Reynolds-Nix finally summed up "the sense of the meeting," which was the third alternative: wait for "the Coldbrook type" (and for the missing to return, of course). There were nods and murmurs of approval from around the room, and she promised to report regularly to the community "if there were any interesting developments."

"Meanwhile," she said, "we can be thankful that even as we were losing Doctor and the others, we *got back* Nat—and Sara, and Ludi, and Marigold, and Sully, and Coke." (Earnest, sincere clapping, with further nods and smiles.) "Even though I think most of us will agree that they chose a pretty extreme way to avoid the first cycle of tests and to keep their names off the duty rosters"—(appreciative laughter)—"we can also agree that it's just *great* to have them safely back among us. Whatever you were doing out there, gang, it sure seems to have agreed with you!" (Laughs, whistles, more applause.)

On the way out, a lot of people were saying that Sandra Reynolds-Nix looked like a pretty cool Director, although as Robert Fritchman (one of the better students) said, "Yeah, sure, and so did Gerald Ford. . . ." He moved his eyes toward heaven.

Chapter Twelve

B Y THE TIME of the next community meeting, two weeks later, the people in Group 6 had undergone a major change in role. At first they were celebrities: the local Mowglis, Ishis, primitive backwoodsfolk, survivors of a bureaucratic plane crash, you might say. Everyone just *had to* meet them, talk to them, ask them how "it" was, and how they liked the school.

On second glance, it seemed (to almost all the other kids) that the people in Group 6 were really rather extra cool and fit: "together," yes, "mature." So, to all of their surprise (excepting Sara's, probably), they all were seen as leaders by the others, and were asked for their opinions on all things. Whenever one of them would say, "Do you see what I mean?" people seemed to see real easily.

At first Group 6 had gotten together every night in Nat's apartment (formerly Homer Cone's). It wasn't anything that they'd decided on, or like a regular "meeting," it was more of a thing that everyone happened to do, and liked to do, a lot. But by the second week, there were already conflicts—not with each other, but with different things having to do with the school: activity meetings, homework, social stuff in the dorms. Something had to give way: "There just aren't enough hours in the day," people said. Everyone felt bad if he or she went a few days without getting over to Nat's, but it seemed as if it had to be that way.

Ludi was always there, at least. She'd bring her books and study there, as a regular thing, even if Nat wasn't home when she started. But she always went back to her dorm before midnight, and because everyone liked both of them so much, a story started going around that they'd known each other for years, that their families lived next door to each other, as a matter of fact, and that's how come they were such good friends. They both had a load of work to do, to even catch up with their courses, and Ludi was bound and determined to make him proud of her.

The agenda of this next community meeting had been circulated by Sandra Reynolds-Nix to all the dorms ahead of time. She wanted to do some "brainstorming," she told them, about the Basic Coldbrook Way of Doing Things—"our *modus operandi*, so to speak." Could it be possible (she asked) that Coldbrook was trying to "win the battle of the eighties with 1960s' weapons?"

It turned out to be the longest community meeting in recent memory and, in general belief, "by far the most constructive." Yes, as Matt Wampler (History, Hamilton College '78) observed, "It caught us up with Exeter."

Essentially, the students and the faculty (most of the kitchen and the maintenance people had drifted out quite early on) voted to impose four changes on themselves.

First of all, they voted in a grading system: now a kid would get, six times a year, not just a written evaluation from a teacher, but also "Honors," "Pass," "Marginal Pass," or "Fail." Sara felt she had to be an "Honors" student, because of that "awful you-know-what" at home.

Next, they all agreed that students had to go to

class. As Marigold said: the teachers had to go, and they'd prepared the class. It wasn't fair to them if kids could cut at will.

Then they said that people had to take a certain mix of classes, during their careers—a *specified* mix, in fact; it was safer from a college point of view and probably . . . *better,* too. A person could always take psych and anthro in college if he wanted to. Coke pointed out that he'd taken some stuff that he'd *hated*—and forgotten right away, right after the exam—but it hadn't *killed* him. Probably been good for him, in fact.

And, finally, they decided that, as Sully said, if people didn't really want to "do" the school, the way it was set up and organized, they should give up their places in it to people who did. To that end, it was decided to elect two community members by secret ballot—one student and one teacher—who would more or less help the Director to help any kids to make that decision, who should. Seeing that these were the first elective offices the school had ever had, they were perceived to be a tremendous honor, and a sign of the community's affection.

The results of the balloting were announced at breakfast the next morning. Louisa (Ludi) Locke and Nathaniel Rittenhouse were very much the people's choice. Everybody cheered and faced around toward where they sat.

Their chairs were empty. Nat and Ludi (both) had disappeared.

Sandra Reynolds-Nix found the note under her office door when she opened it that morning. She read it with a mixture of relief and professional concern. At least they hadn't *just* disappeared.

But what was this garbage about their "feet not fitting the dance"?

What the hell could that be meant to mean?

Epilogue

IT WAS the eleventh of November, Veterans Day, and Nat and Ludi had planned a big spaghetti dinner with hot sausage in the sauce and a bottle of cold rosé to go with it. They'd more or less decided to stay at Spring Lake Lodge until the beginning of deer season, which was in about a week. After all that they'd been through, there wasn't any point in getting shot by accident. And also, it was time for other things, like "adding on to their lives." That was Nat's way of talking about any new thing that either of them might undertake—like Ludi's going to college (which they both looked forward to) or his starting some new work, learning some new skills, even making some money.

Between them everything was excellent. At the moment when they left the school, Nat was able to stop thinking of Ludi as a kid altogether. It just felt natural to have joined his life with the best other person that he'd ever met, and he must have looked pleased about it, and more, because when they got up to the Lodge that day, she turned to him and said, "I know what you're thinking. You're thinking that *this* is the time. Well, to hell with you, mister."

He'd widened his eyes at her, and pointed to his breast.

Then she'd scratched her head, extremely thoughtfully, and smiled and said, "Now, *I* kind of

279

think that *this* is the time. How about you, big boy?"
And then she'd run and made him catch her.

And that was that—having no expectations, they
had no problems. They worked on the Lodge and the
root cellar and the fireplace and the Lake itself, and
what they called "the grounds" in general. They ran
in the woods and dunked in the water and lay in the
sun when it let them, and by being happy, they felt
their love grow even stronger. They did the same
things some of the time and different things some of
the time, and they welcomed their differences, instead of picking on them. They never blamed each
other.

So, on that afternoon of Veterans Day, when Marigold appeared (she'd warned them with a "Yoo-hoo!
Ludi! Nat! Yoo-hoo! Guess who-who's here?") they
both were very glad to see her. And vice-surely-
versa.

"I knew you'd be here," Marigold exclaimed. "I
just knew it. Oh, God, I'm glad to see you!" There
were hugs, a lot of them. "And, boy, do you look
great!"

Nat was sure she'd come to talk them into going
back. They asked for news of her, and the rest of the
Group, and how the school was going.

Marigold said that everyone was fine, and doing
well, extremely well, in fact, as far as the work was
concerned, by far the best that they'd ever done, except for Sara, probably. Nat and Ludi told her that
was wonderful.

"But there is one thing . . . ," said Marigold, and
grinned her most seductive one.

Ludi smiled; she already knew what was coming.
Nat also smiled, the smartie, because he thought
that he knew, too.

"I want to come up here and live with you," said
Marigold. "And guess what?" She did that whistle of
hers.

And there, through the spruces, came the other three, all of them looking just a little bashful and a little worried, but a little hopeful, too—and wearing big old backpacks. And Coke was dragging Marigold's, as well.